# ROUGH CLAY

Chrissie Loveday

CHIVERS

| British Library Cataloguing in Publication Data available |
| --- |

This Large Print edition published by BBC Audiobooks Ltd, Bath, 2010.
Published by arrangement with the Author.

U.K. Hardcover ISBN 978 1 408 49211 6
U.K. Softcover  ISBN 978 1 408 49212 3

Printed and bound in Great Britain by
CPI Antony Rowe, Chippenham and Eastbourne

To the memory of my Mother and Father.

To Mark, Peter and Tim and their families.

To John, to thank him for encouraging me to
write this and for putting up with all
my moods!

To everyone who gave me such valuable
information about the Potteries.

# CHAPTER ONE

## 1917

'Archie,' his mother called. 'You'll have to go down the cellar and get some coal. I daren't try the steps. Not in my condition.' The skinny boy sighed. He got up from his freezing perch on the back step and went inside. The temperature wasn't much better inside, this November day. The meagre fire in the little iron grate was almost dying. The coal bucket was empty and his mother was sitting huddled under a knitted blanket in the one easy chair. Her stomach bulged in front. Archie thought it looked awful. Ugly. Revolting. If he ever had a wife, he'd never let her get like that. Babies. Who wanted them anyhow? He picked up the zinc clad bucket and went down into the dark cellar. He knew the steps so well that he moved quickly into the pitch black darkness. He gathered up the bits of coal and dropped them with a clank into the bucket. The slack on the ground was easy to pick up and he added a good few shovels to the lumps already gathered. Once the bigger pieces were alight, the slack was shovelled on top to keep the fire going. If you let the big stuff burn too quickly, the fire was finished too soon.

'It won't always be like this,' he hissed to

himself angrily. 'One day, I'll have enough money to make a difference. Always skimping and struggling.'

He gritted his teeth and continued. They were lucky to have coal at all. There were several houses in the street who never even had a fire some days. Every weekend, the local mothers and kids clambered over the slag heaps at the pits, hoping to gather enough bits of unused coal to make a fire to cook hot food for the Sunday lunch. It was the one day of the week when everyone tried to sit down together to eat a decent meal.

Archie's dad, Ralph, was a miner. He was a ripper working right at the coal face, doing one of the most dangerous of jobs. He was allowed a bag of coal most weeks as part of his wages. Being a miner was considered a good job. The pay wasn't so bad but when you knew the conditions they had to work in, even an absolute fortune would never have been enough. The thick, dirty air deep in the mines polluted everyone's lungs. Few miners lived to old age and many never even saw forty. The men came out blacker than the coal itself and every cut or nick in the flesh became stained forever with a dark line. The black crescents all over his father's arms and chest fascinated Archie. Caused by the chips of rock as they flew through the air, they looked like irregular tattoos. No amount of washing could ever remove them. Dad did his best to flush away the worst of the grime each evening at the pit head but there was only a cold pump in the yard. Dirt this ingrained needed soap and hot water and a good deal of scrubbing.

'What you doing down there?' called his Mum crossly. 'Sitting in the dark, dreaming away. I don't know what's the matter with you. You're not normal.'

Archie gave a sigh. It was dreaming that kept him going. Dreams of bright colours and intangible, beautiful things he could not really define. They kept him fighting against his dismal prospects and ever critical mother. He climbed back up the steps. They were steep and it was all he could do to haul the heavy bucket up. His little legs made the journey upwards, back into the gloomy light of the living room.

'There y'are, Mum. That'll soon get you warm again.' Even at the tender age of nine, he sensed there was nothing that could ever make his Mum warmer. Her heart was frozen, her mouth a tight little line from years of clamping it together. He didn't understand why she was always so miserable. He knew there had been other babies on the way but as he was still an only child, something must have happened to them. This baby inside his mother seemed to be growing well but it didn't make her any more cheerful. 'Did you want me to back up the fire then?'

'Thanks, son,' she muttered. 'I'll have to get

3

something hot for your Dad's tea. He'll be home soon enough. Can you put that big bone in the pan for me and bring it in? I'll put it over the fire and it can begin to heat through.'

'Will I put an onion in as well?' he asked.

'Don't think there's one left. It'll just be the last few potatoes tonight. I'll have to go to the shop tomorrow, God willing.'

Archie looked in the meat safe in the back scullery. He picked up the virtually bare knuckle bone left from the roast on Sunday. He put it in the blackened iron stew-pot and poured water over it. At least there was water inside the house, even if you had to work hard to pump it out. The miners mostly had their own pumps, to help wash away the colliery grime. The fortunate few who had water inside always helped the other locals when the water froze in the communal pump outside, as it did so often in winter.

'I've put some salt and pepper in the pot, Mum. It should make a good soup, a bone like that,' he lied as he placed it on the iron pot stand over the fire.

'You're a good boy, Archie,' his Mum said, though her face never relaxed its grim expression. He smiled and wondered if now would be a good time to tell her what the teacher had said.

'Mum,' he began. He saw her expression of utter weariness and decided against speaking. The trouble was, time was running out and his entire future depended on it. He had to give his teacher an answer by the end of the week. 'It's all right. It's nothing. Now, am I to put the kettle over the flame, as well? Make you a nice cup of tea?'

'Thanks, love, but I'll wait a bit longer.'

'OK. I'll be out the back.' The boy went back to his position on the back step. He pulled out the last inch of a Woodbine and stuck it in his mouth. The illicit treat was his reward for completing Billy Machin's sums. Billy was the son of the local corner shop and had access to all manner of such treats. He wasn't the brightest of boys and Archie regularly helped him out with his school work, for a modest price. Trouble was, one Woodbine never lasted long enough. He would ration himself so it lasted for a bit longer than the five minutes he could have taken. Though both his parents smoked, they'd have been very shocked to discover Archie's addiction at so young an age.

The boy looked up at the smoke laden sky. He sniffed the familiar smell. It was always the same. There were heavy fumes hanging over the chimneys of the cramped lines of houses. The coarse, unrefined coal they burned gave off a smell that clung inside the mouth. Apart from the domestic users, there were many others who polluted the atmosphere. If it wasn't the pottery kilns belching out smoke and chemicals, it was the treatment plants at the collieries. Everyone round here who was capable of working was employed in the potbanks or down the pits. Life was grey and dusty, summer and winter alike. Only a few weeds struggled through the cobbled yards when it was spring but that was a long way off. They'd laid out a city park a few years before, at the top of the hill where the gentry lived. He'd been to look with some of the other lads when he was much younger. The workmen had told him to *bugger off.* They didn't want such urchins making a mess of their beautiful parks. There was a lake with boats for hire before the war. And best of all, there were places to play football.

'One day, I'll have my own garden with flowers and all. One day, I'm going to be famous.' He spoke fiercely to the grimy bricks in front of him. He picked up a bit of old slate and drew a design on the brick wall. It was a fluid shape, a vase outline with a flat bottom and perfectly matching second side. He drew a handle on the side, more flowing lines which gave him utmost pleasure to look at. He scrubbed at it with his sleeve, knowing he'd get a cuff round the ears if he left it for his mother to see. He was always drawing when he had the means. In school, his slate was always filled with squiggles and lines when he should have been practising his handwriting. He developed a signature with masses of curlicues and the letters joining together to make a design. One day, the signature was going to be known all over the world, he promised himself.

'Where are you, Archie?' called an angry voice. Mum had got up from her seat by the fire. Time for him to move. 'What are you doing out there in the cold? Get in here at once you stupid child. It's cold enough for snow. You'll catch your death.'

He dragged on the final bit of cigarette and stabbed it against the wall. He hated the way his mother always bossed him around. One day, he'd stand up to her but for now, he knew from experience it was best to do as he was told. He went into the cramped house, the glow of the gas lamp making it look warmer and more inviting than usual. But the lights only showed up the immense ugliness of the place. The drab walls were a dirty brownish grey from the constant fumes of heating and lamps. There was a grubby rag rug on the floor, the only concession to warmth on the pitted quarry tiles.

'Lay the table, son,' his mother ordered. He picked up the ugly earthenware plates and the coarse knives and forks. When the baby was older, he'd need his own set to eat from. Some of the factories made the most beautiful, delicate china. Plates, cups and saucers for the gentry to use. He'd seen some of it in the shops when he went into Burslem, the nearest town. He spent hours staring in at the windows, wondering how anything so lovely was meant to be used every day. How could anyone be so rich? Surely it was only the King and Queen who could have anything so perfect on their tables. He thought about it some more. If it was really only the King and Queen ate their meals off fine china, who else would buy it? There must be a few very rich folk around here, he thought. One day, I'm going to be like them, he promised himself.

With a sigh of longing for things beyond his reach, Archie put the scarred wooden bread board next to his mother's place. The three enamel mugs were still in the sink, supposedly soaking away the dark stains from hundreds of earlier brews. As he tipped out the water, he recognised the futility of even asking if he could sit for the school scholarship, as his teacher wanted him to do. He was supposed to take a note from his parents giving their permission. Truth to tell, he wasn't exactly sure if his parents could even write. But the note was only the first hurdle. If he got anywhere near winning the scholarship, that would be the time to bother his parents with any details. He heard the back gate slam and the rattle of metal studs on the cobbled yard.

'Dad's home,' he called to his mother.

'Put the kettle back on the hob,' she called.

'Hallo, love. How ya doin'?' he asked.

'I'm feelin' a bit poorly, truth to tell. Not much longer now, though. I reckon it's another lad. Ready to play for the Vale any minute!'

'And has Archie been a good lad? Helped your Mum have you?' The boy peered round the scullery door and looked at the big man. His father leaned down and ruffled his hair.

'I did, Dad. Honest. Got the coal up and everything.'

'Good lad. Now. Where's my slippers? Got 'em warming by the fire have you?'

The child ambled over to the grate and lifted the old worn boots that Dad called slippers. The toes had worn through and the tops had been cut down so Dad could slide his feet into them. There was no money to spare for such luxuries as a second pair of shoes or even a first pair, for all of them. Dad had to have sound boots to work in, so he was the exception. What ever would it be like when this new baby came into the family? Archie assumed they'd manage somehow, just as they always did.

The kettle came to the boil. He picked up the fat brown teapot and poured water onto the tea leaves. They were the same leaves that started the day at breakfast time, a few new fresh leaves added to make the thick, black, treacly brew that his parents loved. The last drop of sterilised milk gave the accustomed orange tinge to the concoction. He drank down his own share, never imagining that tea could ever taste any different. He believed whatever his parents did was the same as everyone else and the only way to go about

9

living life. Despite his inexplicable love of beautiful things, it never occurred to him to question routines that had always been part of his life.

Once his dad had washed his hands, as well as he could in the conditions, they all sat down. The meat bone had produced an insipid stock into which potato and one lone piece of carrot had been added. His father had the lion's share, a little was poured onto his mother's plate and the last drop was poured over the thick slice of bread on his own dish. He ate hungrily, wiping every last drop from the plate.

'Good eh, son?' Dad said. Archie smiled and nodded. He wished there was at least twice as much. He could have eaten that and more.

'Can I have another slice of bread?' he asked.

'We'll be short for breakfast if you do. Go on then. You can have a thin slice.' He took it hungrily and tried to chew it slowly, to make it last. All too soon it was gone. If their family was among the better off, the poor folks must really be suffering, Archie thought. It wasn't fair. None of it.

'They say the war's going to drag on for yet another year,' Ralph Barnett said, as they began to clear the table.

'How terrible for the poor sods stuck in the trenches. I've heard some of the women talking,' said Frances. 'Thank God you haven't

10

been called up.'

'And nor will I be called up. They need every scrap of coal they can get. They're not likely to send any of our lot to France. They're saying as mining's a reserved occupation.'

The boy sat quietly, listening to his parents. The war sounded like some far away story that had been going on for as long as he could remember. It was a situation too far removed for him to understand much about it. As everything was in short supply hereabouts, war or peace was all the same to him. Every day seemed exactly the same. With a start, he remembered the date from the blackboard at school. Wasn't November the sixteenth his birthday? He waited for a break in the conversation so he could ask. But there never seemed to be a right moment. He had a sudden thought. If he mentioned he was now ten years old, his Dad might start talking about his future again. He had no intention of following the sort of future his dad had in mind for him and kept quiet about the possibility of a birthday.

The weather worsened as November turned into December. The baby was due any day now and Archie had still felt unable to mention the scholarship that could lead him to the grammar school and a proper education. Not that he had left things to take their natural course. He didn't dare risk that. In a moment of madness and longing, he'd written the note himself, the one supposed to be from his parents. In his best handwriting, a pencil stub he'd picked up from Machin's one day and using a brown paper bag he'd saved, he wrote the words.

*Dear Teacher. I give my permission to Archie to sit whatever exams you think fit. Yours faithfully, Frances Barnett. (Mrs)*

He'd signed it with something less fancy than the signature he'd been practising for himself. The teacher had stared at the paper bag and the words on it. The writing was childish and rather familiar. If he guessed the truth, he said nothing. He well understood the longing and needs of the child. That the boy was special and gifted, he had no doubt. He knew a little of his background and the grinding poverty of the whole area. He could hardly blame the boy for trying to better himself, though he suspected that the future held no easy route out of it for this particular child. He put the boy's name forward for the scholarship and kept his fingers crossed.

'You'll have to do some extra work at home, you know. Will it cause any problems?' he asked.

'No, sir. None at all, sir. Only thing is,' he hesitated.

'Yes?' encouraged the teacher.

'Well, sir. We're a bit short of paper. You know, the sort you have to do homework on.' His face burned at his admission. It felt like letting down his Mum and Dad.

'I'll see what I can do.' He smiled at the boy. The teacher knew what poverty meant to everyone in this area. If he hadn't been sickly himself, doubtless he too would have been sunk deep into the hell of the trenches. If he hadn't been poorly as a child, he would probably have been a miner himself, just like his father and brothers. He'd had to fight to learn everything just as Archie did. But strangely, ill-health had given him the opportunity to educate himself and eventually to become a teacher. He glanced at the old, used brown paper bag that contained the few words, supposedly from the boy's mother. With such determination, there had to be a way.

'What do you want to do with your life, son?' the teacher asked.

'Make something beautiful and be famous. I want to be rich enough to eat me dinner off them best, proper china plates, like they have in the shops in Burslem.'

'I see. And how will you become famous exactly? What do you want to be remembered for?'

'I dunno yet. Probably for making summat beautiful. Summat people can keep for ever, just to look at and enjoy. But I reckon I have to learn a lot first. That's why I want to sit this exam. Why my Mum wants me to sit it,' he corrected.

13

'You're a bright enough lad. Now, go on with you. I'll see you tomorrow,' he said, as the child went out. He watched as the poor little lad went out into the cold. His patched jacket, an old cut-down one of his father's no doubt, was all he had against the icy December blast. His shoes slopped about on his feet. They probably belonged to his mother. How on earth could Archie cope at the grammar, even if he passed his scholarship? All that would buy was his education fees. He'd be expected to wear uniform and provide text books as well as his own exercise books. Something might turn up, he sighed desperately but he couldn't quite think what it might be.

Archie ran all the way home. He was late leaving school after his talk with the teacher. His Mum would be fretting. He'd have to get the coal up from the cellar for her. He ran down the back entry, his mother's ill-fitting shoes clattering over the cobbles. He pushed open the gate and stopped in his tracks. There was something up. The lights were shining out of the back scullery and he could hear water running down the sink. He opened the back door and peered inside.

'You'll have to wait outside, love,' said the strange woman who seemed to have taken over the house. 'Won't be long. I know it's cold outside, but your Mum's having her babba. New little brother or sister for you. You'll know real soon.'

14

'Didn't think it was coming awhile yet,' Archie said miserably. Everything was going to change now. 'Is me Dad home yet?' he asked.

'Not yet, love. Best wait there and I'll give you a call when it's all over.' She bustled off and Archie sat in his favourite place on the back door step. He barely noticed the cold. S'pose his Mum died? Women often did when they had babies. His Mum had been feeling poorly for a few days now. He hugged his bare knees and sat waiting, waiting. He heard a scream from upstairs. His blood froze.

'Don't go and die us, our Mum,' he begged. The screams continued and he felt tears filling his eyes. Why did it have to hurt so much? There must be some better way of bringing babies into the world. A new sound filled the dusk. It was another scream but this time, a thin, little sound. Then everything went silent. The boy got up and pushed his way into the scullery. It was deathly quiet upstairs. He padded through the kitchen, leaving the oversized shoes by the door. He opened the door to the stairs and slowly climbed up. He could hear low voices muttering and the sounds of movement. He was terrified. He wanted to go into the room but he was too scared of what he might find. At last he pushed open the door of his parents' bedroom and peered round. The bed-sheets were on the floor, covered in blood. There was a newspaper package, also blood-soaked, near

15

the door. He gripped the side of the door, feeling light-headed and weak. The midwife was bending over the bed, dipping some rags into a washing up bowl of steaming water. His mother lay back against the pillows, white faced and covered in sweat. The midwife wrung out her cloth and wiped his mother's private parts. With shock, he realised he could see all of her private parts. He gasped and stuffed a fist into his mouth to stop himself from crying out. The midwife turned as she heard the sound and began scolding him.

'I told you I'd call when we were ready for you.'

'Is she dead?' he managed to stammer. 'Only I heard the screaming and . . . thought . . .' His voice tailed off.

'I'm all right, love,' his mother said weakly. 'You've got a little brother.'

'Are you all right though, Mum? You aren't going to die are you?'

'Course she isn't. Now, do something useful and get a brew going. Your mother's worn out and so am I. Go on with you. And put a good spoonful of sugar in it. We both need a bit of energy back in us.'

Given something positive to do, the boy went down the stairs with a sense of importance. He'd have some tale to tell the others at school tomorrow. New brother eh? At least that was one better than a sister or even a new kitten. You could play with a brother and not have to fuss round like you did with a girl. He could scarcely imagine what life would be like with a brother. He'd been the only child for so long. He stopped on the bottom step and sat for a moment. He bit his lip as new thoughts struck him. He was always hungry, it seemed. What would it be like with another person sharing the little they had? Mind you, the way things looked upstairs, he doubted his mother could possibly survive, not after the horror of all the blood he'd seen. He tried to pull himself together and went into the scullery. Whatever happened in the future, he, Archie, was important at this moment. He had something to do. He pushed the pump handle energetically and filled the kettle. He put it on the fire hob and turned to the cellar. They'd need some coal fetching up. He'd need to get some supper going as well. Having babies was probably hungry work and his Mum would need some good food inside her. He fetched the coal and stoked the fire. The memory of all the blood came to him and he gave a shudder. Then he went to look in the larder. The shelves were empty. Damn. His mother said she'd go shopping today and she must have forgotten. He stood wondering what to do. His dad would soon be home. He'd expect a meal on the table, new baby or no. There was only one thing for it. Archie would have to go and talk to Mrs Machin at the corner shop. Maybe, under the circumstances, she would give him some credit. His Mum never believed in putting anything on the slate but she was in no position to complain at the moment. He shivered again as he thought all about the blood everywhere upstairs. If giving birth was such a messy business, he wondered how anyone could do it at all and especially not twice. Some families even had a load of kids. He must make sure that his own wife, if he ever had one, never had to go through it all. Still, by the time he was old enough to have a wife, they'd surely have found some better way of getting babies.

'You see, me Mum's just had my baby brother and she musta forgot to go shopping this morning. And me Dad'll be home from his shift soon and there's nothing in the house. So, I was wondering if I could have something for tea. And put it on the slate. Mum'll settle up with you in the morning, I'm certain.'

'Well, I'm not so sure. Your Mum doesn't like having things on tick. But I expect it'll be all right under the circumstances. What did you want?'

'I dunno. Something to feed us all. And the baby. What do babies eat? Will I need to get something for his tea as well?'

'No, love,' laughed Mrs Machin. 'Your Mum'll have all he needs for a few weeks. Now, what can you cook?'

'I can do jacket spuds. Put them in the oven and have 'em with a bit of butter.'

'Right then. Spuds it is. And I'll give you a bit of cheese to melt on top. That'll do your Mum good.' The woman packed a few items into a piece of paper and made a rough parcel. She tied a piece of string round it and handed it over.

'How much is that?' asked Archie, so he could tell his mum what she owed.

'I'll sort it out with your Mum when I see her,' she said. Then she took a deep breath. 'Tell her it's a present to welcome the new baby.' She couldn't bear to think of any of them going hungry at a time like this.

'That's everso good of you. Ta, Mrs Machin. I'll tell her.'

He ran back. The midwife was burning the bloody package he'd seen in the bedroom. He watched, fascinated. The kitchen was filled with steam. He'd forgotten about the kettle. He washed the potatoes quickly and put them into the little oven at the side of the fireplace. They'd take a long time to cook. Mum sometimes left them in all afternoon so he hoped they'd be in time for when his Dad got home. Funny to think, his Dad had another son and he didn't even know it yet.

Archie poured the boiling water over the old tea leaves, adding a few extra, as usual. Once it had time to brew, he poured a mug to take up to his Mum. He was worried at the thought of what he might find. Everything was very quiet up there. He opened the door

19

leading out of the kitchen to the upstairs and climbed the steep steps. However carefully he was carrying the mug, he still managed to spill some on the bare wood. He knocked at his parents' door and went in when he was called. His mother was sitting upright now and the colour had returned to her face.

'Hallo, love. You come to see your little brother?'

'I've brought you some tea, Mum. Are you all right? You gave me a right scare before.'

'You didn't choose the best moment, son. But I'm fine now. A bit sore but I'll be getting up later. I'll see to your Dad's tea.'

'It's all right, Mum. I've put some potatoes in the oven and there's a dab of butter and a bit of cheese to go with them.'

'Where's all that come from? I never went shopping this morning. I was too poorly.'

'I went to Machin's. She let me put it on the slate. But then she said it didn't matter and that we could have it as a present to welcome the new baby.'

'We'll see about that. But it's OK, love. You did well. Now, are you going to look at this new baby of ours?'

Archie went over to the big drawer, lined with a blanket, that served as a cot. He peered in and stared at the wrapped bundle.

'Ugly little sod, isn't he?' he said without thinking. 'All sort of squashed in and wrinkled.'

'He's lovely,' his Mum said defensively. 'All

new babies look wrinkled. You were no great beauty yourself.'

'Boys aren't s'posed to be. But he's a right ugly one. Uglier than most, I'd say.'

'Oh, and you're an expert are you?'

He was spared from replying as they heard the back gate rattle.

'Dad's home,' he said and rushed down the stairs.


## CHAPTER TWO

Archie's new brother was called Ralph William. Rapidly *Ralph* was dropped in favour of his second name, to avoid the confusion of father and son sharing the same name. For Archie the daily chores remained the same. The routine grind of school, hauling the coal from the cellar and helping with the evening meal continued. His extra work in preparation for the scholarship exam was fitted in at odd times. He worked during the school lunch break, helped by his teacher. The night before the test, his teacher told him to try to get an early night so he awoke refreshed and ready for his big chance. He still hadn't told his parents about the exam, partly because they were too busy with the new baby and partly because he knew there was no chance of him ever taking up the scholarship, should he be lucky enough to win it.

At nine o'clock, he muttered his goodnights and went up to bed. His parents barely noticed his absence and he lay awake, dreaming of the opportunities education could provide. It was the first stage in his plans for the future. He wanted to learn to design something but his limited experience left the actual subject somewhat undefined. He heard his parents come up to their room, bringing the baby with them. It was midnight before his excited mind allowed him to doze off and by the time morning came, he was feeling the exact opposite of bright and alert.

Downstairs, his father was lighting the fire. Usually, a good shovel of slack last thing would keep the heat in. For some reason, the whole thing had gone out and had to be started from scratch. It wouldn't have mattered but today, Archie wanted to get to school in plenty of time for a last minute chat with his teacher. There were four boys sitting the exam and he understood that competition was intense.

'I've got to be at school early today, Dad,' he said. 'So I'll have to miss the tea. Kettle'll take too long on that fire.'

'What's your hurry, lad? I'm afraid your Mum isn't feeling well. She wants you to stay home and help her with the baby.'

Archie's heart sank. Today of all days. This was his only chance and there could never be another.

'But, Dad, I can't. There's something special going off at school today and I can't miss it. Please, Dad.'

'Someone has to look after her. I can't take a day off. I could lose my job and then where would we be? No, son. There's no choice.'

Archie felt tears of frustration and loss filling his eyes.

'But Dad,' he began. Then he stopped. There was no point even trying to explain what it meant to him.

'Archie? What is it, lad?'

'Nothing, Dad. I'll get the kettle filled.' Scrubbing away the tears that were threatening, he went into the scullery and began to work the stiff pump. His father watched him. He was a good lad. Bright. Most sons followed their fathers down the mincs. Another few months and Archie would have his place booked beside his father. The boy returned and put the kettle on thc hob. It would take a long time to boil as the heat was slow today. Thc boy's already pale face was drained. He looked as if he was in pain.

'What's so special about school today then, lad?' Ralph Barnett asked kindly.

'Just a test. A special sort of exam.'

'And you were s'posed to be taking it? Whatever for? I never had any tests in my life and I've never missed them.'

'No, Dad. It's for boys who want to go on to the grammar.'

'Fat chance of that, lad,' his father said gloomily. 'You'll have to be working soon. Earning a wage. Once your little brother starts to grow, we'll need more money coming in. Have you given thought to the pit? I can have a word with Mr Copestake. Dare say he'll even keep you a place for a few months, till you're a bit older.'

'No, Dad,' Archie said calmly. 'I'm never going down the pit. Never. I'll maybe try for something in one of the pot banks.' His father stared at him.

'Pot banks? What do you know about making china?'

'I could learn. My teacher says I'm a bright lad. He was the one put me in for the exam. He thinks I'll pass, easy.'

His father's face softened.

'Go on then. Get off to your precious exam.' Archie stared in surprise at the unaccustomed turnaround. Usually, once his Dad had spoken that was it. No amount of cajoling would make him change his mind.

'But what about Mum? Who'll see to things for her?'

'I'll see if Maggie next door will pop in a couple of times during the day. Mind you get home as soon as you can. Oh, and good luck, son. Not that it'll do you much good. You'll never be able to go to any grammar school, you do know that, don't you?'

'Thanks, Dad,' the child said as he ran out

24

of the door. He didn't see the troubled look on his father's face as he watched him go. Grammar schools. Pottery worker. He wasn't his father's son at all. The mines had always been good enough for him as they were for his father before him. He looked down at his scruffy, filthy clothes. He looked at his hands, rough and marked with the black scarred evidence of his life's employment.

'Maybe you should have some ambitions, son. Make a new life and get out of this hell hole.' There was no-one to hear his words but he made a solemn promise to help his lad as best he could. Somehow, they had to find a way to put the boy through school. If that's what his teacher thought was possible, somehow, he had to make it so. If Archie had known of his father's change of heart, he might have felt better about his escape from a day's housework. As it was, he felt consumed with guilt. Maybe he could get away carly, as soon as the test was finished. His teacher would have to understand.

At nine o'clock sharp, four boys sat at individual desks, placed at one side of the classroom and right away from the rest of the boys. Proper ink and pens had been supplied, instead of the usual slates and slate pencils. The ink was in a little pot fitted into a wooden hole in the desk. It was the first time any of them had used these desks and the scratchy pens seemed to need dipping into the ink every couple of words. Archie felt cross. It would have been so much quicker if they could have used pencils. He was more used to them and he would have finished much earlier. Once he got into it, he began to enjoy the tests. He even began to like the smell of the ink, a special smell that he would always remember. The maths was easy and he'd always loved writing stories. He was usually the hero, a successful, wealthy man. He had proper china plates on his table, ones with painted flowers on them. He scratched away with his pen and soon the pages were covered in blots of ink and spidery words, containing Archie's childish, hopeful ambitions of a better life to come.

He was all ready to go back home at dinner time and went to say goodbye to his teacher, explaining that his dad had only let him come to school for the morning.

'Hang on, lad,' the teacher said. 'You can't go yet. You haven't finished. You have to have a talk with the headmaster of the grammar this afternoon. He's coming over to see all the candidates. If he thinks you'll benefit from the grammar school, you'll get your chance, providing your tests are good enough.'

'But me Dad'll belt me if I'm not home. Me Mum's ill and with the new baby and all . . .'

'I'll put you in first,' the teacher promised. His heart was heavy. If the lad succeeded the way he knew he would, the future would be fraught with difficulties. It was the custom in this area that whenever there was a crisis at home, the children were kept off school. There was nothing they could do about it. And once the parents needed their children to go to work, that was the end of schooling for any of them. The system had to change, he told himself.

Archie kicked a few stones around with the other boys, in the school yard. His stomach rumbled. He felt weak with hunger as he remembered he'd missed breakfast. He'd had nothing for lunch either. Such was life. When the time came for the interview, all Archie could think about was his scruffy jacket, cut down from one of his dad's, and his mother's shoes. He tried to scrub his face a bit cleaner but with nothing to use, he merely drove the grime a little deeper. The head of the grammar was most intimidating. He spoke with a very posh accent, the boy thought. He wasn't from this part of the world. He tried to think more about how he spoke himself and managed to give quite a good impersonation of his interviewer, or so he believed.

'And what do you hope to become, Archie?' the head said seriously.

'I don't know, sir,' he replied. 'But I'll not go down the pit. However much my Dad thinks I should. I want to do something with beautiful things. Like I wrote in my story this morning.'

'For example?'

'I don't know. Maybe work in the pottery. I'd like that. Designing things.'

'And do you have any connections with the pottery industry?'

'No, sir. I've seen things though. In the shops. Beautiful things. Real china plates like royalty must eat from. And beautiful flowers, made out of fine china, and ladies in frilly skirts. They're so lovely you could cry just looking at them.' His eyes shone with enthusiasm. 'There's loads of colours and even some with real gold on 'em. I want to make something like that. Oh, and I'm going to be famous. I've practised my signature for when I am.'

The austere man relaxed. He smiled briefly. All too often his potential pupils had grand ideas of the future. Few of them had the confidence and certainty to dare speak of them. This child had something quite different from the usual stream of boys passing through his school. He was undoubtedly a dreamer but his deep certainty about the future was refreshing. He deserved to be spared from the mines with their black and ugly darkness, however necessary they were to the locality. He saw the ill-fitting shoes and the cut-down, threadbare jacket. This boy would find nothing easy in his attempt to better himself, but in spite of his thoughts, he began to speak.

'I'd like to see you starting at the grammar school next year. I can't promise you a place at this early stage, of course. There are still a number of boys to interview. But I think you might be optimistic.'

'Right, sir. Thank you, sir.' He got up uncertainly. Was that it? Could he get back home now? The man nodded his dismissal.

'Send in the next candidate, please. Goodbye, Archie. I look forward to seeing you again soon.'

'How did it go?' asked his teacher anxiously.

'He said I could be optim . . . something. And he looked forward to seeing me soon.'

'Optimistic?

'Aye, that was it.'

'That's really good, Archie. I think it means you have a very good chance of success. Well done. Now, you can go home, if you want to.'

It was almost Christmas. There was little to suggest that this would be a good Christmas for many of the families of Longport. The war that had become known as The Great War was still rumbling on. Soon it would be 1918. Archie and his family still had food of sorts on the table and coal for the fire so were luckier than many. There had never been anything to spare for presents but each year, they looked forward to a day off work, often in the middle of the week, and a day when the family could be together.

'I think we should all go to church on Christmas morning, this year,' Mum had said. The family never went to church.

'What do you have to do there?' Archie asked curiously.

'Sing some hymns. Well, carols they're called at Christmas, and say some prayers and listen to what the vicar says.' Archie immediately lost interest. It didn't sound very special at all. He quite liked singing though, so didn't raise any great objections. He hoped he'd know some of these carols his mum was talking about. They sometimes sang at school and he wondered if these carols might be some of the songs they sang.

'It's going to be a good Christmas this year, after all,' Frances told him. 'Your Dad's had some extra shifts and we've managed to put a bit by.'

'Eh, that's good,' Archie said. 'Does it mean we'll have a proper Christmas dinner? Like we used to?'

'That's right, lad. And maybe, there'll be a little something in your stocking this year. Not much mind, but just you wait and see.'

Archie grinned happily. He'd like to have some paper and a new pencil most of all. Maybe if he dropped a few hints, his Mum would get some. The corner shop sold exercise books. Maybe he should drop a hint there, too. If his Mum went in the shop looking for something, Mrs Machin might suggest it. And a proper Christmas dinner. Good old Dad. Even the baby was behaving itself. It was still red and ugly but he was beginning to smile

30

when Archie talked to him. Sometimes, his Mum left him nursing his brother while she did the cooking. Now she was recovering from the birth, she seemed to be in a better temper some days. Archie could put up with anything if it meant there was food cooking when he came home. Life was looking good when the bombshell hit him.

'There's jobs going at the pit,' his dad said one night near Christmas. 'They're looking for some likely young 'uns to help out. We've lost so many lads around here for the war effort, they're taking them on younger than usual. Pay won't be much but it'll be a start. I've put your name forward. You'll be old enough soon.'

Archie's heart sank. He didn't mention the fact that they'd all forgotten about his birthday, last month. During these days of war, even the very youngest children were allowed to work above ground.

'But, Dad. What about me schooling?' he said at last.

'I never needed none of that rubbish. Fills you full of ideas. 'Sides, this isn't an underground job. Mostly running with messages, up at the head. You can read well enough and you've got a good memory.'

'But I don't want to work at the pit. I told you. Besides, there's good chance I'll get a place at the grammar. The teacher told me.'

'Where d'ya get these ideas from? Beats me,' Ralph Barnett burst out.

'I'm good at sums and all that stuff. And I can write a decent story.'

'Aye well. Maybe. But that sort of stuff doesn't put food on the table nor pay the rent.'

'Maybe I'd get a better job in the end. Pay might be better than the pits.'

'I suppose you think you're above such things. Well, mark my words, lad. As long as the pits are open, there'll always be work round here. We don't do so badly, do we? Things have really bucked up in the last few weeks. There's good food and warmth from the fire. You can forget your high and mighty ideas, my lad. Come Easter, you'll be well established as a runner.'

Archie went outside to his perch on the step. He rubbed his eyes on the back of the worn sleeve of his coat.

'I'll not do it. I won't do it,' he muttered over and over. Somehow, he had to find a way to stay on at school. If mining was so good, his Dad could continue to keep his family and Archie would get his chance at high school. Maybe he could get some sort of job on Saturdays and Sundays. Somehow, he had to make it possible.

It snowed hard the day before Christmas Eve. The streets lost their grimy grey-black pallor and looked mysteriously even and light. Houses had white roofs and window sills were piled high with soft sparkling snow. Once a few coal carts had gone down the roads, the snow

32

was dirtied and began to look grey and uneven. Several of the occupants of the houses had shovelled away narrow paths to their houses, heaping up grubby mounds in the gutters. Archie went to knock at some of the doors down the street to ask if they wanted their snow shovelled away. A few said yes, rewarding him with a sweet or an apple. No-one paid him anything. Money was much too scarce in this street. By Christmas Day, most of the snow had gone. Grey-brown slush lined the gutters and water dripped from most roofs. But the damp dullness could not quash the spirit in the Barnett household. Archie had got his stocking, hanging over the hearth. There was no pretence of Father Christmas in the household. There never had been. Besides, a ten year old was far too old to believe in such childish nonsense.

After breakfast, the boy solemnly put his hand inside the old sock. He pulled out a long thin parcel wrapped in a piece of brown paper. Two pencils. He gave a delighted grin.

'Thanks, Mum. Dad. Great.'

'Go on. There's more.' He looked up shyly and delved into the sock again. This time he found a thin, flat package. Inside was a small red exercise book. He flicked it open and was just a little disappointed to see it was lined. Not so good for drawing but it was paper and it was his own. He knew there was another object in the sock and slowly, at his mother's

33

urging, put his hand down again. She nodded and smiled at him. He felt something round and squashy. It was wet and sticky. When he pulled it out, the tangerine had a large hole in it where his finger had stuck into the soft peel.

'It's an orange,' he said with a smile. ' 'Cept I've stuck me finger in it and made a mess.'

'Best eat it then,' Dad laughed.

'I'd like to save it,' he began. 'Maybe not. It might go horrible.' It took only seconds for the fruit to disappear. 'Oh, sorry,' he said. 'I should have shared it with William.'

His parents both laughed. His dad spoke.

'Don't worry, son. The baby's much too small to eat anything like that. Now, next year, maybe he'll give you more than a bit of competition. Now, if we're going to this church of yours, we'd better be off. Are you ready, love?'

'Aye. I've put the chicken in the oven and it's cooking nicely. I'll just get my hat and we'll be off.'

The usually austere chapel was lit by candles and the bleak walls had taken on a glow of light which seemed to permeate everyone's mood. The dreadful war must end in the coming year. They'd said it would never last, soon after it began, but they were all still suffering the deprivations. People who never spoke to each other normally smiled on this festive occasion and nodded their greetings. It was the family's first visit to church since

Ralph William had been born. Several of the women came and peered at the bundle and cooed over the child. Archie was bored and shuffled on the cold stones in his worn out shoes. His father stood stiffly uncomfortable in the unaccustomed high collar. He was ill at ease in this place but felt he owed it to his family to share the occasion. Archie thought the whole service thoroughly boring and only looked up when the minister berated the sinners for their lack of support for God's house. He banged against the wooden pedestal he was standing on. Archie wondered why he was yelling at all the people in the church. They'd come, hadn't they? He was yelling at the people who weren't there. Mind you, he thought, he was yelling loud enough for most of Longport to hear him. Somehow, he got the impression that the minister seemed unaware of the hardships faced daily by his flock. The flock looked down and studied their feet as his words stirred feelings of guilt. At last, the congregation stood to sing the final carol. As the harmonium played the introductory bars, Archie gave a small grin. It was one of the carols they sang at school and he joined in with great gusto. His mother eyed him curiously and even dad looked impressed as his voice rang out. One or two others turned round to see where the voice was coming from. Archie thoroughly enjoyed himself and felt quite sorry when it came to an end. He hoped someone might comment about his fine voice but he saw only faint grins from those around him.

'I enjoyed that,' he said as they left the chapel. The minister shook their hands as they left.

'And was that your voice I heard during the final hymn?' he said unsmilingly to the boy.

'Yes, sir. That is, I don't know, sir,' he replied uncertainly.

'Someone teaching you to sing are they?' he continued.

'Not really. We sing at school a bit. I knew that one. So I could sing out.'

'Do you always try to sing in harmony?' the minister said with a severe expression.

'I dunno. I don't think so. I don't know what a harmony is.'

'I see. Well, once you have learned the melody line thoroughly, you might find harmonising something you could try. Until then, I suggest you practise the melody a little more. You might sing quite well one day. You could even join the church choir. Good day to you all.'

The minister turned back inside and shut the door behind him.

'What was all that about?' his mother asked. 'All I heard was you bellowing out of tune. I think the minister was trying to be kind. You'll sing in tune in future, son. None of your fancy harmon-a-thinging. Never felt so embarrassed in my life. Everyone turning round and all.'

'I didn't know,' Archie said sadly. He went pink and looked down at his scruffy shoes. 'Anyway, that's how I sing at school. They don't seem bothered. Are we going home now?'

'Aye,' his father nodded. 'Let's go and get to that roast dinner. I can smell it cooking from here.' Archie looked at his dad in amazement.

'Can you really?' He sniffed the grimy air but could smell only the smoke from the hundreds of fires, stoked up far beyond their normal heat to provide hot ovens to cook special Christmas meals. He shrugged and lost himself in his private dreams, where he could make pictures of beautiful things, shapes, colours that lived only in his imagination. He might do a drawing when he got home. In his new book. Mum would be busy and Dad would probably go to sleep so he'd have the chance.

'Christmas is all right, isn't it?' the boy remarked.

New Year's Day blew in with a ferocious wind.

'Aren't you working today, Dad?' Archie asked. His Dad rarely took holidays.

'Bad luck, son. Miners don't work New Year's Day. Not that the managers like it but it's a tradition, sort of.' It was a bit like having an extra Sunday that week.

January was bitterly cold. The wind blew mercilessly along the backs of the houses in the Barnetts' terrace. It whistled through every gap in the window frames and under doors. They stuffed anything they could find across the doorways but the temperature never seemed to rise above freezing. Archie was used to it and seemed a sturdy enough child. Little Ralph William was less fortunate. He caught a cold and spent several days gasping for his breath. Frances was desperate to know what to do. She put a brick in the oven to warm up, wrapping it in an old sheet before putting it into the drawer that acted as a cot for the baby.

'Goose grease is what we really need. A piece of brown paper to wrap round him and goose grease.'

'Someone must have had a goose for Christmas,' Dad said.

'Isn't there a bit of chicken fat left?' Archie suggested. 'It might work.'

Doubtfully, his mother spread a little of the fat over the baby's chest. It stank. She put a brown paper bag over it and wrapped the thin shawl over the top. Despite her efforts, his sniffs seemed to keep all the family awake at night. All the same, somehow the sickly child survived.

'He's a fighter all right,' Mum said.

In February, Archie was called into the headmaster's office.

'I'm sorry, sir,' he said, just in case he'd done something wrong.

'Sorry, lad? I'm not. Do you know what

you've done?'

'No, sir. But I didn't mean to. Honest.' He was so busily racking his brains to remember what he'd done wrong that he didn't even hear what his teacher was saying.

'Relax, lad. Archie Barnett, you've only gone and won a scholarship to the grammar school. Well done, my boy. I'm proud of you. There's not a lot of lads around these parts can make it to the grammar but you've done it.' The head was showing a degree of emotion none of the boys had ever seen before. Archie stood there, unable to speak. Not only had he survived the interview without getting a beating, he had got his scholarship to the grammar school. He grinned. He'd done it. He'd achieved his first ambition. The head was holding out his hand to the pupil and Archie shyly shook the proffered hand.

'I'm sure you'll be a credit to your school. Good luck.'

Archie left the room and went back to his class. Despite his own delight, the dingy room looked exactly the same as it had before.

'Well done, Archie,' Mr Gladstone said proudly. 'I can tell you all now. Archie has gained his scholarship. He's the first pupil from this school of ours ever to gain this honour. Shall we give him a round of applause?' Uncertainly, the rest of the class clapped. Archie blushed to the roots of his hair. He didn't know where to look.

At the end of the day, he ran all the way home, anxious to tell his parents the good news. He was the first boy to gain a scholarship from the school and the teachers were proud of him, he rehearsed the words. He decided to save his news until after tea, when both parents were ready to listen. At last, the time came.

'Mum. Dad. I've had a bit of news today.'

'Have you now. Well, I've got some for you,' replied Dad. 'I had word with Mr Copestake last week, and he's willing to give you a try out at the pit. There now, what do you think of that?'

'But . . .'

'You say thanks to your Dad. Be grateful you'll be able to do a bit to help this family.'

'Yes, thanks, Dad. I still want to do something else, though. I don't want to work at the pit.'

'I know, lad. But it's steady work and the money gets better once you get to work in one of the teams.'

'I know but . . . Well, I've heard today that I got that scholarship. Nobody from our school's ever got one before. The teachers are all very pleased with me.'

'Oh, lad. How could you? I thought you'd given up on all that stuff. You need to bring in some money.'

'I thought the war'd soon be over and then things'll be all right again. I could go to the

40

high school. Just for a bit. See how I get on.'

'It's not just the school. You'd have to have books and paper and all that. And clothes. You couldn't go in your Dad's old cast-offs. They have uniforms there and you'd stand out like chapel hat pegs if you didn't have the right things.'

'I'm sure summat could be found,' Archie said helplessly. He could see all his dreams fading away into his father's precious job at the pit head. He'd have to become a miner like his dad. It was what people did, round here.

'S'pose I'd better tell them I don't want to go, then,' he said sadly, rising from the table.

'Clear the table, lad,' his Dad said. 'Can't leave it all to your Mam to do.' Obediently, Archie picked up the dirty plates and cutlery. If he went to work at the mine, what chance did he ever have of making beautiful things for people to have in their homes? Fine china with flowers and gold patterns. Models of fine ladies and animals. He'd do animals. If big vases were too difficult, he'd make tiny ones. Miniature ones. But it was all just a dream. His future lay at the mine. He could hear the dull murmur of his parents' voices as they talked. He couldn't hear their words but he could guess what they were talking about. His dreams were disappearing into the dirty black grime of life as a miner. His body would carry the black crescents of coal dust, just like his father. Black crescents so deeply carved into

41

his skin they looked like tattoos covering his arms and chest. One day he'd grow up and discover he'd got some girl pregnant and be saddled with a family. Some of the older lads talked about it. Billy Machin said his big brother had got some girl from Burslem in the family way and they had to get married. He'd laughed when Archie asked him what he meant and if it was such a problem, why had he done it?

'I don't know much about anything, do I?' he said angrily to himself. Maybe the high school was an impossible dream. What else could he do? He could damned well get a job in one of the potteries. It may not be well paid but at least he'd be working with some of the beautiful things he admired so much.

'I'll do it,' he promised himself. 'I'll damn well do it. If I can't go to school, I'll get me own job. I won't go down that awful mine and get black bits stuck all over me body like me Dad.' His voice whispered back to him in the dark, cold bedroom. He heard baby William snuffling in his drawer cot near to him. He pulled his blanket over his head in an effort to get warmer and finally fell asleep.

# CHAPTER THREE

'I s'pose I have to tell the teacher I can't go to the grammar, do I?' Archie said to his mother next morning.

'Leave it a day or two. I don't s'pose they have to know right away. Let's take time to think about it a bit. No promises mind, but we'll have to give thought to it. You're a clever little lad. You've done well, boy.'

Archie stood still, shocked at his mother's words. It was the first time in his life that he could ever remember her saying anything complimentary to him. He almost blushed with pleasure. Did this mean they were thinking it over? Something swept through his entire body. An unaccustomed feeling that he couldn't begin to describe. If this first step came true, who could know what else he might achieve? As he walked to school, his head was held just a little higher and he barely noticed the pad of brown paper wedged into the hole in his shoes. His mind was already seeing him going to the high school, along with the elite of the area. He didn't even understand why he was so driven to go to the school. After all, this was only the beginning of his education. It would take years for him to understand all the things that fascinated him.

'Well, Archie? Were your parents pleased

with you?' asked his teacher the next morning.

'I reckon so,' he replied numbly. He hoped the teacher wasn't going to ask him anything more.

'And will you be taking up the offer?'

'I expect so,' he mumbled. 'But nothing's fixed yet. There's stuff to be sorted out.' He turned and went to his place on the bench next to Billy Machin.

'I told me Mum about you,' the child whispered loudly. 'How you're going to the posh school and all. She's going to send me there, she says. So you'll still be able to do me sums for me.'

'Fat chance. You haven't got the brains.' Billy glared at him.

'Show off,' he snarled. 'I'll show yer one day. Just yer wait.'

'Quiet, you boys,' called the teacher. 'Now, let's see what you remember from the last lesson.' He set them some work to do from the board and stood silently, watching his protégé. He desperately wanted to help but could think of nothing. He could possibly provide him with the odd few books. Lend him some from his own collection but that was a mere drop in the ocean to a family like this. Maybe he should call round to see Archie's parents. He made up his mind. If this was the only thing he could do, then surely, it was his duty to do it.

'Tell your parents I'd like to call round to see them. Tomorrow night. No, tonight,' he

44

corrected. If he gave them the opportunity to refuse or postpone his visit, they might decline to see him at all.

'Yes, sir. I s'pose it'll be all right. I'll tell them,' Archie replied doubtfully. Their house was not the sort of place that teachers visited. His parents would have a fit. It might just be sensible to forget to tell them. His mum would rush round like a mad thing, trying to tidy up, getting more and more angry with everything.

When the knock came on their door, Frances cursed and asked who on earth that could be. Quick as a flash, Archie chimed in.

'Oh, I expect it's my teacher. He said he might call. I'm sorry, Mum. I forgot to tell you.' He was not put off by the withering gaze. He opened the door and ushered in the young man. He hesitated.

'I get the feeling Archie didn't warn you of my visit,' he said calmly.

'Sorry, sir, I forgot.' Archie's eyes met his and the teacher interpreted his anxious gaze.

'Hope he hasn't been causing trouble,' Ralph Barnett muttered.

'On the contrary,' Mr Gladstone replied. 'We're all very proud of him, as I expect you are. I came to ask you to allow me to offer my support and help.'

'We don't need anybody's help,' Ralph began. 'We don't accept charity.'

'I'm not offering charity. Even if I wanted to, I couldn't afford to do much to help. No, I

45

was merely going to offer the loan of a few books. I have a number which may be of use. I'm sure you're going to find it very difficult to manage and I couldn't bear the thought that he may be unable to take up this wonderful offer, all for the sake of a few pounds.'

'Aye well. We've every intention of doing our best for the lad. It's a struggle but we shall be letting him go to the school. Never had much of a chance myself, but that's no reason for him to do the same.'

Archie sat disbelieving what he was hearing. Dad sounded as though it was all arranged. The boy got up from his seat on the floor and went and stood beside his father's chair. He put a shy hand on his father's shoulder and whispered, 'Thanks, Dad. I'll make sure you're proud of me.'

'That's splendid,' said Mr Gladstone. 'Splendid.' He was wondering, perhaps uncharitably, if the result would have been quite so satisfactory had he not made this visit.

After he had left, Archie once more stood beside his father. His mother had said scarcely a word during the whole evening. She raised one eyebrow and looked expectantly at her husband.

'Aye, well I was going to tell you but hadn't got round to it. I had a talk with Mr Copestake today. He's willing for me to exchange shifts and go on to nights. That way, I'll be earning a better rate. It doesn't bother me. It's always

46

dark down the pit so what's the difference?'

'You always said you hated working the night shift,' Frances said sharply.

'It isn't so bad. Not once you're used to living back to front. Once you're down the pit, day or night is all the same. It's better money, love. The boy deserves his chance.'

'I suppose so. Take some getting used to though. You going to work when I'm going to bed. And the kids'll have to keep quiet during the day when you want to sleep. I hope you appreciate what your father's doing for you,' she snapped.

'Does that really mean I can go to the grammar?' Archie asked in a trembling voice.

'Aye, lad. But you'll have to do your bit at home as well. Like your Mum says, you'll have to keep quiet during the day and help with young William.'

'Oh I will. Promise. I can't hardly believe it. Me, at the grammar. My teacher'll be dead pleased. There's only one thing. How will I get the uniform?'

Frances's face paled. He'd have to have the real thing. Cut-downs were no good. And shoes. He'd have to have proper shoes. It was a long walk to the school and he needed proper shoes to make it there.

'Oh, Ralph. What shall we do?'

'I've given that some thought. One of the foremen has a boy at the grammar. He was saying t'other day how the lad's shot up. Had to get him new kit all round. I thought I could ask if the old one's for sale. And we can get him some shoes on tick.'

'I could get a Saturday job. They're always wanting delivery boys. I bet I can get summat.'

'Looks like it's all settled then,' Frances said with a grim look on her face. Her thin lips pursed and Archie knew at once she hated the very idea of him getting an education.

The war ended the following year, a few days short of Archie's eleventh birthday. He had been attending the grammar school for two months, clad in his handed down uniform and his first proper shoes bought from the tally man for a few pence a week. For Archie, they had been the happiest months of his life. He read avidly and was one of the most frequent visitors to the small library in the school. He began to learn Latin and quickly mastered every sort of mathematics that was put in front of him. His ambitions were always prominent in his mind and if anything disappointed him, it was the lack of time spent developing any artistic skills. But this was a small price to pay for what he saw as opportunity.

At home, things were very different. Archie's young brother, William, was a sickly child. Although quite big for his age, the baby did not thrive the way Archie had done. Perhaps it was due to the poor diet of his mother. Since the older boy had begun his grammar school, money had become even tighter. The miners still had work but they had all been put on short time. The war no longer demanded huge amounts of coal for the manufacturing industries. Despite the early optimism, life in the back streets of the Potteries certainly missed out on any sort of long-term prosperity. The Barnett family were not alone. Most folk in the street were feeling the pinch.

'We'll have to get the doctor to look at our William,' Frances said desperately to Ralph one evening. 'He's coughed and wheezed all day long and his little forehead is that hot. I'm at my wits' end. He's cried for days now and I just don't know what to do.'

'You've tried steam from the kettle?' his father asked.

'Course I have. That's the only thing we can do that doesn't cost money. Mrs Machin even gave me a bit of proper goose grease to rub on his poor little chest but it doesn't seem to have done much good.'

'Camphor,' Archie said suddenly. He was working in the dim light on his homework. 'Someone said they'd had their chest rubbed with camphor. Didn't half pong.'

'Aye, well that's as maybe. But we don't happen to have any cam what ever it is lying about the place.'

'Let's try him for one more night. If he's no better in the morning, we'll have to get the doctor round. Though how we'll pay him is

49

another matter. The child must be given his chance.'

Archie carried on with his writing. He began to feel guilty and pushed the thoughts away. If he got his education, who could tell where it might lead? Maybe his Dad could retire or at least find a job that didn't mean he had to go down the pit into whatever hell lay at the bottom. He had made few friends at his new school. Most of the boys lived close by, at the posher end of the grimy town. As soon as the bell rang at the end of the day, he had to run to get home before it was dark.

There were a mere handful of scholarship boys at the grammar, most of whom were better at their academic work than the majority of fee payers. For Archie, any new information was something to be devoured. He listened to his teachers with a rapt attention, trying to store away every word for later use. Most of the other boys thought him a swot, perhaps a bit too keen on pleasing the masters. There was, however, one boy with whom Archie had begun a sort of friendship. He was Ernie Draper Junior. They had found themselves thrown together during music lessons. Though he had never before even seen a piano close to, Archie had shown a surprising aptitude for playing. He was fascinated by the sounds and sat for several of the breaks each week, playing the keys. The music master had listened to him and had even offered to give him a few lessons. Ernie was also having lessons, though his were on an official basis, paid for by his father.

'No, Archie, it goes tum-tum-te-tum-tum,' Mr Dixon said, singing and clapping his hands together at the same time. Archie tried again and sang as he did so.

'He's got a nice voice, 'asn't 'e, sir?' Ernie said.

'Not bad. Quite untrained of course. What do you think, Archie? Would you like to attend choir practice after school?' the teacher asked.

'I would like to but I can't. I have to get back to help me Mum. There's a young'un at home, see,' he explained. ' 'E's a bit poorly and I have to help out. And besides, it's a long way to our side of the town.'

'You should try and stay, Archie,' Ernie told him later. 'It's good at choir. They give us a cup of tea and a biscuit some nights.'

'Like I said, I have to get back.'

'Maybe you could come for tea at our house one day?' the boy said suddenly. 'Mum's always asking if I want to bring someone home. I don't have any special friends though.'

'I couldn't ever ask you back to ours. In return like.' Archie felt a chill at the thought of any of the other pupils knowing the poverty in which they lived.

'That doesn't matter. Not at all. Come round on Thursday. You can come home from

51

school with me and we can do our homework together. Then we can have something to eat and maybe do a bit of music practice.'

'I dunno,' Archie replied. 'I'd have to ask me Mum and Dad. But I don't think they'd let me.'

'Ask anyhow. You can see my piano. Well, it's my Mum's really, but she doesn't play much now.'

'You got your own piano? Blimey. Are your parents very rich then?'

'I don't think so.'

'Sounds like it to me. I've got to go. I'll ask me Mum soon as I get home.' Archie skipped away and ran quickly back to the smoky, grimy place that was his home.

His parents debated his request for some time.

'It's only natural the boy would make some friends from the other end,' Ralph said. 'It's part of going to a posh school.'

'I said I was against it from the start. Giving him ideas he shouldn't have. He'll be turning into a right little snob. Mark my words. What if he wants to bring his posh friends here? How do you think we'd manage? Not likely.'

'It's all right, Mam. I'll say I can't go.' Archie turned away, almost glad to have an excuse to refuse the invitation. He wouldn't know if he was doing the right things and it might be very embarrassing. What was the good of meeting new people if your background always held you back? He made a new promise to himself. He would never be ashamed of what he was and where he came from but he was going to make every possible effort to improve himself. The way he spoke; the way he looked. He may have second hand clothes but there was no reason on earth why he should look dirty. There was plenty of water for free and even if he didn't use much soap or anything, he could wash himself thoroughly with water, at least once a day.

Ernie was waiting for him at the school gate the next morning.

'Me Mum's looking forward to seeing you. She says it's OK straight after school. And it'll all be like we said. She's getting us a nice meat pie made for tea.'

Archie listened to his new friend's words. He desperately wanted to make the visit, if only to see what it was like in someone else's house, someone from this end of the town.

'Me Mum wasn't too keen to tell the truth. She needs me to help mind me brother. He's sickly, see. Nearly drives her mad some days and if I look after him, it gives her a bit of a break.'

'Oh, go on. Just for once. Me Mum's dead set on meeting you. I've told her all about you. And me Dad'll come home early, just to see you.'

'What does your Dad do?' It was a total mystery to the boy to know how someone could simply leave work early because a friend of his son was coming for tea.

'He works in his Dad's factory. You must have heard of Draper's? They make china for the table.'

'He's a potter?'

'Well, the manager more like. He has to work hard. My Grandad's getting on a bit now. He must be nearly sixty. Me Dad'll take over properly one day soon, I expect.'

Archie knew he had to go to meet his friend's parents. He had to go. Whatever his Mum and Dad said, he knew it was the biggest chance he'd ever get to glimpse the world he longed for.

'I'll come,' he decided suddenly. Whatever it took, he had to go. Besides, the very thought of a good meat pie was making his mouth water.

That evening, Archie tackled his parents separately. First, he took his Dad on one side, while he was washing himself after work.

'I think I've offended my friend Ernie. His Mum says that you must think he isn't good enough to be my friend. When really, it's the other way round, isn't it?'

'Come on, son. That's not likely is it?'

'Well, Ernie said she was a bit put out that I said no to the invitation. They're doing a meat pie, special, like.'

'I see. You must be an honoured guest then, mustn't you? Meat Pie eh? Would that be with potatoes under the pastry?'

'I expect so,' Archie replied, mystified by his father's question.

'Seems like it's too good a chance to miss then, doesn't it?'

'Does that mean I can go?' Archie asked incredulously.

'You'll have to ask your Mum. Depends if she's willing to let you off your baby minding.'

'Do you think she will?'

'I reckon you'd better ask her.'

'Right. An' I can say you'll let me go, if it's all right with her?'

His Dad smiled and ruffled his hair. He pushed him away from the sink and Archie went into the sitting room. He repeated his story and his mother frowned. He stood twisting his hands together, almost praying that she would say yes. He didn't even know why the visit had become so important to him. Somehow, it had assumed life or death proportions.

'I s'pect you'd better go. But don't go getting any more fancy ideas. And for God's sake, don't go inviting him 'ere.'

'Oh I wouldn't. Honest. Thanks, Mum. Thanks, Dad,' he called excitedly, as he clattered up the stairs to change out of his uniform.

When Thursday came, Archie was in a state of nerves. Suppose he made an idiot of himself? He'd heard that some folks had a

55

whole lot of plates and knives and forks when they had a meal. Suppose he used the wrong things when he finally sat at the table? He'd be that embarrassed. He'd learned by now, that china on the table was much more common than he'd realised. If Ernie's Dad was a potter, they'd be sure to have loads of proper china plates from which to eat.

Ernie's house was a large, detached house in a quiet road not far from the school. They walked home, talking about things that had happened during the day. Archie looked up at the ornate roof with shiny grey tiles and decorative reddish trim on the ridge. The front had several different colours of brickwork, making patterns over the doors and windows.

'It's a very smart looking house,' Archie said conversationally. 'Very nice.'

'Come on. We'll do our homework first and then we can play the piano a bit. We'll have supper when Dad gets home.'

A maid let them in and Ernie called out to his Mother, as he dragged his friend up the biggest staircase he'd ever seen outside of the school buildings. An elegant lady came out of one of the rooms.

'Ernie, please. Where are your manners.' Her voice was soft and there was little trace of the local accent.

'Sorry, Mother. This is Archie. Archie, this is my Mother.'

'How do you do, Mrs Draper,' Archie said

carefully. He tried to remove some of his own natural accent, mimicking that of his hostess. 'I'm Archie Barnett. Pleased to meet you.'

'And I you, dear. Now would you both like a drink of milk? I think there may be some fresh scones, too.'

'Do you want some, Archie?' Ernie asked impatiently.

'Yes please,' he said, his stomach rumbling at the very thought. How often his stomach longed for food when he got home from school but he always had to wait until the evening meal was ready.

'Go into the lounge then. I'll ask Perkins to bring something on a tray.'

Archie sat uncomfortably on the edge of one of the many chairs in the room.

'Where's your piano, then?' Archie asked after a few minutes.

'Oh that. In the other sitting room. Mother calls it the drawing room. I think it's a stupid name for a room. You never draw in there.' Ernie laughed at his little joke but it was quite lost on Archie. The maid came in carrying a large tray. There were two glasses of milk and a plate of the most wonderful looking scones Archie had ever seen. There was a dish with jam and two smaller plates.

'Wow,' Archie said later, having eaten three scones and emptied the jam dish. 'That was so good. Really taken the edge off my appetite.'

'Hope it hasn't spoiled your supper. There's

a meat and potato pie and I know there's a treacle tart for afters.'

Archie grinned. Nothing could spoil his appetite. He'd already eaten as much as he normally did in an evening, and this was only the start.

'Shall we get to the homework? Old Scratcher'll kill us tomorrow, if we haven't done it.'

By the time they sat down for supper, Archie had got over his nervousness. He gazed longingly at the delicate china plates and fingered the pattern on the side plates. He picked one up and peered at the maker's stamp underneath.

'Draper's Fine Bone China,' he read aloud. 'Smart looking stuff, isn't it?'

Mrs Draper frowned almost imperceptibly. Ernie's father laughed at the boy's enthusiasm.

'The best. Well, the best for the price. We don't match up to Doulton's of course, but who knows, one day?'

'How do you get the colours to stay on?' Archie asked, staring at the fresh looking flowers that adorned the edges of his plate.

'Well, it's special paint and it's fired on. Put in kilns and cooked until it's done.'

'I didn't realise that. I knew it was fired to make it hard but I've always wondered about the rest of the processes.'

'You must get Ernie to bring you for a look round one day. He can give you a guided tour.

Would you like that?'

'Oh wow, yes please. I'd like it more than anything.' The boy sat with shining eyes. He'd known it was important to make this visit. Now he began to see why.

'If you come one Saturday morning, you'll see plenty happening. We finish at dinner time. We usually go to watch the Vale in the afternoon. You could come along with us if you like.'

Archie's eyes were nearly popping out of his head. Port Vale footballers were the local heroes. To actually go to a football match was something unheard of in his family. Visit a potbank and then go to the match. It sounded like heaven. Then he remembered his delivery job and his world crashed back to reality.

'I do a job on Saturdays,' he admitted miserably. 'I can't let them down.'

'All right, lad. Maybe you could see round the works one day in the holidays. Pity about the match but I understand. I like a lad who puts duty before pleasure. Now, who's for a bit more of this pie?'

It was almost nine by the time Archie returned to the dark back-streets that were home. The air was thicker, dirtier and smelled much more of soot at this end of town. He walked over the cobbles of the back entry and pushed open the battered back gate. It stuck on its rusty hinges as usual, as if trying to make a point and bring him back to his own world.

His Mum was sitting in the dim light, staring into the fire.

'Dad gone to work?' he asked.

'Course he has. Wherever've you been till now? I was about to send out a search party.'

'Sorry,' he muttered. 'I thought I might as well make the most of it. Mr Draper's invited me for a look round his factory. And you should see the china plates they have for eatin' off. So thin you can almost see through them if you hold them up to the light. And they've got lovely patterns on them. Flowers and real gold at the edges. I thought only royalty ate off stuff like that. Still, if you're in the trade, I s'pose you have to.'

'What a lot of nonsense, Archie. I knew it was a mistake to try and let you mix with toffs, not our sort of people. I s'pose you want all this fancy stuff on our table. Rubbish. Why waste money on things like that?'

'Just 'cos it's lovely, our Mum. Like having real flowers on the table.'

'Aye, well. For them as got money to waste. D'ya want owt?'

'No thanks, Mum. I couldn't eat another thing. In fact, I think I feel a bit queasy. I'll just go up the yard, a minute.' The larger than usual quantities of food were beginning to lie rather heavily in his stomach.

'Crikey,' he muttered as he groped his way along to the outside lavatory, 'I hope I'm not sick. It'd be a terrible waste of all that good food.'

## CHAPTER FOUR

After the war was finally over, everyone had expected things to return to the way they always had been. As the soldiers returned back home, they soon realised that things would never be quite the same again. Many of them were wounded, if not in body, then in mind. A few were fit enough to return to their former work but many of them were forced to take less demanding jobs. The excitement of war ending and new beginnings for everyone never seemed to live up to the promise. For Archie, school remained fascinating but as money grew tighter, the family had to face the inevitable.

'Your Dad and me have to talk to you,' his mum said a few days before his fourteenth birthday.

'What's up, Mum?' he asked cheerfully, expecting her to ask him to do a few extra chores. William was still suffering from very poor health and now he was almost three, he needed extra medicine and even the occasional doctor's visit.

'We'll wait for your Dad. Now, have you done your homework?'

'No. Just going to do it.' He stared at his

mother. Usually, she tried to get him to do anything, rather than suggest homework. 'Oh, Mrs Draper's asked me round again, by the way. On Friday. Is it OK?'

'We'll have to see, son,' Frances replied. She looked upset but took a breath and snapped at him in her usual way.

After tea that evening, William was put to bed and Archie sat down between his solemn faced parents.

'This is hard for me to say, Archie. You must have realised things have got much tougher lately. The thing is, I've been taken off night shifts. The colliery's going on to short time now the war's over. The night shift is the first to be cut back. They've tried to make it fair and cut everyone's time so they don't have to sack too many but it means that we're going to be very strapped for cash.'

'I see. Maybe I could get some more errands?'

'It's more serious than that, lad,' his mother said. 'We need more than a few pennies.'

'How d'ya mean?'

'I'm sorry but there's nowt for it but you leavin' that posh school you're so fond of.' The words came out in a rush and Archie almost failed to understand.

'I'm sorry, lad. So very sorry,' Dad said. 'I know how much it means to you.'

'What d'ya mean? I'll have to stop going to school for ever?'

'I'm afraid so,' Ralph replied.

'It was never a good idea in the first place,' Frances snapped. 'I was always against it. Giving you ideas that you're summat special. Better than the rest of us. You start work Monday.'

'On Monday?' Archie echoed. 'Next Monday.'

'Aye, lad,' his Dad said gently. 'Mr Copestake's come up with a job for you. Don't worry, you won't have to go down the pit. It's on the surface. You'll be working in the office. I told him you've got a real feel for numbers and he's going to give you a chance to help the clerks out. It won't pay much but it'll make up the difference between what I was getting and my wages after the cut backs.'

'But Dad. Mum. I can't work at the pit. I just can't. Everything's so black there. The air's grey and so are the people. Everything's dirty and . . .' The boy's voice failed him. All his dreams of working in the china factory, were disappearing. His visions of beautiful things to lighten their drab, grey lives were vanishing.

'Don't talk rubbish, boy,' his Mother said roughly. 'Your Father's worked there all his life and he doesn't complain. Besides, the pot banks are hardly clean, are they? Just 'ave to look at the smoke pouring out of them kilns. Filthy places.'

'I didn't do very well in maths this term,'

Archie lied rebelliously. 'I doubt I'd be any good at working in the offices.' He scrubbed fiercely at his eyes, trying to stop the tears from streaming down. He bit hard at his knuckles. His Mother would pour scorn on him if he broke down now.

'I'm sorry, son. I've really let you down, haven't I?' Archie looked hard at him as his Father spoke. The kindly man looked as if he were about to burst into tears as well. Poor Ralph. He'd always tried so hard to keep his first son at school and his efforts had failed.

' 'S'all right,' he managed to stammer. 'But I'd still like to go to the Drapers' on Friday.' With that, he turned and ran upstairs to the small, cold room he shared with his little brother. He stared at the sleeping toddler and cursed him. Then he felt very bad.

'Poor little sod. You didn't ask to be born, did you? It isn't your fault if you're always being ill.' He leaned over and gave him a guilty peck on the cheek. Then, fully clad, he lay back on his bed, staring up at the ceiling. It was almost dark. He put his mind to thinking, thinking harder than he had ever done in his life before. He dreaded the next two or three days . . . his last days at his beloved school. He'd had such high hopes that it would make all the difference. But this wasn't the reality. He must leave it all behind and forget his dreams. At least he'd be spared the unkind taunts and gibes of some of the other boys.

Because there were rarely any faults in his work, they found other things to ridicule. The blazer he had worn so proudly was now threadbare. They laughed at his socks which were definitely not regulation but his mother's old stockings, folded down into his shoes. They too were becoming worn out and more than once, he'd padded out the soles with pieces of old card. But he could cope with any amount of derision knowing he was better at most things than they were. And he had his friend Ernie. Their friendship had continued over the months and Archie had become a regular visitor at their home. He and Ernie played the piano together and sometimes they even sang some of the popular songs of the day, learned from records played on the brand new wind-up gramophone recently bought by Mr Draper. He had an ability to pick up a tune and play it on the piano, a talent envied by Ernie who often struggled with his lessons.

The factory owner had kept his word and shown the boys round the factory one day during the holidays. Archie had never forgotten it. The magical smells of paint and turps, linseed oil and the huge numbers of paintbrushes set at the desks of the paintresses. He marvelled even at the palettes, in reality tiles, covered in heaps of multi-coloured splodges, making their own statement. The rest of the factory had been interesting but it was the decorating shops that really enthused and inspired him. He had stood for as long as he was allowed, watching the women putting the delicate swirls of colour on the pottery. He was fascinated by some of the odd colours before they were fired.

'You can hardly believe that funny brown colour will come out bright blue when it's cooked . . . fired, I mean. And the reds look almost black sometimes.'

Some of the plates had what seemed like real pictures painted on them. Birds, fruit, flowers; each was a unique work of art, like a painting. Only the master painters were working on these and the 'girls' would fill in the simpler parts of the borders or some blocks of colour. Some of the plates were edged with transfers, strips of tissue-like material that were burnt away in the firing. These plates were much quicker to make and so were cheaper to buy. When Archie saw them, he promised himself that when he worked in a factory like this one, he would buy a set of plates for his Mum. Then, she might begin to understand why he wanted to follow his dream.

He gave a start and returned to the reality of a dark room and lying on his bed in his clothes. The house was silent. He must have fallen asleep and now his parents had also gone to bed. He felt once again his anger at his parents' plans for his future. He almost wished he'd never attended the wretched school in the first place. Perhaps his parents were right. It could then have remained a dream of what might have been. This was his punishment for being proud, for thinking himself so much better than he was. He'd thought himself better than his own father, a man who'd always worked so hard for his family, never even considering his own wishes. Maybe, once his dad had also had dreams. Maybe he'd wanted to make something better of his life. He got up and removed his school clothes. He'd cop another scolding in the morning when everything was creased and there was no time to press anything. What did it matter? There would only be a few more days. He rubbed his eyes hard to remove the tears that were gathering. His mother would be very scornful if she knew he was crying. She didn't believe in it or any other emotions, come to that.

He dozed on and off through the night. Each time he awoke, he felt the heaviness of disappointment tumble over him. He tried not to go to sleep at all, so that he didn't have to keep waking up and feeling so bad all over again. At six o'clock, he got up quickly and dressed. He could hear his mother downstairs. The fire was riddled noisily, a sign of her bad temper. He heard the kettle banged onto the hob. At least he'd get a cup of tea. He ought not to grumble. He was coming up to fourteen that year. He'd had more schooling than many of the lads around here. But to go to work in the pit. He couldn't face it.

'You look a mess,' his mother announced as he came down the stairs.

'Sorry. Is the kettle nearly boiled?'

'I reckon so. D'ya want a piece of bread and dripping?' she asked.

'Yes please,' he said enthusiastically. 'I'm starving.'

They said little more to each other, each busy with their own thoughts. They were like two strangers who had run out of pleasantries.

'You'll have to send a letter to the headmaster,' Archie said, at last.

'You can tell 'im, can't you?'

'It will have to be official, like. He might not believe me.'

'Why wouldn't he?' she said with a blank expression.

'Cos some lads try it on all the time. 'Sides, there's the scholarship I won. The school has to give it to someone else. And we might have to pay the money back,' he added out of sheer devilment.

'Load o' rot if you ask me.'

'Well, if you want me to leave, you have to say so in writing.' Archie spoke firmly, gazing at his mother with clear green eyes. She stared back, undergoing inner turmoil. She and her son both knew she could neither read nor write legibly. The boy was quite intelligent enough to recognise that her bluster was designed to cover her own inadequacies.

'You'd best ask your Dad this evening. Now get off with you. You'll be late and then they'll be givin' ya the push anyhow.'

Archie set out on the long walk to school. It was early spring and a bright sunny day. Even the heavy layer of dark cloud which usually hung over the whole area was penetrated by shafts of sun. Ernie was waiting at the school gate.

'Wotcha,' he called. 'How did you get on with that Latin homework? I got stuck. Wished you lived a bit nearer so I could ask you.'

'I didn't do it,' Archie admitted. Once the dreadful conversation had begun last night, all thoughts of homework had totally left his mind.

'Old Scratcher'll kill ya,' Ernie exclaimed. 'Blimey. Not like you to miss out on your homework.'

'I'n't worth it. Don't tell anyone will you?' His friend shook his head. 'I'm leaving at the end of this week. Have to get a job. Me Dad's bin put on short time.'

'Crikey. I'll miss ya, lad,' Ernie said, a look of horror on his face. How on earth would he manage without Archie? The other lads teased him and called him names, just because he liked music and hated sport. 'Where you going to work?'

'Me Dad's fixed something at the pit. Above ground, thank heavens.'

'But I thought you wanted to work in the

69

potbanks.'

'Course I do but who'd take me on? I don't know anything. I can draw a bit but I'm not good enough for any of the decent firms.'

'D'ya want me to have a word with me Dad? He might tek yer on.'

'D'ya think he would? That'd be a blinkin' miracle. I'd do anything. I'm big for my age and quite strong. I'm growing all the time so it wouldn't be long before I can lift the saggers, if that's what he'd want me to do. I wouldn't care.' Archie's eyes were bright at the thought of any chance of reprieve from working in the coal mines.

Somehow he survived the day without getting killed by Scratcher, the Latin master. As he was leaving, he cornered Ernie once more.

'You will ask your Dad for me, won't you? I'm depending on you.'

'Course I will. You'd better come round for tea tomorrow and then he can talk to you. You should be OK. He likes you, ya know.' Ernie knew than if his dad employed his friend, there was a good chance they'd be able to stay friends. Their backgrounds couldn't have been more different but they had a deep affinity. Neither of them made real friends with the other boys and they had formed a close bond.

'Thanks, mate. You're a good pal. I'll come round after school tomorrow, then. I can tell me Mum tonight. Sure your Mum won't mind?

She did say Friday and it'll only be Wednesday tomorrow.'

'She won't care,' Ernie assured him. 'She likes yer as well. Cheerio then.'

Archie went home much more slowly than usual. It was as if he wanted to savour each little part of his routine, which was to end so soon. If only Mr Draper could have faith in him. He knew he could or would do anything for this chance.

'Your Dad'll send a letter with you tomorrow,' his Mother said brusquely. 'He's getting some paper and an envelope from the shop on his way home. You finish school Friday and start work on Monday, like we arranged. I don't want you carrying on about it. It's all over and done with. Right?'

'Right, Mum. How's William today? Is his chest better?'

'You'll not get round me with your soft soap. He's better. Not much mind you, but his breathin's a bit easier. Now, get out from under my feet. I've work to do.'

Archie wandered into the grimy backyard. He stood staring at the black walls and grey slates of the roofs. This was an awful place to live, day after day. We should paint our door red. Bright red, he thought to himself. He gave a rueful smile. When would there ever be any money for paint? The rooms inside were just as bad. There may once have been a pattern on the wallpaper but it had long ago faded into uniform brown with occasional darker brown blots. One day, he would live somewhere where there was light. Bright sunshine getting into every window. On top of a hill. High over the town, looking towards the country. The sound of his little brother wailing as usual brought him back from his forlorn dreams. Whatever else happened, he was leaving school on Friday. He wondered if Ernie was talking to his Dad yet. He went back inside and picked up his parcel of books. Quietly, he sat at the kitchen table and began to do his homework.

'Don't know why you're botherin' with all that rubbish,' his Mother scolded. 'Ain't worth it as you're leavin' any'ow.'

But the boy plodded on with the irregular French verbs and Latin translation. She was right, his Mum. French and Latin would be of no use to him ever again. But there was a sort of ritual in his working, as if he were trying to lessen this period of impending bereavement.

'You'll have to move in a few minutes. Load a rubbish. Givin' you fancy ideas. Set the table for tea.' Why did his Mother always resent him working on school things? He made a promise to himself. Whatever happened, he'd find some way of continuing his studies. Somehow, he had to try and keep learning new things.

'Me Mum and Dad say it's all right for you to come round tonight,' Ernie announced at the school gate. Archie gave a jump. What with everything else, he'd forgotten to tell his Mum. He'd have to run home first or she'd be very angry with him. Anything to do with school or the Drapers made her angry.

'Thanks, Ernie. Did you ask your Dad if he'd got any jobs going?'

'I did. He wants to talk to you when you come round tonight. He didn't say *yes* but he didn't say *no* either.'

'Sounds all right. Look, I'd better go in cos I have to see the Head. I've got me Dad's letter.' He touched his pocket, unwilling to show his friend the ink blotted envelope with his Father's scrawl written on it. His Father may have been able to read and write a bit, but even his writing was little better than that of a small child.

'Eh, Archie, this place is going to be grim without ya, ya know.'

'You'll be all right, lad. Keep on graftin' with your head down and you'll come out right. You're a bright enough lad.'

Ernie looked down. His own eyes were just a little tearful and he daren't let anyone see him or he'd get teased even more. Get accused of being a mummy's boy, the worst thought possible.

'Right. We'd better get to it then. I'll see ya later.'

At the end of the day, he left Ernie to walk slowly home while he ran back to his own home to tell his Mum that he would be out for tea. Unusually, she wasn't at home when he arrived. The back door was open as normal but there was no sign of either her or his brother. He cursed and pulled out a bit of paper from his exercise book. Quickly, he scribbled a note and left it on the table, before running out again and to his friend's house.

Mrs Draper welcomed him, as always, and commiserated on the change in his circumstances.

'Such a pity when a bright young man is forced to abandon his studies,' she said with a sympathetic smile. 'But let's hope this isn't the end of your friendship with Ernie. I know how fond of you he is.' Archie felt embarrassed. Nobody in his family ever really mentioned how they were feeling about anyone else. It simply wasn't done.

'Reckon I'll miss old Ernie as well,' he mumbled.

The two boys went up to Ernie's room and listened to some records. Somehow, Archie could not enjoy the lively tunes or even talk much. He was busy with his own thoughts and however much his friend tried to take his mind off his gloomy future, he continued to sit staring into nothingness. They heard the front door shut and looked at each other. It was Mr Draper returning home and the hour when Archie might learn his fate. They sat motionless, quiet as they waited for a summons from downstairs. It would either come as a call for tea or a request for Archie to go into the study. Tea came first, almost to Archie's disappointment. The tension of sitting through a meal was almost too much. As usual, Mrs Draper had laid on a good spread with a pork pie, ham and salad and a huge crusty loaf. There were several kinds of cake to follow, all of which Archie would normally have devoured with an appetite approaching greed. Today, he toyed with his generous plate of food, as Mrs Draper watched him anxiously.

'Aren't you feeling well, dear?' she asked.

'He's worried,' Ernie said confidently. 'Knows he's having to leave the school to make a living and he doesn't know where it's coming from.' His parents stared as they heard his words.

'I'm sorry, lad,' Mr Draper said kindly. 'Didn't realise it meant so much to you. Think our Ernie'd be off and away from school tomorrow, if I'd let him. Eat up your supper now. And don't worry. I reckon as we can work summat out.'

'Really, sir?' Archie burst out. 'Do ya really think ya can give me a job?'

'I reckon so. But come on now, eat up or my wife'll think there's summat wrong with the food and she'll be that upset, I'll not know what to do with her.'

Archie stared at Ernie's Mum. He couldn't imagine anyone being upset about food being left but then, in his own house, there was rarely enough food for one meal, not to mention leftovers. The boy's grin was enough to cheer all the Draper family and the rest of the meal became a happier occasion. Once the plates were emptied and the final drop of tea drunk, Mr Draper rose to his feet and, looking serious, asked Archie to accompany him into the study. It was the first time he'd entered the rather dark room, which was always kept locked. It was business-like, with a large desk dominating the space. Bookshelves lined the walls and boxes of loose papers filled the lower shelves. Archie had never seen so many books in one house. Mr Draper followed his eyes.

'Always been a bit of a soft touch for buying books,' he muttered. 'You'll be needing to read a few of them if you're to get on in the pottery trade. All sorts of technical stuff here. Now, down to brass tacks, as they say. It's all a bit hard going at the moment. But I think we're getting over the worst. I'm prepared to offer you an apprenticeship. A proper one. Papers an' all. You'll no doubt want to be working on the decorating and design side eventually, but I'd like you to have a thorough grounding first. No good starting in one place without knowing what's involved in the rest of the works. I've said the same to Ernie, though he shows little enough interest in my business. Maybe with you working there, he'll change his ideas in the future. Now, lad, fire away with your questions. I can see by your face that you're nearly bustin'.'

'Thank you, sir,' Archie stammered. He was so overcome he was almost speechless. 'Thank you. I can hardly believe my luck.' His eyes were wide and he knew that tears weren't too far away. Even if men weren't supposed to cry, he felt pretty close to it. He wasn't used to people being kind.

'It's all right, me boy. Don't think I'm doing you any favours. You'll have to work. Work bloody hard, I can tell you. And if you don't come up to scratch, you'll get your cards like anyone else. It'll be the usual five year apprenticeship before you decide exactly where you'll be working.'

'Er . . . well, thanks a lot. You've been more than kind but you do understand that I have to earn some money. That's why I've got to leave school. Me Dad's been put on short time and we haven't got enough coming in. Me brother's always being poorly and we sometimes even have to get the doctor in. Expensive business being ill, me Mum says.'

'You'll not be getting much of a wage, not while you're learning. The pay's usually eight shillings and sixpence a week for the lads. I'll start you off on that and we'll see how you go on. That satisfactory for you?'

'Thanks very much, Mr Draper. I think that should satisfy me Mum. I haven't given much thought to actual wages. But they'll be saving

77

money anyhow when they don't have to keep me in clothes for school.'

Mr Draper looked at the boy's shabby, worn clothing and bit his lip. Poor little tyke. He'd had to *make do* with everything in life, so far. If he'd thought the family would accept it, he would even have sponsored the boy's stay at school himself. If nothing else, it would have been worth it to keep his own son happy. But he knew that for one thing, the parents wouldn't allow it and for another, it would smack of the sort of charity that would never be acceptable these days. He hoped that, at least, a new start would herald the beginning of something better for Archie. The boy had guts and he was obviously determined to make something of himself. One day, he'd probably end up at least as a manager in the decorating shop or even better.

'Right. Well, I'll get the papers drawn up and you can start on Monday. Now, you'd better get back to my son or he'll complain he's hardly seen you. I hope you two will stay friends. You'll have to come round for your tea on a Sunday in future. I shall want to keep in touch with how things are going. I should warn you. Don't talk about your friendship with Ernie to the other men. It won't do you any favours if they think you're too much at home with the bosses.'

At eight o'clock, Archie took his leave of the family who had become his benefactors.

He shook hands with the parents and even with Ernie. Two more days at school and he'd become a working man. He ran all the way home, much happier with the prospect of his new future. He arrived home, only to have his bubble of happiness burst.

'Where the bloody hell have you been till now?' his Mother yelled as he clattered in through the door.

'At the Drapers'. I came home to tell you but you weren't here. I did leave you a note.'

'What's the use of that? I can't read, you smart arse. Just trying to show me up, were you? Never could read, so now you know. I didn't have expensive schooling like some as I could mention. Going off to your posh friends and leaving me with the baby to cope with. I 'specially needed you this evening to sit with him. Mrs Harris next door was taken poorly and I had to go and help out.'

Archie stared at his mother. It was the first time she had ever acknowledged the fact that she couldn't read.

'I'm sorry, Mum. But it wasn't just for tea. Mr Draper's offered me an apprenticeship. In his factory. I can work in the potbank, just like I always wanted.'

'Potbanks? Rubbish. Your Dad's sorted you a job and you start on Monday. That's an end to it. Ya can hold ya tongue 'cos I don't want to hear any more of it. Now get up those stairs and I don't want to hear another sound out of you. You're lucky I don't take a broom handle to your backside.'

'How much would I be gettin', at the pit, like?' Archie asked, crossing his fingers. It was the one sure fire thing his Mum would know to the last halfpenny.

'Seven shillings a week. Make all the difference that will.'

'Mr Draper's offered me eight shillings and sixpence and a proper apprenticeship with papers and everything.' The eight and sixpence was his trump card. Frances Barnett stopped and stared.

'Eight and sixpence eh? S'pose that's cos he knows you.'

'No, Mum. All the lads get that rate. He said so. And if I turn out to be any use, he'll probably review it. That means increase it. Oh, Mum. Please. It's just what I want to do.'

'I don't think it's that simple.' She continued. 'Your Dad has gone to a lot of trouble to get you the position. His own job could be lost, if you mess him about. Then where'd we be? You can hardly keep a family on eight shillings and sixpence a week.'

Archie felt his world crashing around him once more. His life seemed to flit from one crisis to the next. Just when he'd thought things were going to work out, this new situation arose. How on earth could he tell Mr Draper that he couldn't, after all, take up his offer? Probably the same difficulty as his father faced with his boss. There was nothing to be done for the moment. Once Dad came home, he'd tackle him, man to man. His Mother didn't really understand business. How could she? Women had nothing to do with such matters.

## CHAPTER FIVE

'I really don't know,' Ralph Barnett said later that evening. Although he was back on days which were the lower paid shifts, occasionally he was offered overtime to cover for absence or if there was extra work on. It was almost eleven o'clock when he returned, exhausted. In just a few more hours, he would be on his way back through the grimy streets. He was bone weary and longed for something to eat and his bed. Instead, he faced an angry wife demanding that he 'tell the lad straight' what he was to do. The *lad* in question was still sitting at the bottom of the stairs, quite unable to sleep or even go to bed. His wonderful offer of a job had been belittled by his Mother. She simply didn't understand. To her, work was work. You did it for the money, whatever it entailed.

'It looks to me as if our lad has shown a bit of initiative and got himself sorted with a job he'll like. I can't quite see why meself, but I

81

can understand he doesn't want to go down the pit. It's now a matter of who we tell and what we tell them. I'll have to see Mr Copestake or else Archie has to go and see his friend Mr Draper. On balance, I'd say he's got better prospects with the Drapers.'

'Yes,' whispered Archie in some triumph. 'And it's one and sixpence a week more money, Dad,' he pointed out, slightly more loudly in case his mother hadn't taken it in.

'I'm more sorry than I can say, that it's come to this, lad. Leaving school and all. I had such high hopes for you. You go and get yourself to bed. I'll have another word with Mr Copestake tomorrow. I reckon he'll just have to continue to manage without you on the books.'

'Aw thanks, Dad,' the boy said. 'I'll make you proud of me, Dad. Honest I will.' He turned and rushed upstairs. He too had an early start the next day and not much night left for him to try and sleep. He may have to give up his learning at school but he was going to make a start on his adult life. He had the chance to work somewhere he was sure he was going to like.

The last two days of school flew by for Archie. Surprisingly, his teachers expressed sorrow that he was leaving. Even old Scratcher shook him by the hand, telling him never to stop learning. 'There will always be something new to discover, every single day,' the old teacher told him.

Ernie was distraught. No longer would he have anyone to chat to at play times. And who would support him against the other boys? His own life was about to change for the worse. Once Archie was working, he'd be sure to lose interest in his friend and there would be no more collaborating on homework. How would he ever manage mathematics without Archie's good sense to put him on the right track? They walked home together, for the last time.

'You'll be a working man, come Monday,' Ernie said sadly. 'No more time for us schoolkids.'

'I'd sort of hoped we could still be friends. I know it'd be difficult, your Dad being me boss and all that. But maybe we could meet up sometimes. You can tell me about what you're learning and I might even keep up a bit with me education.'

'You'll be making new friends. Workmates. You'll soon forget about me, mark my words,' Ernie replied wisely. 'But, I s'pose you can still come for your tea sometimes. Maybe on a Saturday or Sunday? Wouldn't do for you to be seen coming home with my Dad, after work. I reckon you'd get some stick from the other lads at the factory.'

They shook hands, marking a formal end to their school friendship. Archie returned home, sad and not a little daunted at the prospect of becoming a working man. His parents were also aware of the change that was about to happen. On the table stood a can with a handle over the top and a lid. It had once been enamelled but most of this had worn off, leaving the bare metal beneath.

'What's this then?' asked Archie, blushing slightly. He knew very well what it was. All the workers round these parts had one. Known as mashing cans, they carried the worker's lunch or liquid refreshment for the working day. If there was a stew or some soup, the mashing cans were stood against a stove or if they worked in the potbanks, against the kilns to keep hot.

'It's for you, son,' his Mother said. 'I got it down the market. You'll need it, working in that hot place.'

'Thanks, Mum. I appreciate it. I'll be a proper wage-earner come Monday, with me very own mashing can. I'd best get upstairs and take off me uniform, for the last time.'

It was a strange weekend. He did his Saturday errands, handing over the pennies to his Mother as usual. He was very surprised when she gave him a penny back to spend on himself. He could buy sweets or even a comic or maybe a Woodbine from Mrs Machin's. He knew she split the packs and sold the cigarettes singly to those who couldn't afford a whole pack in one go. It was a hard decision. He finally bought a comic as it would last longer, and sat on the back step, laughing at the crazy antics of the characters. The pictures were simple, crude even. He knew he could easily copy them and possibly make his own improvements. He still had a few sheets of paper left in his old exercise books and was determined to have a go. Come a few years, he'd be a professional designer and the more things he could turn his hand to, the better. He sat for several hours on the Sunday morning trying and trying to get the figures to look the way they did in his comic. He quite changed his mind about it being easy. It took skills he didn't have to make the figure seem to move rather than be a static, lifeless picture. He persevered until finally, just before tea, he was satisfied with his results. He propped up his best picture against the window where he could see the light shining through it. He realised with a start that this time tomorrow, he'd have finished his first day at work. It was a very scary thought.

Archie would never forget his first day. He walked into the factory, half fearful and half excited. The smell hit him as he went in through the factory gates. The bottle kiln had just been opened after cooling over the weekend. The heat wafted across the yard and he could see the fiery glow of the heated pottery still inside. He walked towards the office, unsure about where he was supposed to be starting. There was a smart woman sitting behind the desk. She wore a pair of spectacles perched on her nose and she raised an irritated glance towards the scruffy child.

'What are you doing in here?' she demanded. 'This is the office. Not a place for the workmen.'

'If you please, Ma'am,' Archie said, doffing his cap. 'If you please, Mr Draper said to report to work this morning. And I didn't know where to go.'

'What's your name, boy?'

'Archie Barnett, if you please.'

'Oh. Yes.' She gave a disapproving sniff. 'I believe Mr Draper may have mentioned that you were coming. You're to report to the clay shop. Like as not they'll set you on fetching the clay up.'

Archie stared. He hadn't given much thought to this side of things. Fetching clay up sounded like hard work. Dirty work as like as not. His Mum had insisted he went to work in the best clothes he had. He twisted his hands as he stood in front of the high desk. The woman pushed her glasses to the end of her nose and peered over them.

'What are you waiting for?' she demanded.

'It's just that . . . well . . . I don't know where the clay shop is. And what do I do about overalls? I didn't know what I'd be doing this morning. I've come in me good stuff.'

The woman sniffed, looking even more disapproving.

'Even more stupid than you look,' she snapped. 'You supply your own overalls, naturally. Are you sure they're the best clothes you have? Looks like they're ready enough for the rag and bone man.'

'That'll do, Miss Baines,' said a familiar voice behind him. 'Mornin', Archie. Glad to see you bright and early. I'll see the boy in my office, Miss Baines. We'll get his indentures sorted and signed. And I'll have a cup of something hot. Dare say Archie would like something too, wouldn't you, lad? See to it please, Miss Baines.' Archie caught sight of the glare from the woman as he followed Mr Draper through a door at the side of the front office. He did not know it yet, but he had made his first enemy. Elsie Baines considered herself far too good to fetch and carry for some brat.

'Right, lad. Let's get you sorted,' said Mr Draper, walking round his large desk. Archie gazed at the untidy room, taking in shelves of books to do with the various manufacturing processes, law, taxes and dozens more subjects that left him guessing. On the desk itself, apart from the clear space round a large leather blotter, there were several pieces of unfinished pottery, drawings and strange, glass-like objects that bore signs of being subjected to some great heat. He could have spent hours just looking. His heart thudded in his chest. This was the real beginning of adult life. This was where he wanted to be.

'I've got your papers here, if you'd like to

look over them and then sign at the bottom.'

'I thought you wanted me to work for a trial period first,' Archie said doubtfully.

'Aye, well I decided there was no need for that. I know you well enough, lad. I know what you're made of. I hope we shall be working together for a good few years, long after the apprenticeship is over and done.'

'But won't the others think it's a bit strange? I mean to say, I expect they've all had to wait for a time before their apprenticeship began.' Archie was worried that he'd be seen as the boss's pet and given a hard time as a result.

'Let's say it's your education that has pushed you forward a bit. Ah, here's Miss Baines with our coffee.'

The secretary came into the room with a tray of coffee and wearing a scowl enough to turn the milk sour, Archie thought. She banged the tray down and turned to leave.

'Thanks, Miss,' Archie said loudly. She hesitated and gave another of her disapproving sniffs.

'That'll be all thanks, Miss Baines,' Mr Draper said to her retreating figure. She reacted with the merest ripple running through her skinny shoulders. 'Now, Archie, how do you like your coffee?'

'I don't know, sir. We usually has tea. I have that with milk.'

'Then I'll pour you some with milk. This is just to celebrate your first day, you

88

understand. It certainly isn't the normal thing for new employees. Only I promised Mrs Draper that I'd see you right. Insisted on it, she did. Now then, this is the plan. I shall start you in the clay shop. You'll learn how the clay is prepared first off. I shall expect you to be an expert in everything to do with the clay, by the time you're done. We'll move on to the rest of the process later. Understand?'

'Yes, sir. Thank you, sir. What sort . . . I mean, how should . . . oh hang it. I've only got me best clothes to come out in. What am I supposed to wear? Me Mam wouldn't take too kindly if me Sunday suit was covered in white clay dust.'

Mr Draper smiled.

'How's your coffee, lad?'

'Very nice thank you.'

'Then why is it going cold in the cup? You don't like it, do you?'

'It's like pussy pee and pepper, to be honest. Sorry, sir. Shouldn't have said that.'

'Don't worry about it. Now. About your clothes. I reckon you should have a proper set of overalls. I'll see what we can do. Don't worry about it for today. I expect you'd like to have a look around. See where everything is. I won't take you myself. The men'd give you stick afterwards. Don't worry. I'll organise something. You can start properly tomorrow. Don't look so worried. I'll still be paying you the full week.'

'You're being really good to me, Mr Draper. I'm ever so grateful.'

'Think nothing of it. You've been a good pal to my Ernie. He's going to miss having you to stick up for him at school. Oh, and don't say anything about the overalls. They'll all be demanding to have them supplied, if they know. Right then. Just you cast your eyes over these 'ere papers while I see who's available to give you the grand tour. Once you've been round, you can spend the rest of the day somewhere that interests you. Watch the men and women at work. You'll learn by what you see.'

As Mr Draper went out into the reception area, Archie sat looking at the large, impressive looking document and decided he could make neither head nor tail of it. He picked up the pen Mr Draper had left on the desk to sign the bottom line. If Mr Draper was prepared to take a gamble on him, he reckoned it must be OK for him to sign something without really looking at it. No-one need know.

'Right. Young Ned Reed's coming to take you round. Nice lad but a bit simple. He's everyone's gofer. They're always sending him for something stupid. Brushes to paint stripes, cat's whisker paint, rubber hammers, you name it. He's harmless though and knows his way around. I'll be seeing you then, lad.'

Archie got up and went out into the

reception. Miss Baines was still sitting at her desk, looking disapproving.

'I hope you don't think you'll get this treatment every day. I thought as how you'd come here to work, not sit around like management drinking coffee all day.'

'Thank you for making it,' Archie said, at a loss to know how to treat this woman. He decided she was probably a dried up old spinster with a fancy for her boss. Only he was married, and had a kid, so she was left with no chance of her own happiness. He was surprisingly accurate in his estimation, except for her age. She was only in her early twenties but was the type of woman who had looked and acted middle aged, ever since she left school.

'This is Ned Reed. He's come to give your highness the guided tour. You have to watch what you say to this one, Ned. He's a special pal of the boss's.' Ned looked over Archie's clothes and down at his shoes. He looked into his face and at his untidy hair.

' 'E dunna look much like th'boss.'

'You're right, Ned Reed. Maybe he just hopes he'll be th'boss himself someday. Now, get out of my sight the pair of you. Some of us have got work to do.'

The two boys, much of an age, began their tour round the factory. They crossed the yard to the clay end and Archie watched as a cart came in through the tunnel, the only way in and out of the factory. Workers and raw materials came in; finished goods went out. Dust hung in the air. The buildings were a uniform greyish colour from the smoke and clay dust. The boy gave a small rueful smile. He'd complained at the dirty, dismal life of the miners but this wasn't really so much better. All the same, there was a world of difference between the end products from here and those of the coal pits. The large man who looked after the Lodge was going back into his room, holding his sheaf of papers as he clocked everything that came in and went out. Nothing escaped his eye and woe betide anyone who tried to take anything out that they shouldn't.

The clay workshop was noisy. The steam engine ground along, filling the air with clanking sounds as the clay was prepared. Bemused, Archie watched the various machines as the clay was processed. Some of it was made into a liquid for casting into moulds. That was called slip he was told. Other clay was kneaded and worked until it could be pressed into solid lumps for the potters to shape into flatware, using various machines and sometimes, the potter's wheels he'd expected to see.

'I didn't know they pressed stuff on machines,' he said to the man he would be assisting, once he started work proper. 'I thought it was all made by hand.'

'It's the finishin' that's all done by hand. But

don't let it fool yer. There's real skill in getting the clay just right and putting the exact amount on the jig. Get it wrong and the plate or saucer or whatever won't be up to standard. That's money off your wages. All piece work here, you know. You get paid for each piece. The more you makes, the more cash in the wage packet.'

'Oh. I thought I'd be getting a regular wage.'

'Oh I see. One of the apprentices are you? Who are you with?'

'I don't know. You to start with, then I move to the next shop. Get a picture of the whole job, start to finish.'

'I see. Sounds like you're aiming for the top. What the 'eck made you want to start here?'

'Well, I know Mr Draper like, well his son, really . . .'

'I hope you're not some sort of spy. Don't like them sort, do we Ned?'

'No, Mr Clough. Miss Baines says as how you've got to watch him.'

'But you haven't. I'm not any sort of spy. I just want to learn everything I can about making pots. Honest. I want to paint and make designs. I shall do one day, just you wait and see.' He scrubbed angrily at his face, scared that he might shed a tear in his passionate desire to be a part of this world. Nobody could understand how very much it meant to him.

'We'll see, lad. You'd best get round to see the rest,' Mr Clough said more kindly. 'Make the most of it. I'll be working you very hard after today.'

Though Archie had visited the factory once before, guided by Mr Draper and Ernie, he didn't remember it very clearly. Ned was called away to do his own work, so Archie was left to look round on his own. He spent much of the day in the paint shop, watching the girls painting delicate patterns on the edges of plates. The gilders added dark brown stripes to cup handles and spun dishes on small, heavy wheels. He was amazed at their skill. Always exactly the right amount of the gold pigment to complete a circle and perfect symmetry of the brush strokes. It looked very easy but at once he recognised the skill behind the simple actions. Many of the dishes arrived with transfer patterns already made and they had to be finished with touches of hand painting. On first sight, it looked like cheating, he thought. Once he had seen the patterns made from engraved copper plates, he realised that the process was very hard work. Paint was rubbed onto the copper and tissue paper placed over the engraving and rolled, to pick up the paint. He watched some girls as well as men, rubbing down with enormous effort to make the printed pattern transfer to the china plates. If the paper tore when it was being applied, it was useless and all that energy was wasted. Even worse, it had to be scrubbed off and the whole process started again.

94

'There's a lot more to it than I realised,' he said to friendly looking woman.

'Aye, lad. It's hard work. There's some as can do it and some as can't. My Florrie can't for one. Useless she was. But look at her gilding in the paint shop and you couldn't fault it.'

'Who's Florrie?' Archie asked.

'My eldest. Two more of 'em work as cup handlers. Me youngest son starts soon down the clay end.'

'That's where I'm going to be. What's his name?' Archie asked. The woman pursed her lips and suddenly looked less friendly.

'What you doing here if you're working at the clay end?' she asked suspiciously.

'I only started today and I'm getting a good look round so I know everything that's going on.'

'I bet my Charlie doesn't get that sort of treatment. You someone special then?'

'No. I'm just Archie. I want to work in the decorating shop eventually but Mr Draper says I should see how everything's done. I'd best leave you to get on,' he said awkwardly. Being a friend of the boss's son wasn't the advantage he thought it might be. In fact, unless he was careful, it could turn right against him. When the siren sounded for the end of the working day, he made his way to the tunnel, crowded with the workers clocking off.

'You Archie Barnett?' the Lodge man asked

him.

'Yes, sir. How did you know?'

'They told me to look out for you. There's a parcel waiting for you.' He handed a package wrapped in newspaper to the boy.

'What is it?' he said, awestruck with the novelty of being given anything at all.

'How do I know? I just 'ave to do as I'm told. Hang on a minute. Betty Prestwick. What you got in that bag?'

'Only me mug for me tea. I'm taking it home to give it a good scouring.'

'Show us,' demanded the Lodge Keeper.

The woman, not much older than Archie, blushing to her roots, fished out a grimy mug from her shopping bag. The man turned it over in his hands and gave it back.

'All right then. Just checking up on yer. You're OK this time.' She stuffed it back in her bag and scuttled out. Archie clutched his parcel, something soft and squashy. Something clicked in his brain and he realised it was the promised overalls.

'Thanks, Mister,' he called to the Lodge Keeper and went over to the clock, found his card and clicked it through the machine. It gave him a sense of pride and he really felt like one of the team. It was a mucky, dirty environment but at least something bright and colourful came out at the end. Not dirty black coal which made everything else as black as itself. This was his future and not some filthy

96

coal pit. Though he hated himself for thinking it, what was good enough for his Dad, certainly wasn't good enough for him.

Two girls were standing just inside the main gate. One must have been about the same age as he was; the other was much younger. He smiled at them as he went out into the road. The young one giggled and hid behind her sister. Must be the Lodge man's kids, he thought. Fancy being able to live here, in the middle of all this.

It was beginning to rain. The gutters were soon running with a greyish liquid as the clay dust was washed down. Rivulets of the dirty water filled the gaps between the cobbles and Archie's feet were wet through. He added another item to the list of things he would buy as soon as he could afford it. A pair of decent boots.

# CHAPTER SIX

The next day was the hardest day's work Archie had ever done in his life. At the end of the first proper working day, he could hardly move. Heaving up great lumps of clay from the plug machine and kneading it into the right sized pieces had made every muscle in his body ache. His arms felt like jelly and he thought he'd never get up again if he should bend over. He dragged his feet as he toiled home and collapsed into a chair as soon as he could.

'Not such an easy ride then, your posh job in the factory,' his mother said with some amusement. 'Not as fit as your Dad, are you?'

'I'll get used to it,' Archie replied as normally as he could.

'Come and play with me, our Archie,' demanded William, his little brother.

'Get lost. I'm not playing with you,' the weary boy retorted. 'Go and find someone your own age.'

The child began to cry.

'It's not fair, Mum. Our Archie never plays with me any more.'

'He's much too grand for the likes of us, with his posh job at a factory. Leave him be, lad. Why don't you go and see if your mates are playing out? You've got an hour before supper time.'

William ran out and Archie dimly heard the gate bang shut before he fell asleep. He awoke to the sound of his mother clattering pots down on the table. He jerked awake and almost fell off the straight chair. His limbs felt like lead and it was all he could do to stand.

'Your Dad'll be home any minute. Get yourself washed. You've got more clay in your hair than your Dad gets coal dust. Strikes me you haven't quite got the bargain you were looking for. I bet your Dad'll stay healthy a good bit longer than you ever do.'

'Don't keep going on at me, Mum. You've made your point. I'll go and wash before me Dad gets home and wants the sink.'

He caught sight of his reflection in the window. He gave a wry grin. No wonder Mum had gone on at him. His dark hair looked completely grey and he was covered in a film of dust. Good job he'd had them overalls, he thought to himself. And it wasn't as if he'd always be working at the clay end. A couple of months, Mr Draper had said, then he'd move to the casting shop. He liked that idea. There was something amazing about the way the pieces of ware came out of the moulds, all soft and fragile. It didn't take long for them to dry enough to be handled and then it was fettling and sponging to get all the rough edges off and make them smooth and ready for the kilns.

'You finished yet, Archie? I need to get to the sink for the vegetables.'

'Almost,' he called back, making a start on his ablutions. When he had his own big, grand house, he'd make sure there would be a proper bathroom so that anyone could get washed without the benefit of vegetable preparation. Hot water as well. He'd insist on having plenty of hot water, just like the Drapers had.

'Let's be 'aving you, lad,' his mother chided. 'Daydreaming again I suppose. I'd hoped as working hard would knock a bit of sense into you. There's plenty of space in that head of

99

yours for a bit of sense.' He wiped himself dry and went into the living room. 'And give our William a call. Don't know where the lad's got to.'

Archie sniffed. There was some meat cooking. It was good to think he was helping out with money. At least it meant there'd be some decent food on the table again. However hard the work was, he had made a start on where he wanted to be. He watched the grey sludge as it swirled down the sink. He was a working man.

The next few months flew by. The new apprentice worked hard and was quick to learn. The hard, manual labour was gradually building up his strength and he could manage a bit more each day. He toiled round the yard on the days when the plaster was delivered, hauling the hundred weight bags off the cart, while the horse stood quietly chewing something in a bag hung over its head. The plaster was in hessian sacks, all of which had to be returned when the plaster was emptied. It was a dry and dusty job, folding the bags, and Archie was gagging for a drink of water by the time he'd finished. He carried buckets of slosh, the waste plaster dregs, to the factory's refuse area, called the shraff. The two heavy buckets had to be carried down at the end of the morning and in the evening. It was an exhausting process at the end of a long day, especially for a skinny lad like Archie. He was growing taller and his lanky frame was only just beginning to develop a bit of muscle.

He gradually made his progress through the factory, always willing to listen to the various managers and workers alike. He sweated with the stackers in the bottle ovens, tipping buckets of water over himself just as they did when emptying the huge kilns after firing. Even after two or three days, the ovens retained heat greater than most ordinary people could sustain. It was hard, grim work and only a few of the men lasted out till retirement age. When he was a boss, he would never make people work in these sort of conditions, he promised himself.

'Pass us your can, lad,' said Joe, the man he was working with, one lunch time after he'd been working the kilns for several months.

'It's got tea in it,' Archie replied.

'The lid'll do,' the man told him. He passed the lid over, wondering what was happening. Out of his can, Joe spooned some of the most delicious looking stew with meat and vegetables, piping hot. 'There you go. It's lobby, lad. It's lobby. The mainstay of all of us blokes working the kilns.' The boy had seen the cans standing round the sides of the ovens. He'd stood his own tea there to keep hot for during the day. The men all had the local stew in their pots. It simmered away all morning and they had a good hot meal to eat at lunch break. It was the most delicious thing he had

101

ever eaten. He described it to his Mum that evening.

'All the potatoes mix in with the juices and thicken it. It tastes of all the vegetables at the same time. I think lobby's just about the best thing I've ever eaten.'

'Course I know what lobby is. Everyone in the Potteries knows what it is. I'll make you some one day. Now we can afford a bit of decent steak and kidney. Best cooked overnight in the oven, when the fire's got low.'

'Great,' Archie replied, but when it came, it tasted nothing like that first lobby, shared with his mate Joe. Maybe his own mother hadn't quite got the hang of it.

Archie reached his eighteenth birthday and was beginning to feel more like the working man he truly was. Through the years, Archie and his old school friend Ernie had got into the habit of watching the Saturday football matches at the Vale. William always begged to accompany the two young men but Ernie always met his friend straight from the factory to save time. They called in at one of the local pubs for a half pint of bitter and a pork pie. Ernie was attending a course in art at one of the local colleges and learning about the industry from a different angle. His heart wasn't truly in the business but it was expected of him and he was still somewhat in awe of his father.

'Me Mother's been complaining that she

hasn't seen you for ages. She asked if you'd like to come for your tea one day soon? What d'ya think?'

'Tell the truth, I'd feel a bit awkward now, working for your Dad an'all. Wouldn't do for me to be seen socialising with the boss's family.'

'Dunna be daft. We've been friends for years. Everyone knows that.'

'Being friends with you is different. When you come to work at the factory, we'll have to be very careful not to alienate everyone. I could never work with the lads if they thought I was some sort of spy. That Miss Baines made it tough enough at the start. Treating me special, she thought your Dad was doing. He should never have got her to make me a cup of coffee on me first day. She's never forgotten it, you know.'

'I see. Well, just get this straight. You're me friend and I'll never forget that. I won't make things tougher for you but I'm not giving you up just because the factory girls might tittle tattle. Now, are you coming for your tea tomorrow, or do I have to thump you?'

'All right. Ta. It's not because I don't want to, you realise. I like your Mum. And your Dad of course. But he is my boss you know. Makes things more difficult than when we were just kids.'

Archie's mother sniffed her disapproval, when he announced he'd be out for tea the

103

following day.

'Your Aunt's coming over to see you, special like,' she told him. 'You've no right to make plans without telling me. It's not convenient.'

'But, Mum, I can't just not turn up. They'd think I was ever so rude.'

'And what about your Aunt Clarrie. Don't you think she'd think you were *ever so* rude?'

'You should've told me, Mum. I didn't know she was coming. I'm sorry but I'm going to see the Drapers. I have to.'

'You'll do as you're told me, lad. I say you're stopping here. I suppose you think you'll get a better tea at the Drapers'. We're not good enough for you nowadays. You and your smart friends and their posh house. China on the table. I don't know who you think you are. Summat better than your own parents? You'll be here for tea tomorrow or you can realise you're not too big for a good hiding.' Archie stared at the woman standing in front of him. He realised that he felt no real affection for her. He did as he was told because she was his mother and that's how he'd been brought up. She was jealous of everything he could do that she couldn't. Burning with anger, he went up to his bedroom, where his little brother was fast asleep. His Dad would be home late tonight. He usually went for a pint with his mates after he finished his long shift. His supper would be kept hot in the oven for him for when he came in, usually well before

104

closing time. His mother usually sat glowering at him, jealous because he'd been out enjoying himself and she'd been stuck at home with the child. Maybe Archie was being too hard on her. She didn't have much of a life, after all. He glanced at the sleeping child. He wasn't strong, not like Archie. He was tall and very skinny. He needed to build himself up and get plenty of good food inside him. Somehow, there must be a way out of all this poverty. His family were better off than many around here. Two men earning. His own wage packet had more in it now and he was promised another rise soon, when he started in the decorating shop. He was to be given time to do some of his own designs as well as learning some of the intricacies of painting on plates. He was going to work with one of the master painters, the one who painted beautiful pictures directly onto special plates. Fruit, flowers, animals and birds were all in his repertoire. He was even allowed to sign the plates himself and it was said that people from all over the world collected his work. Archie sighed. His mother would never understand his need to experience colour and shape, not only with his eyes but with his hands too. He needed to feel, to touch and to smell. Looking at a finished object, he could begin to sense the processes and skills that had gone into making it.

'Archie? There's tea on the table. Your Dad's home.' His mother's voice held a note of impatience and he knew that to fail to appear downstairs would only bring recriminations the next day. Besides, he needed to enlist his father's support for the proposed outing the next day.

'Hallo, Dad,' Archie said as lightly as he dared. 'Good match today. We won one nil.'

'I'd 'ave liked to see that,' Ralph said wearily.

'Maybe you can come with us, one day when you have a different shift.'

'Maybe, son. Work all right this week?'

'Yes. I'm moving to glazing next week. Then after that I go to the decorating shop. Can't wait for that.'

'Sounds like you're getting a good grounding in all departments. You're a lucky chap. Strikes me that knowing the boss isn't a bad thing. The Drapers have certainly done you proud.'

'You're right, Dad. They've asked me for me tea tomorrow. I haven't been for ages 'cos I didn't want to make things awkward. But Ernie says his Mum thinks I'm avoiding them.'

'Good for you, son. I'm proud of you. You always knew what you wanted to do and you've stuck to it. Enjoy yourself tomorrow.'

'I would, only Mum says I can't go. Auntie Clarrie is coming for tea.' Archie sneaked a glance at his mother. Her mouth was clamped together in a tight thin line. She was glaring at the teapot and stirring tea at the same time.

'Clarrie's coming here? First I've heard of it. When did you hear from her?'

'You remember. You must. She said she'd be coming round in a week or two when we saw her after church the other Sunday.'

'I didn't know she meant this week.'

'Course she did. You should know your own sister. Anyhow, it isn't right that the lad goes trying to socialise with the likes of some company boss. Getting above himself, he is. Not right at all. Looks down on us, his own parents.'

'That's not right, Mum. You know it isn't. I just want to make something of myself. I don't want to settle for some dirty back street and a no hope job.' He glanced at his Dad as he spoke, hoping he didn't take it badly. He wasn't meaning to criticise. His Dad had always done his best to provide for the family. It was never his fault that things went so wrong. Ralph was looking down at his feet and trying to hide the look of defeat that swamped his feelings. The boy was right to try and better himself. Somehow for him, it had never been worth the effort. Whatever he'd done, Frances had criticised him. Even when he'd worked like stink to take home a decent wage, she grumbled that it was a pity it wasn't a bit more so they could make the house half decent. Her so-called improvements doubtless meant a few extra fags at the end of the week.

'Good luck to you, son,' Ralph said wearily.

'I hope all your wishes come true. Enjoy your tea with your friends.'

'But . . .' began Frances. 'Oh, please yourself. You'll do what you want anyhow. Doesn't matter what I want or think.' She took Ralph's dirty plate and dumped it noisily into the kitchen sink.

'Thanks, Dad,' Archie said softly, turning to go back up the steep wooden stairs. His mother's discontentment with life was something to be overcome rather than challenged.

He changed into his Sunday best ready for church, before they had breakfast. The family attended church regularly now, not through faith but more from superstition. The dangers of mining were always present in their thoughts and somehow, a weekly church visit seemed to lessen the odds against an accident. Most of the other miners in the area felt the same way and divided their loyalties between the Church of England and the Methodists. Archie preferred the church they attended as he was able to sing in the choir. He enjoyed the singing much more than any of the service and he had developed a good tenor voice. His early instincts for harmony had stayed with him and now it was a more controlled, structured sound. He had also progressed in his piano playing, since the early days at the Drapers' house. Though he never managed to practise since he started work, he did sometimes stay behind after church service and was beginning to learn to play the organ. He still couldn't read music but developed his ability to play by ear, once a tune was firmly fixed in his mind. Today, he was hoping to impress his friends with his progress.

'What are you doing all dressed-up before doing your mucky jobs?' Frances demanded. 'I suppose you think yourself too grand to help with the fire and fetching the coal up.'

'I thought our William could maybe help out,' Archie said defensively. When he'd been William's age, he'd been fetching and carrying for several years. His younger brother did nothing at all to help in the family home.

'Don't be soft. He's not well enough to do the chores. You know what his chest's like. One puff of wind and he's in bed for a week.'

'Maybe he needs to toughen up a bit,' Archie suggested hopefully.

'His time will come,' Frances said impatiently. 'Now go and get your work things on and fetch up the coal. I want to get the breakfast cooking. We're having a few rashers today.'

As soon as lunch was over, Archie helped stack the dishes in the sink and went back into the living room.

'You can help Mum with the washing up today. I'm going out.'

'That's not fair,' moaned William. 'What about me weak chest, hanging about in the scullery?'

'Won't hurt you. It's about time you started helping a bit. I go out to work, don't forget.'

'But it's your job to help out. Mum says so. She doesn't like me getting cold.'

'You're keen enough to play out, and it's even colder outside.' Archie was determined to off-load some of his chores onto the boy. Besides, William would grow up expecting everything to be done for him all the time. Archie had no intention of staying here at home forever and his Mum would be left with everything to do if William didn't begin his training pretty soon.

'Give my love to Auntie Clarrie,' he called, as he left the house.

'Is Auntie Clarrie really coming?' William asked.

'I doubt it,' Frances replied bitterly. She was getting her own way in absolutely nothing these days.

The welcome Archie received at the Drapers' was enough to dispel all his remaining bad humours.

'You've been depriving us of your company for too long,' announced Mrs Draper.

'I'm sorry,' Archie replied shyly. 'It's just that it seemed a bit sort of wrong to come round. Mr Draper being the boss, like. But I did miss seeing you. Honest.'

'I quite understand, but let's make sure it isn't so long next time. Now, come and sit by

110

the fire and tell me all about everything you've been doing.'

Tell her, he did. He talked about the pottery, the workers, the factory and how he coped with all the jokes they played on him. She laughed with delight.

'You know, Archie, you've told me more about my husband's business in half an hour than he's told me in all the years we've been married. Now I think it's time I rang for some tea. You must be parched.'

He sat back in the comfy chair. Why couldn't his mother show such consideration? Show such interest in the things he did? She could hardly bear to ask if he'd had a good day. He looked round the room, feeling at ease, at home, as if this was the sort of place he was meant to be.

'After tea, I've got something to show you,' Ernie told him. 'I think you've gassed long enough to my Mother.'

'There was a lot of catching up to do. I do like these plates. They're Mr Stafford's work, aren't they?'

'I think they are,' Mrs Draper replied. 'Seconds of course. When did a manufacturer ever get the best for his own home?'

'Doesn't show,' Archie said, inspecting the plates hanging on the wall. 'I suppose it says something on the back?'

'Don't ask me,' she laughed. It was a light, tinkling laugh, a very feminine sound. When he thought about it, he could scarcely remember his own mother laughing at all. When tea was over, Ernie took his friend upstairs.

'I can't wait for you to see what I'm getting for my birthday.'

'That's not for another two months, is it?'

'No, but I wanted to get my order in early.' In his room, Ernie had a large desk, untidily covered in papers, sketches and magazines. On top of the pile was a car magazine, left open to show the latest models. 'There,' he said excitedly, 'what do you think of that?' Archie stared at the picture.

'You're getting a car? But you aren't old enough to drive it.'

'No, but I will be when I get to my birthday. There's a long waiting time for orders to get filled, so I've got to persuade my Dad to get the order in quickly. Think what a difference this is going to make to our little jaunts. We can go out to all sorts of places. No more hurrying home in case we miss the last bus. We'll have the girls flocking round us. All begging for a trip in my car.'

'It's nice of you to include me, of course, but it's going to be your car. You won't want me tagging along.'

'You're my friend. We share things. I don't want to be the one to get the girls on my own. Come on Archie. You should know me better than that.'

'But don't you realise Ernie? We could be from different countries. Different worlds. My Dad's a miner. A coal ripper. He works right at the coal face, in the worst part of the mines. We live in a back to back terrace with a netty up the yard. We wash at the kitchen sink. I have to fetch coal up from a cellar every day before I go work. We don't always have enough food on the table. I'm wearing my Sunday best today and look at the state of it. It was handed down from some cousin or other and it's years old. It fitted me once, when I was fourteen.'

'I'm sorry Archie. I'm sorry you even find it necessary to talk like that. You're my best friend. My only friend. I wouldn't care if you turned up in your father's nightshirt. It isn't clothes or houses I care about. It's you.'

'How could you know what it means to care about houses or clothes? Just take a look at yourself. Your mother rings a bell and someone brings in the tea. We have to stoke the fire to make a kettle boil. You've never had to go without anything. I'm sorry Ernie. But you just don't understand. When I'm rich, I shall buy a house just like this one. I'll have fancy plates on the wall as well as on the table. You've never been to my house, so you've got no idea of what it's like to live the way we do. No idea at all.'

'Come on lad. Don't go all soft on me. I'm sorry I never realised as you felt this way. To me you're still my friend, Archie. My very good friend and I hope you always will be. Now, let's hear no more. Let's go and have a bit of a sing round the piano till it's supper time. You are staying for supper aren't you? Me Mum's expecting you to.'

The two young men went down the stairs to the drawing room. Archie was still nursing his grievances and Ernie was doing his best to make him forget there was any difference between them at all. The room was empty and they sat at the piano together, playing the well-remembered, childish songs that allowed both of them to forget that they were now almost grown ups. To Archie's relief, Mr Draper did not appear until supper was served, around seven. Though Archie admired his boss a great deal, he felt shy with him now that their relationship had changed from being merely his son's friend. His fears of awkwardness quickly disappeared with the accomplished social graces of Mrs Draper. The meal was as delicious as ever and the company friendly and hospitable. It was almost the end of the evening before Mr Draper spoke of work.

'Have you seen what some of these new folk are producing, Archie?' he asked.

'Not exactly, sir,' Archie replied, glancing at the other two at the table.

'Suzie Cooper and Clarice Cliff. They're really beginning to make an impact. Very bright colours on basic cream-ware. I'm not sure I like it much but it seems to be selling. And shapes. They're moving from the traditional shapes. Lots of geometric shapes. Triangles and such. Have a look round the shops. See what you think, Archie. I'd like you to see what you can come up with.'

'What, design summat meself?' Mr Draper nodded.

Archie blushed and looked uncomfortable. These days, he never had the time to look in shops. His only free afternoon was on a Saturday and going to the match was sacred.

'I'll try, sir, but it isn't easy. Shops are all closed by the time I get off work.'

'Up to you, lad. Now, how about another slice of that excellent ham?'

Archie's brain was buzzing as he walked home. Mr Draper must think something of him, if he asked such a thing. Somehow, he'd have to get to some shops and have a look round. Bright colour was the fashion, was it? Sounded right up his street. He was always saying there should be some colour in people's lives. Mind you, it wasn't exactly what he had planned. He wanted to learn some of the skills of the master painters. Paint pictures on plates that people could hang on their walls. Whatever direction he took, it was important to follow Mr Draper's suggestions. He was being given chances that others in the factory weren't. Maybe it was time to stop worrying that they thought he was getting favouritism.

Maybe this was just the chance he needed to get on. He promised himself that he'd go and do a spot of window shopping the very next evening after work.

Clad in his working clothes and weary beyond words, it was a huge effort for Archie to make the trip into Burslem the next evening. The shops were all closing and he looked into the darkening windows to see the displays set out. To his eye, most of the pots looked crude, garish and though the colours were bright and cheerful, he knew he did not care much for this new craze. Art Deco they were calling it. Cups with triangles for handles. Square plates. Still, at least he now knew what they were talking about. He'd certainly enjoy coming up with some designs. He remembered the mathematical shapes he'd been learning about at school and knew that the sharp angles and intersecting circles would make for some interesting designs. Meantime, he should get home to face his mother's wrath. He had said nothing about his proposed trip to town because she'd been in such a foul mood when he got home last night. She'd made sarcastic remarks the moment he had come into the house. He'd gone up to bed right away. He didn't even hear whether Auntie Clarrie had turned up. He doubted it. She had simply been a fictitious weapon Frances was using to get at him. She was plain jealous. Again, he could feel a slight sympathy for her and her boring, unchanging life. What did she have to be pleased about? What did she have to look forward to? He sighed. It was no-one's fault. His mother had no particular talents, ambition or even the will to improve herself. Even the neighbours had given up trying to be friendly. She'd made a career out of being difficult, unfriendly and bad-tempered. Not for the first time, he wondered why his Dad had married her. He wondered how long they'd been married but they never mentioned anything like anniversaries. In fact, they rarely remembered birthdays. He wouldn't be getting a new car for his next birthday, that was certain. One day though, he'd have a suitably large car to park outside his big house.

'I'm home,' he called as he went into the scullery.

'Your tea's ruined,' announced Frances. 'Completely dried up. Been off with your posh friends again? Hope it was worth it.'

'Sorry. I had an errand to do for Mr Draper.'

'I should've thought he'd have plenty of people he could ask to do his errands. I bet he didn't offer you any extra money.'

'Something I wanted to do. Never mind about my tea. I'm not that hungry anyhow.'

'Ungrateful brat,' his mother snapped. 'You could at least try to eat it.'

'Sorry. I thought you said it was inedible?' He sat down at the table and with very bad grace, Frances took the plate out of the oven. It was quite edible, as much as any of her cooking was edible. 'Thanks,' he said over-politely. 'It doesn't look too bad at all.'

The following week, Archie spent every spare moment he could sketching, planning and looking at possible shapes he might show to Mr Draper. Knowing the various machines they had available for manufacturing, he tried to work out how new shapes could be produced. It was not as easy as he'd thought but he came up with several possible schemes. He felt shy about making the suggestions and wondered how best to present his ideas. There was no way he could just walk into Mr Draper's office. Nor could he ask the dragon lady, Miss Baines, to pass them on. Finally, he decided on the mail as being the only way he could do it. He carefully rolled up his sketches, using an elastic band to secure them. He wrote an address label and put them into the mail box at the factory gate. He took care that no-one was watching him as he did it. This way, no-one would see the package was from him. Mr Draper would know. For the first time ever, he used the signature he had practised so many times before. It gave him a peculiar sense of pride.

The next week seemed to last forever. He heard nothing. No summons to Mr Draper's office to discuss his designs nor any comments from the decorating shop, where he lingered as

118

often as he could manage. He tried to show interest in the glost process, watching the skills of the dippers as they drew the pots through the thick glaze. They managed to entirely cover each item, flicking their wrists to shake off the excess glaze and placing them down again without leaving the faintest blemish. He thought it looked very easy and was just a matter of getting the knack. When he tried it for himself, he made a total mess of the piece. He returned to his job of fetching and carrying for the skilled men. He lost count of the number of times he went from one department to the next with trays of ware. He was fascinated by the under-glaze designs, where pattern was applied to the biscuit stage of the pottery, after the first firing. Patterns were applied to the highly absorbent body of the pots and then the glaze put over them. The result after the firing was the all over printed pattern, the favourite being Staffordshire blue tableware. It was like magic to Archie, seeing the magnificent patterns when they finally emerged from the kilns. He was surprised to discover that many of the workers never saw the finished results. He couldn't imagine what it was like to work in one department, never knowing what went on in the others, nor even seeing the finished results.

'I really like these plates, don't you?' he asked one of the other apprentices, one day.

'They're just plates,' the boy replied.

119

'But they look such a lovely colour after they're finished.'

'Dunno. Ain't never seen 'em,' he replied.

'You must have done.'

'All we want to know is how many we've pushed through at the end of the week. If it's bin a good week, we get a decent wage packet.'

Archie couldn't imagine being disinterested in any part of the work. It was what made it all worthwhile. He heard no more about his designs and questioning Ernie at the next football match gave him no information. Suddenly he realised he wasn't anything special to Mr Draper. He was just another employee who also happened to know his son.

## CHAPTER SEVEN

Archie had spent several months learning various techniques in the decorating shop. He worked hard to understand everything that was going on, especially the chemistry behind the colouring processes. The whole industry had undergone many changes as the need to improve working conditions was gaining ground. Glazes contained less of the poisonous lead than they used to and the colours they were using contained less harmful metal oxides. All the same, the rate of toxicity meant that greater control was developed over the way they were handled. More modern gas fired kilns were being used and the great bottle kilns were throwing slightly less pollution into the air.

He did little actual decorating and was still considered the lad who was sent to fetch and carry. Inevitably he was sent to find cat's whisker paint or horses' hoof paint and even a tin of elbow grease, until he realised they were sending him up. By the time he was asked for striped paintbrushes, he'd learned to smile and nod and didn't fall for their tricks. They accepted him and settled down to work. He got used to carrying the long planks of finished ware to the room next to the kiln. He was careful and steady as he went, knowing that an accident would result in a huge loss to everyone in the department if there were any broken pieces. He watched the men who etched the copper plates to make transfers and spent some time working alongside the men and women who spent long days and enormous energy in scrubbing the flimsy paper down onto the pottery. He was constantly fascinated by the workers who could paint the same design, day after day with so little difference it was hard to believe the items were all individually hand painted. At lunch break, he would often try out his own skills on damaged pieces that were to be thrown out. Gradually, he learned how to apply the paint smoothly. Some pottery was air-brushed, where a larger area of colour was needed and then it was hand-finished when the paint was dry. It was everything he wanted. At last, he felt at home. This was where he wanted to be.

'Could I have a go at painting a plate, for me Mum?' he dared to ask one day.

'You can, as long as you fit it into your own time. You can come and work with me at dinner, provided you make me a good cuppa before you start.' Archie nodded happily. This was Thomas, one of the top painters in the company, one of the masters who was allowed to sign his own name alongside the manufacturer's name on the bottom of the plates. 'So, what do you fancy having a go at?'

'I thought I'd do some flowers. We never have flowers in our house or in the back-yard, so I thought it'd cheer things up a bit.'

'Does your Mum like flowers?' he asked.

'I dunno. I dunno if she even looks at them. But everyone likes flowers, don't they?'

'I reckon you're right lad. Now, how about a test run with that teapot before we start?'

Archie went over to the grate where a fire burned to warm up the room. It was the only place in the factory where such consideration was given. It was a sign of how highly these skilled craftsmen were ranked in the business. He filled the blackened kettle and looked for the teapot.

Thomas Bryant arranged a space at his bench and started Archie to work on his first

122

ever attempt at painting a plate. These china plates were specially designed for hanging and had no rim. It was a smooth, slightly concave surface, glazed and fired and ready to be turned into a masterpiece.

'You need to work out some idea of what your design will be,' Thomas instructed. 'Then you lightly draw the main lines with the finest brush. Use the light grey pigment, then it will cover over if you change your mind. That's it. Go on. Be confident.'

Tongue hanging out in concentration, Archie carefully painted the first lines. His hand shook slightly and the lines wobbled.

'Doesn't matter, lad. Get the feel of your tools. Feel how the paint flows from the end of the brush.' Archie tried again. This time it was better, though the lines still tended to go in slightly the wrong direction. 'OK. You know what colours the flowers will be?' Archie nodded.

'Nice bright pinks and yellow. There has to be plenty of yellow.'

'OK. Now you need to decide on the background colours. What will show off your flowers best?'

'Green, I s'pose? Or brown, like soil.'

'Look at my plate. Can you see how I've made the background dark, mixed colours to make the flowers stand out well? Neither brown nor green. You need to colour that in a bit first, so you don't have to paint right up to the flowers. You can always wipe it away before it dries, if you get it wrong. Like painting a wash over the paper before you paint a picture.'

'I haven't ever used paints to make a picture. I missed out on art at school 'cos I had to do Latin. I've only ever drawn with a pencil.'

'Maybe you should try painting on paper first.' The artist looked thoughtful. This lad was so keen but he really didn't have a lot of idea about the job. 'Let's see how you do with this first, if you like.' Archie shot him a look of gratitude. He couldn't wait to get started properly. He didn't have time to draw stuff on paper, like planning essays at school. It was always much better to get right on with the job. This was all a sort of planning and he wanted to spread the colours properly, on his mother's plate.

By the end of his dinner break, his stomach was empty but his mind was full of colour and designs. He'd made a start on his plate but there was nothing like enough time for him to really get the feel of the job. Towards the end of the day, Thomas beckoned him over again.

'You can clean off my palette if you like. There's some good background colours there.' To Archie's delight, the craftsman stayed with him for an extra half an hour while he painted round the edge of his plate. 'Right,' he said after the paint was almost gone, 'you can clear up the table for me. Leave your plate on one side to dry off overnight. Tomorrow you can begin on the flowers. What sort will you paint? Roses, maybe?'

'I hadn't thought,' Archie admitted. He didn't know a great deal about flowers. He only knew the ones that he'd seen at work when he was watching the flower makers at work one day. The carefully made china shapes were put together and magically turned into exquisite looking tiny blooms. They looked fragile and ghostly in the dull grey clay. When they'd been assembled into pots, fired and then painted, they looked as if the dew should still have rested on every petal. Yes, he'd paint roses. He knew exactly what they looked like and Thomas wouldn't think him a total idiot. He really must look carefully at the flower beds in the park, if he went again. Usually, his eyes had caught only the blocks of bright colour, without noticing individual flowers.

Each day for the next week, Archie worked away at his painting whenever he had a moment. If it looked uneven, he would carefully remove the paint using a piece of cotton wool wrapped round the end of the brush and dipped in some sort of spirit. Gradually, the picture grew and though slightly out of proportion, was quite passable. Thomas was struck by young man's enthusiasm and recognised that he had the makings of an artist. Most of all, he was impressed by the boy's dedication.

'You'll make a painter, lad,' he told him at the end of the second week. 'I reckon that's probably as good as we'll get it. Leave it on one side and I'll set it in with the next firing.' Archie felt his heart leap. It would be ready well before Christmas. He could hardly wait to see his Mother's face when she got a proper Christmas present. His Dad would be proud of him as well. It was the solid, tangible proof that he had made the right choice in his career.

A couple of weeks before Christmas Ernie invited his friend to accompany him to a dance.

'I can't dance,' Archie protested. ' 'Sides. How can I go to a dance with nothing but my tatty old clothes to wear.'

'We're around the same size now. Maybe you're a bit skinnier. You could have one of my suits. I've got a couple to spare that don't really fit me any more. Come on. I can't go on my own and anyhow, it's high time you got out and met a few girls. We're wasting the best times of our lives. Come round to our house after work one day. Friday. You can have some supper and then we'll kit you out. I can teach you a bit of dancing. Enough to manage with. Come on, lad. It's time you branched out a bit. Enjoy life for a change.'

Archie was very tempted. But Friday night. That was pay night and his Mum expected him home with his wages.

'I don't think I can make it Friday. How about after the match on Saturday?'

'I s'pose. But we usually go for a jar then. Can't miss out on that.'

'Oh all right. I dare say I can manage Friday, just for once.' His Mother would have to lump it, he thought. She probably wouldn't desperately need his money till Saturday anyhow.

When he told his Mother he would not be home till late on Friday, she exploded.

'I've got the club-man coming round at half seven. How am I supposed to pay him? It's out of the question. You're a selfish sod, aren't you? Think of nothing but yourself.' Archie thought of the hours he'd spent on painting his plate. She knew nothing about it, nor that he'd used his lunch times and stayed after work for some time each day.

'What's the club-man being paid for?' he asked curiously.

'Maybe you haven't noticed we've got some new furniture. The chairs. Your Dad and me have got a new bed. 'Bout time too after all these years.'

'And it's my wages that have bought it all, is it?'

'Who do you think you are? You've got food on the table waiting whenever you come in. You get your money for the match every week and you waste money on beer with that friend of yours. How I spend the money in this house is my business.'

'I don't think you do too badly out of me,' Archie said quietly as he left the table and went up to his room. He felt angry. He worked bloody hard and gave almost his entire wage packet to his mother. He never begrudged it before but she never thanked him or offered to buy anything new for him. Damn it. Why should he always have to make do with cast-offs? Apart from his decent boots, he'd insisted on buying at the beginning, he'd had nothing new. Why shouldn't he have some new clothes for himself? Each time he'd had a pay rise, she'd taken his money without comment, handing back the same few coppers for his own use. He hadn't yet told her that he was to get another pay rise. A good rise, in fact. If he kept giving her the same money, he'd be able to keep a few shillings to himself each week. It wouldn't take that long to save up for a new suit of his own. If she was being so selfish, it was about time he made his stand. Besides, if he and Ernie were starting to do a bit of socialising, he needed to have something in his pocket to entertain the young ladies.

'I shall be out on Friday evening,' he announced at breakfast the next day. 'If you need my wages that desperately, you'd better send our William to meet me from work.'

'I'm not letting him get his hands on my money. God knows if I'd ever see him home again.'

'Then you'll have to wait till Saturday morning.'

She looked as if she was about to say more but she held her tongue, shooting venomous looks at him. If she got into trouble with the club-man, she could find her own way out of it. The things she had bought were for her own comfort so why should he worry?

The Drapers provided the usual lavish spread. Archie could never get used to the idea of so much food being available at one meal. Not wishing to appear greedy, he tried to hold back politely but obviously Mrs Draper was aware of the home circumstances. They didn't seem to have improved, despite Archie's contribution to the family purse. He still looked extremely scruffy and wore shoes that she would have insisted were thrown out long ago.

'I understand you've been doing some exciting designs, Archie?' she asked as they drank coffee at the end of the meal.

'Have I? I did send some stuff in ages ago, but . . . well, I haven't heard any more,' he replied, casting a slightly embarrassed look at Mr Draper.

'Er yes, well, we've been thinking about things. I think we might go with some of the ideas. Maybe you could try out a few designs on the actual plates we make at present. Try a cup and saucer. I'll make sure they know in the decorating shop. What have you been working on?'

'Mostly fetching and carrying. But I have done a plate. Mr Thomas let me have a go during dinner times and after work some nights. It's ready for firing. I thought I could buy it off you. For me Mum for Christmas, like.'

Mrs Draper smothered a smile. Her husband knew all about Archie's plate, having initially suggested to Thomas that he gave the boy a chance to see if he had any talent.

'I'd like to see what you've done when it's out of the kiln. Get it sent to my office will you? And make a start on the designs on Monday. Right, now if you'll excuse me, I have a date with my paper. Haven't had a spare minute to read it today.'

'Excuse us, Mother, will you?' Ernie asked. She nodded and the two young men went up to Ernie's room. He had taken a record player up and several of the most recent dance records. He wound it up and the music blared out.

'This is a quickstep,' he announced. He pranced around, clutching an imaginary partner until Archie ended up roaring with laughter.

'What do you look like? I'll never manage that. Not sure I want to, actually. You look a right prat.'

'You'll get the hang of it. Anyway, from what I hear, the Town Hall dances are so

130

crowded, no-one can see what anyone else's is doing. Right now. You can be the girl and I'll show you how the steps go.'

For the next half an hour, the pair struggled to get the rhythm and steps to coincide. They tried waltzes, quickstep and even the foxtrot, all with the same appalling results.

'I don't think this is a good idea. I don't want to make even more of a fool of myself.'

'I'm not letting you get out of this one. I've got us a pair of tickets for next Saturday. We're going to have to make our lads' night out on Fridays from now on. Saturdays are definitely hunting nights. We're going to get us some girls.' Archie stared at his friend. He'd never given much thought to girls. He was used to being teased by all the girls in the factory but as for socialising with them, it was quite a different territory.

'I'm not sure I want to hunt for girls,' he said thoughtfully. 'What do we want girls for?'

'Good grief, man. Don't you know anything? I think I'd better begin by telling you the facts of life. How old are you?'

'You know damned well. Same as you, give or take a couple of months.'

'Right, then unless there's summat wrong with you, eighteen is more than old enough to be looking. Now then, the next job is to sort out some clothes for you. You don't mind do you? Having second hand stuff? Only my Mother thinks I need at least one new suit

131

every year, besides the half a dozen other outfits I scarcely even wear.'

'No, I don't mind anything. But won't she be cross if you give your stuff away?'

Ernie didn't bother to reply. He was busy pulling out heaps of clothes from his wardrobe. He picked up a suit and held it against Archie. It was navy blue with a fine stripe.

'Try this one for size.'

'But it's brand new. Not a thread pulled anywhere and it hardly looks as if it's been worn.'

'It hasn't. Well, only once. For some wedding. I hate it. On me, that is. If you like it, it's yours.'

Archie had never seen anything quite so smart. He took off his own battered jacket and tried the navy one with the fine pinstripe. It could have been made for him. Trying to hide his lack of underpants, he took the trousers to one side of the room and pulled them on quickly. They were a bit loose but Ernie offered him a leather belt to pull them in.

'By the heck. You look better in that lot than I ever did. Now, we need a shirt and tie to go with it. I reckon I'll never stand a chance with the girls until you've got yourself sorted. Take a look at yourself in the mirror.'

Archie could hardly believe the transformation. He looked so grown up. He looked like a man. He looked like one of the managers at the factory. He was almost beginning to look something like the person he had always wanted to be. Someone of importance. He wanted to go somewhere to show himself off. For the first time in his life, he knew what it meant to have self-confidence. The white shirt and striped navy and red tie looked amazing. Like something belonging to one of the bosses, which it was, near enough.

'Are you really sure you want to part with these things?' he asked doubtfully. 'Only I've never had anything this good. Not even my Sunday best is anywhere near this good.'

'Take it and know that I'll be glad to see the back of it. Just promise me one thing.' Archie nodded. 'Promise me you'll come to the Town Hall dances for the next few weeks without complaining. Hey, Archie lad. We're going to have us some fun.'

'I'd better change back into my old stuff or your Mum'll be thinking I'm robbing you.'

'She knows all about it. In fact, it was her idea to pass the stuff on. There's a couple more things for you in that bag. Try them on when you get home. Now, let's have one more go at this waltzing stuff. Got to get us ready for the last waltz. That's the time you can get a bit closer to your girl. Have a bit of a spoon.'

'Eh, Ernie. I doubt I'll ever get the knack of any of this lot. But, we'll give it a try. I'll never manage to pay you and your family back, you know. I may not have been able to stay on at

133

school but at least passing that scholarship meant you and I could be friends.' He didn't want to sound soppy but he doubted Ernie would ever realise just how much his friendship had meant to him.

It was late by the time he walked home, carrying his new clothes carefully over his arm. He pushed the back gate open and went inside. His mother was either in bed or she'd gone out. He felt very relieved. He didn't like the thought of having to explain everything to her. He crept upstairs and hung his suit on the back of the door. William whispered something in the dark, making Archie jump.

'I didn't mean to wake you,' he whispered.

'I wasn't asleep. Our Mum's dead mad at you. You're for it in the morning.' He didn't quite keep the glee out of his voice.

'Why? What am I s'posed to have done?'

'She expected you'd be home with your wages but you weren't.'

'I told her I wasn't coming home.'

'She didn't believe you'd go through with it. What's that hanging on the door?'

'Just some new clothes.'

'Good lord. I hope you haven't spent your money on new clothes. That'll really send her flying in the air.'

'Course I haven't. If you must know, Ernie gave them to me. We're going out on the town tomorrow night.'

'Can I come?' the boy asked.

'Course you can't. It's for grown-ups. Now shut it. I need to get me beauty sleep.'

Archie only worked till lunch time on Saturdays. He and Ernie were going to the match and then he'd come back and change before the dance. He arranged to meet Ernie some distance from the house. He still didn't want Ernie to see where he lived, despite everything he'd said. He could hardly bear to face his mother in his new clothes, knowing how sarcastic she'd be. But it was just too bad. Whatever she said, he wasn't going to let her spoil anything for him. He even managed to slip out to work before she was up the next day. He left his wage packet on the table, less the amount he'd decided to take out for his own use. She wouldn't like the fact that it had been opened. She believed it was her right to open it and give him a few coppers back for his smokes and whatever else he wanted. The few coppers she gave him certainly would not be enough for an evening out. Especially not if he did strike lucky and find a girl. He might want to buy her something to drink.

The Town Hall was very crowded. The bar, in a room to one side of the dancing area, was crowded with young men while the girls lined the walls in the main hall. They were jigging up and down to the band, all talking as if what they were saying was very important. They nudged each other as various groups of men came in and looked around, summing up the talent. Archie had never felt so nervous in his life. He'd hoped that the new clothes would be enough to carry him through the evening but he was wishing desperately that he hadn't allowed himself to be persuaded. Ernie looked as if he was enjoying himself, leaning on the bar, a pint in one hand and a cigarette in the other.

'Come on, Archie. Sup up. You'll be fine once you get in there.'

'Wish I could believe you. I've never been so nervous in my life. I tell you, I'm near shittin' myself.'

'Mebbe you need summat stronger than ale.'

'I never drink anything but beer. It can't be much fun if you have to get drunk to get up enough courage.'

They went into the dance hall and stood with other men around the doorway, surveying the talent. They looked round at the girls. No-one was dancing. The band-leader went to the microphone at the end of a number and announced a 'ladies' excuse me.'

'What the heck's that?' Archie demanded.

'I think the girls have to ask us to dance.'

'Blimey. Think maybe I need another beer after all,' Archie said quickly.

A few daring girls asked some of the men to dance. Several couples went onto the floor. Everyone stood watching and eventually, a few more joined in. Archie and Ernie stood watching. No-one asked them to dance, much to their relief. The next announcement was for a Paul Jones.

'You never told me there was so many different sorts of dancing. Who's Paul Jones, any road?'

'I haven't a clue, mate,' Ernie confessed. They watched and realised it was probably the best way anyone had thought of to get everyone on the dance floor. The band-leader called for everyone to join in. The men made a circle on the outside and the girls on the inside. They all danced round and when the band stopped, they had to dance with whoever was opposite them. Trembling, Archie held his partner, the way Ernie had showed him. She smiled nervously at him as the band began a waltz. Fortunately, the floor was crowded and nobody looked at anyone else's dancing style. He could think of nothing sensible to say and he shuffled the girl to the end of the number. The leader called for the circle again and they danced round, everyone now laughing and joining in. It was a quickstep next and the girl he'd got this time was a bit livelier and she asked his name. He relaxed a bit and asked hers in return. All too soon, the circles re-formed. This time, he ended up without a partner. There were far more men than girls so inevitably, always some were left out. He wanted to sink into the ground. Instead, he went off to look for the gents. That way, it made him feel less obvious. When the dances eventually finished, Ernie came to find him.

'You did all right, didn't you?' he asked.

'Didn't get anyone the last time.'

'I saw you talking away to Elsie. She's all right that one.'

'How do you know her?'

'She works in one of the offices at the factory. Don't tell me you haven't seen her? She's been out with most of the blokes. They say she's quite a goer.'

'How d'ya mean?' He caught sight of Elsie and turned away, blushing slightly. The girl had hair much blonder than nature intended and wore bright red lipstick and rather more face powder and rouge than he liked.

'Come on, Archie. You must know what I mean?'

'Yes. Course I do. I was just thinking of summat else. Else. Elsie? Get it?'

Ernie shook his head at his friend.

'We'll get you sorted. Eventually. We're having a Christmas Party at the factory this year. That should give you a chance. My Grandfather's decided to leave at last, so we're having a party to celebrate his retirement and me Dad taking over. Should be a good do.'

'I didn't know anything about it. When's it going to be?'

'The Saturday night before Christmas. Gives me a couple more weeks to get you dancing properly.'

138

Archie felt his heart give a lurch. The thought of dancing with girls from the factory scared him half to death. Everyone would know him and he'd never have Ernie to lean on or chat to. As the son of the boss, he'd have to be on his best behaviour the whole evening. He'd be with all the big-wigs. That really would show him up and where did that leave Archie?

'They're doing a proper sit-down supper as well. Really pushing the boat out, is the old man.'

'I expect you'll enjoy it, being the new boss's son.'

'I hope everyone will. You'll be sitting with me, Archie. I shall insist. You're my best friend after all.'

'But everyone of the factory floor will think I'm something special. Jumped up nobody. I don't think it's a good idea. Besides, I'm not sure if I'll bc ablc to go.'

'That Elsie's looking at you,' Ernie said. The discussion was apparently over. 'Go and ask her to dance. She's smiling at you.'

'I daren't,' Archie said miserably. 'Besides, it's probably you she's after.'

'Get over there, lad. Before I have to drag you. She'll be all right for you to practise on.'

'You're terrible, you,' Archie protested but his friend gave him a shove and he tottered towards the girl. He danced with Elsie for the rest of the evening. She cuddled up to him

139

whenever she got the chance and whispered things he could scarcely hear above the music. He just grinned and hoped he wasn't making too much of a fool of himself. Though he'd never have admitted it, he quite enjoyed it.

'You can walk me home if you like,' he heard her whisper when the music stopped.

'Oh I couldn't do that,' he said hastily. 'I've promised to go with my friend.'

'I wouldn't bank on it,' she said with a grin. 'I think he'll be walking someone else home, by the looks of it.' Archie looked across the room. Ernie was wrapped in the arms of some other girl, not even noticing that the music had stopped. How on earth did he get out of this one?

He was saved by Ernie. He glanced across the room, said goodbye to his partner and came to Archie's side.

'You ready then, mate?'

'Certainly am,' he said gratefully. 'See you around, Elsie.' The two young men left together, grinning as they walked along the street.

'I take it I did the right thing,' Ernie inquired.

'You certainly did. I was bloomin' terrified.'

'Well, I hope you realise what I gave up for you. I reckon I could have scored with that one. You didn't look as if you were doing too badly yourself.'

'Ah dunno what you mean. Innocent I am.

Pure as the driven snow.' They laughed all the way home. The only trouble was, Archie knew he was speaking the truth. He was innocent as far as women went.

After this first dance, Archie was slightly less nervous about the work's social. He was hardly looking forward to it but it was better than he expected. He got a certain amount of teasing from the girls but he managed to cope. He was very relieved that he hadn't taken Elsie home the previous week or he'd have suffered a great deal more unwelcome attention.

'I s'pose we're all too common for the likes of you?' Elsie asked him.

'I'm saving myself,' Archie replied, quick as a flash. 'When I meet the right girl, there'll be no stopping me. Besides, I couldn't walk out with anyone here, now could I? Think about it. You'd all get to know all me secrets!' The girls giggled and good humour was restored.

When Christmas came, Archie went to town and bought presents for his Dad and William. He brought home the precious plate and sneaked it upstairs one evening, wanting to keep it secret till Christmas Day. He had no idea what his mother would think of it but he prayed she would appreciate it. He was very proud of his efforts and it represented a huge achievement in his life. Tom himself had approved it and said it was better than anything he'd ever painted at Archie's age.

'You've got talent, lad. Don't waste it.'

141

On Christmas morning, he put the presents on the table, before anyone else had got up. He'd bought two comics and some colouring pencils for William and some smokes for his Dad. At last they came down and he stood by the fire, waiting.

'What's all this then, lad?' asked Ralph.

'Happy Christmas, everyone.'

'Presents is it? Good to have another working man in the house.'

He waited anxiously until his Mother opened her parcel. She looked at the plate and gave one of her sniffs.

'I did it myself, Mum. Specially for you.'

'It's lovely,' she said grudgingly. 'Very clever I'm sure.'

'Well done, lad,' his Father added, aware of the boy's disappointment at his Mother's somewhat tepid reaction. 'Very clever, our lad, isn't he, Frances? Takes real talent to do summat like that.'

'Oh yes. Very,' she replied. 'Now, I'd best get breakfast. Shame we haven't got four posh plates, then we could use them for eating our toast and dripping.'

'These are plates to hang on the wall, not to eat off,' Archie told her.

'Bit of a waste, then.'

'I thought you'd like it. It's me very first effort. Mr Tom says I show real talent. He's the Master painter. Allowed to sign his name on the back and everything.'

It was several weeks later that Archie noticed his plate had disappeared. He'd put up a piece of wood on the wall so the plate had a proper stand of its own. Frances saw him looking at the space and hurriedly went into the kitchen.

'Where's me plate gone, Mum?' he demanded.

'Thought it was *my* plate. To do with as I liked.'

'Well, yes. But I painted it specially for you. My very first piece. Summat really special.'

'Yes well, I'm afraid it's gone.'

'How do you mean, gone? Broken?' His face was aghast with shock.

'Oh no. If you must know, I had to get some new shoes for your brother. Mr Swinbourne offered me a good price for it.'

'You sold it? How could you? My very first piece of hand-painted china? If you'd said, I'd have given you the money for his new shoes. How long will they last? My plate is the only one that can ever be my first piece. It could have lasted forever. I'll never, ever forgive you, Mother.'

'What did you mean that you'd have paid for his shoes? Where've you got that sort of money from? Have you been holding back on me? I'll see your wage slip next week, my lad.'

'Oh no, Mum. You've really blown it this time. You have to realise I've grown up. I'm not your little lad any more.' He could hardly

143

contain himself.

'What's the use of some fancy plate if you haven't got fancy food to put on it?'

'That wasn't the point. It was summat that can never, ever be replaced. I'm going out. Expect me when you see me.' He went straight round to see Mr Swinbourne at the second hand shop, to try to buy it back. It was no use. The piece had gone and the old man refused to say who had bought it. Archie knew he would never see it again.

# CHAPTER EIGHT

'There's going to be a few changes,' Mr Draper announced to the assembled staff in the decorating shop. It was the largest room in the factory, where people could gather without falling over the growing amount of machinery. He outlined some of the plans for the future. There were some lean times ahead and something drastic needed to be done to increase Draper's share of the market. It was 1928 and the Art Deco movement was gathering pace rapidly. Many of the old lines produced by Draper's simply weren't selling any longer. In charge for some years now, Ernie's father was determined to introduce some new merchandise. He made a number of announcements about staffing, including

Archie's promotion to under manager of the decorating shop. Some of the girls nudged each other and Archie plainly heard some of the whispers.

'Told you he was in with the bosses.'

'Shows what you can expect when you know the right people.'

He blushed to his roots, as Mr Draper spoke of the extraordinary promise he showed and how he would probably be among the leaders of the next generation of potters. He'd suspected that something was in the offing, after he'd been out with Ernie the previous Saturday. His friend had been rather cagey about the future and kept telling him to wait and see.

He was floating high on a cloud. He had arrived. He was almost where he wanted to be and he was only twenty-one. His heart sank suddenly. He'd have to smarten up. Buy more clothes and even keep some stuff for best. Since the incident with the plate, even though it was a long time ago now, Archie had barely tolerated his mother's ways. He paid her what he considered a reasonable amount for his keep and something towards expenses but she had no idea how much he earned. Neither did she know how much he spent each week, nor about the savings account he'd begun. It wasn't much but he felt a glow of pleasure that he had been thrifty enough to put a few coppers by each week. It didn't leave much over for anything else. Maybe Mr Draper would be giving him a rise in wages to match his new job.

'We'll go out and celebrate next Saturday,' Ernie promised. 'There's a special do on at the Town Hall.'

'I'm not much for the Town Hall any more,' Archie said. 'Tell you the truth, I find it embarrassing, dancing with all the girls from work. Especially now . . . well, you understand.'

'Now you're management you mean,' Ernie teased. He punched his friend's arm. 'All right. We'll go a bit further afield. I'll drive us out somewhere different. I'll let you know.'

Ernie was now part of the sales department. He enjoyed the office work and going out on selling trips. He was often away from home and spent time in London meeting with representatives from all over the world. He seemed to have few friends, apart from Archie, but he was liked by most people and respected by the factory workers.

When Saturday came, Ernie collected his friend from work. They drove to see Port Vale playing and then went back to his house.

'I haven't found us anywhere very special to go but there is a dance on at Longton Town Hall. Makes a change from Burslem and at least you won't get our girls there. What do you say?'

'I s'pose so.'

'Don't look so bloomin' enthusiastic. What else is there to do but go dancing? Apart from the pub, that is. You don't exactly meet any decent girls in the pubs.'

'I s'pose not. But I don't know what to say to girls. I can't talk to strangers like I talk to the factory girls, now can I?'

'Whatever am I going to do with you? You're hopeless.'

They went to the dance and for once, Archie was able to relax. There were no familiar faces leering at him from the sides of the room.

'Maybe you're right, Ernie,' he said. 'You do get different girls here. How about those two over there?'

Ernie looked. Pleasant enough types, he thought. If his mate was at last showing some interest, he'd give it a go.

'OK. Mine's the dark one.'

'You're on. I like the one with light brown hair.'

Once on the dance floor, Archie's confidence evaporated. He could think of nothing to say and the girl seemed equally tongue-tied. She was pretty in a conventional way, blue eyes and hair that was obviously cared for. It was carefully waved in the current fashion. It suited her, Archie thought.

'Do you live near here?' he asked her, eventually.

'Not far,' she said. 'I've only come with my

sister because me Dad said I couldn't come on my own. I don't really know what to do. She wants me out of her way. I usually go out with my friend but she couldn't go tonight. My sister keeps telling me off all the time. Says no-one's asking us to dance 'cos I'm too young and look so miserable.'

'How old are you then?' Archie asked without thinking.

'You're not s'posed to ask how old a lady is. Seventeen, nearly eighteen, if you must know.'

'That's not bad. Just about right. I'm twenty-one.'

'You don't look it.'

'Don't I?'

'The music's stopped. Hadn't we better get off the floor? Me sister's waving at me. I'll have to go.'

'Might see you again sometime. Thanks for the dance.'

'Yes. Thanks.'

He went back to Ernie.

'Let's get a drink. What a fast worker that one was.' Archie stared. Ernie had been dancing with his girl's sister.

'Why? What did she say?'

'I don't want to talk about it. Not my type at all.'

'I'm sorry. Her sister was quite nice. In fact, very nice.'

'Her sister? She said she was her friend and she'd had to bring her. Said she was cramping her style something rotten. Wanted to ditch her and could I give her a lift somewhere decent. She'd make it worth my while.'

'I see. Well, the other one is quite shy. I doubt yours will go too far wrong if her sister has anything to do with it.'

A few weeks later, Ernie left a message at work for Archie. He wanted his friend to join him and two guests for a dinner dance at the North Staffs Hotel, the following weekend. Archie wasn't entirely sure what a dinner dance was but he did know the North Staffs was way out of his league. When he protested as much, Ernie took him in hand.

'Now look here. You're one of the managers now. You've done pretty well for yourself. It's time you started to branch out a bit.'

'Who are these guests?'

'Couple of girls from the tennis club. Daughter of someone Dad knows. You should join. Meet all sorts there. Now, are you on for this dinner dance, or not?'

'How expensive is it?'

'Nothing. Dad's paid. We're doing him a bit of a favour, taking these two. Besides, he thinks I should expand on my social acquaintances, as well. Says it's good for business. You will have to dress up a bit though . . . summat a bit special and not my old stuff. Not that there's owt wrong with it, of course. Can't you buy yourself a new suit? You should be earning enough by now. You never spend anything on yourself.'

Archie thought of his nest egg. It would certainly be enough to get something off the peg. Maybe it was time to break it open.

'I s'pose so. But isn't the North Staffs a bit posh? And how does the dinner part fit in with the dance?'

Patiently, Ernie explained it all to him. Archie was not at all sure that this was the right way forward for him. He was only a miner's son, for goodness sake. Wasn't he trying to fly just a little too high? He thought of his childhood dream of a big house with a proper bathroom. The big car he was going to have parked outside. A flood of energy went through him and he renewed his promise to himself. He spoke with conviction.

'You're right, Ernie. It's high time I started trying to better myself. Really started. Take myself in hand. Will you help me choose my new suit on Saturday, for starters?'

Archie didn't go home on Saturday after work. His mother had given up on him and rarely even bothered to ask what he was doing. He felt a bit bad about his father and brother but it was too bad. They seemed to have little to do with his life these days. He got himself changed at Ernie's house, being assigned to one of the spare rooms.

'You might as well stay over here afterwards. It'll be far too late by the time we've dropped the girls off,' Ernie said with a lecherous wink. 'Your mother won't mind will she?'

'Doubt she'll notice. Thanks. I haven't got anything with me though. Clothes and that.'

'We'll fix you up. Don't worry about a thing. This is the night, Archie my boy. I feel it in my water.'

They collected the two girls, a young-looking, giggling pair, and drove to the hotel. There seemed to be dozens of people milling round and Archie felt very nervous. He was worried about making a fool of himself. It was all right for Ernie. He was used to eating in company and always knew which knives or forks to use. Archie was never used to more than one of anything on a table at one time. If he hadn't shared a good few meals at the Drapers' over the years, he'd have been even more lost. Ethel and Ada disappeared into the ladies powder room and he stood by the bar with Ernie.

''Ere you are, mate. Get that down ya. Dutch courage.' Archie took the glass and sipped at the spirit. It burned his throat and made him feel warm all over.

'Not bad that. Not bad at all.'

'We'll stick to beer after this,' Ernie advised. 'It'll be a long night and we don't want to ruin anything by getting pissed, now do we? Here come the ladies. Now then, what can I get for you?'

They both asked for orange juice and stood

151

awkwardly sipping, giggling if anyone spoke to them. Archie was already wishing the evening was over, despite the whisky. He caught sight of someone, reflected in the mirror behind the bar. He swung round. The girl across the room smiled at him and gave a little wave.

'Who's that?' murmured Ernie.

'Just a girl. I met her at the Town Hall do. Longton. You remember? The one with the sister.'

'Oh yes. I remember. You liked her, didn't you?' Archie nodded.

'She's obviously with her boyfriend tonight though, damn him. He's far too good looking for his own good.'

'P'raps it's her brother.'

'No such luck. They're probably engaged or something.'

'Really, you two. Are you here with us or not?' Ethel asked petulantly.

'Sorry, girls. We were being thoughtless. Shall we go and find our table?'

Gradually, Archie relaxed. He couldn't help looking over to the girl. Her hair was crimped into Marcel waves. Very stylish. The bloke she was with seemed to be very casual and there were several other men sitting at their table. He thought she was the nicest looking girl he'd ever seen. He wished he wasn't having to make conversation with the boring Ada, his allotted partner for the evening. He wanted to gaze at the girl of his dreams. He wondered what her

152

name was. He tried to pull himself together and concentrate on dancing with Ada between the courses. Somehow, it felt all wrong to be dancing and then eating again. There was movement at the table where his mystery girl was sitting. All the blokes got up and went behind the curtains. A few moments later, they came onto the stage, as the regular hotel orchestra left for a break. They began to play some of the popular tunes of the day and the boyfriend seemed to be at the front of the band. He began to sing, as he played his guitar. He wasn't bad. No wonder she had fallen for him. Archie excused himself for a few moments and went to the gents. It gave him the excuse to go past the girl who was now sitting alone. She didn't seem to mind.

'Hallo again,' he said to her as he passed.

'Oh hallo. Didn't expect to see you here.'

'I didn't expect to see you. That your boyfriend, then? The singer?'

'Course he isn't. He's my cousin. Started the band a couple of years ago, and just beginning to make his name around here.'

'I see. And is one of the others your boyfriend?' He felt himself blushing at the directness of his questions.

'I don't have anyone special. My friend's with us tonight. She's dancing with someone at the moment. There's quite a few of us go out together. Just friends, sort of. Barry, he's the singer, often lets me come with them. I tell him what people are saying. Any road up, it's better than spending the evening with my 'orrible sister.'

'What's your name?'

'Dora. Dora Marsh. What's yours?'

'Archie. Archie Barnett. Pleased to meet you.'

'Likewise,' she said shyly, offering her hand.

'You've got little hands, haven't you?' he said, holding onto it.

'Have I? I'd never noticed.'

'What do you do?' he asked, forgetting all about his party at their own table.

'I'm a hairdresser. I work at Stanways.' He remained unimpressed. Ladies hairdressers were hardly something he knew about. His Mum occasionally washed her hair at the scullery sink, same as the rest of them. All the same, it explained why Dora was so particular about her hair. He suddenly caught sight of Ernie, waving frantically at him.

'I'm sorry. I'll have to go back to me friends. Tell your cousin I think he's really good. Will I see you again, Dora?'

'I usually go to Longton now, on Saturdays, when I finish work. Sometimes it's Newcastle, with Barry and the lads.'

'Maybe I'll see you at Longton sometime. Hope so.'

'I hope so too. Are you going to the dance next week? It's Bill Davis and his band. Should be a good do. Me friend's coming as well.

154

P'raps your mate can come. Will you be there?'

'I will. For definite. Especially if I know you're going to be there. I'll see you there then.'

'All right. Bye for now.'

Archie was blushing to his roots by the time he got back to his table. Ada was looking thunderous. Ernie grinned at his friend and tried to smooth things over.

'Thought I was going to have to come and drag you away,' he said with a grin. He raised his eyebrows questioningly. As soon as Archie thought the girls weren't looking, he gave a grin and stuck up his thumb. He could hardly wait for the evening to be over. He dutifully danced with both girls, every time looking out for Dora, and when he saw her dancing with anyone else he looked daggers at her partner. He didn't manage to spot her friend, who might be at the dance next week and be a partner for Ernie. Ethel wanted to sit by Ernie in the front seat for the return journey and made Archie sit behind with Ada. Each time they went round a corner, she allowed herself to be flung against Archie. He got steadily more embarrassed as the journey continued, especially when she made little or no effort to return to her own half of the seat. She rested her head on his shoulder and he felt himself growing hot and uncomfortable. She turned her face to his and waited for him to kiss her.

155

He closed his eyes, trying to imagine it was Dora sitting close to him on the back seat. Just as he felt there was nothing he could do about it and that he must kiss the girl, the car swerved and he was thrown in the opposite direction.

'Steady on there,' Ernie yelled at Ethel. 'You'll have us in the ditch if you're not careful. Just hold your impatience till we stop, will you?'

'Who do you think you are?' she protested. 'Think a lot of yourself, don't you, Ernie Draper? Well I don't offer twice, so you've lost your chance. Now drive us home please.'

Archie gave a wry grin. Thank heavens for Ethel. He could now forget all about the tiresome Ada and concentrate on the next weekend when he would see Dora. She was much more his type. Grumpily, Ernie drove to Ethel's house and opened the door for her to get out. He pushed the seats forward to let the two out of the back.

'I take it you're driving back with me?' he asked Archie.

'Certainly am. Thanks for your company, ladies,' he said politely.

'Yer. Thanks for the lift, Ernie.'

'Right snooty pair aren't they?' Ada, or was it Ethel, said loudly as they got out of the car.

'Can't stand these types who think they're God's gift to women. We'll show 'em one of these days. Think they might regret turning us down.'

It was hardly a gracious farewell but neither of the men minded. They would not be offering either of those girls another chance. As they drove away, they both roared with laughter. Sheer high spirits.

'So, how did you get on with the girl of your dreams?'

'She isn't my dream girl,' Archie protested. 'I just think she's nice, decent type.'

'So did you get a date?'

'Well, as a matter of fact, I've arranged to see her next Saturday at Longton Town Hall.'

'I see. Does this mean the end of our Saturdays?'

'Shouldn't think so. You might find yourself a girl, anyhow. She's got a friend. You might like her. Then we can be a proper foursome.'

'Hang on a bit. You're not exactly courting this girl are you? You've only just met her. Any road, I thought you said she had a load of men with her?'

'Her cousin plays in the band and the others were friends, or band members. I thought they were quite good, didn't you?'

'They were all right. Yes. Not bad at all. So, what's her name?'

The short journey back to Ernie's was barely enough time for Archie to recount every detail of the brief conversation.

'I s'pose I do think she's a bit special. Did I tell you she's a hairdresser? Works with her friend.'

'Several times. Oh, Archie. Take it easy. Don't go pinning your hopes on this one. You've only just met her and you don't know much about women at all. You're not exactly experienced, are you?'

'I know what I need to know, thank you very much.'

'You know about girls at work. Crowds of 'em, admittedly. But they're a sight different when they're not all in a gang. You get on with 'em well enough at work but they'd have you for breakfast if they met you out on your own somewhere. I only want you to be happy, Archie. You deserve it for god's sake. You haven't had much of a life, have you?'

'I don't know what you mean.'

'Think on. Home's always been a tough place to be. You've said so yourself often enough. But you've fought your way to get where you wanted to be. Ignored everything your mother's tried to make you do and you've got what you wanted. Don't throw it all away for some crush on a girl.'

'I'm not throwing anything away. You know summat, Ern? I reckon I'm going to marry this one. Yes, I reckon she's everything I could ever want.' He blinked in surprise at his own words. He'd never even thought of it before but suddenly, he knew deep down that Dora Marsh was the girl he wanted to marry.

'I think you've had a bit too much to drink

my lad. We'll say no more about this conversation. Pretend it never happened. Now let's get out of the cold and see if me Dad's left a decanter out for us. There should be a bite of summat to eat as well. How does that sound?'

'Pretty good, mate. I reckon I could take to life at the Drapers' house. There's always food and drink available and you never have to scrub a single pot.'

On Sunday morning, he went to church to sing in the choir straight from Ernie's. He enjoyed singing but he'd long realised that was the only reason he ever went to church. He had no faith and the words meant nothing to him but it was the only place he felt free to let his voice ring out. That particular Sunday, all he could see in his head was a vision of Dora. He arrived home for Sunday lunch with the family. His mother had made a few barbed comments but he ate silently, knowing that to tell them anything about the evening would provoke only nastiness from Frances. He did feel sorry for his Dad. Several times, he caught his gaze and wondered if they'd ever be able to talk again. He was a gentle, hardworking man who did his best for his family and put up with a great deal.

'How about a stroll down to the park this afternoon, son?' he asked suddenly.

Archie stared. It was so unusual he wondered if something was wrong.

159

'Can we have a game, Dad? Will you play football with me, Archie?' William piped up.

'All right. I'd like that, Dad.'

'And what am I s'posed to do while you're gone? Wash up and make tea? I'm nobody's slave you know.' Frances was also surprised by her husband's unusual suggestion. Usually, he liked nothing better than to sit in front of the grate with his feet resting on the fender, once the meal was over.

'We'll do the pots before we go,' Archie offered. 'I'll make a start right away. Come on, our William. Get stuck in.'

'I'm not washing,' his brother announced.

'All right. I'll do the washing. Lazy little sod aren't you? Washing's always the worst job. Especially on Sundays when there's a roasting tin as well.' He cuffed his brother's ear, noticing for the first time in ages just how much the lad had grown. 'You must be coming up for the senior school soon. Have you thought about what you're going to do with yourself?'

'Nah. I'm not clever like you. I reckon it'll be the pit for me.'

'I thought you were s'posed to have a bad chest? The pit'll be no good for you if you have.'

'Dunno. My chest's been all right for ages. Haven't bin poorly at all. Maybe you can get us a job at your place when the time comes? I shan't be staying on at school any longer than I can help.'

William found some of his mates when they got to the park and Archie watched as they kicked a ball around. His Dad stood with him, sucking on his old pipe.

'How's it going then, lad?' he asked.

'Real well, Dad. I love me job and I've got definite prospects. I'm being promoted to under manager of the decorating shop soon.'

'Manager eh? By heck. That'll mean a good rise I expect.' Archie blushed. 'Under-manager, Dad.' He was speaking out of turn. He felt suddenly guilty about keeping back some of his wages for his own use. His dad had worked hard all his life and yet he'd never heard him complain about anything. 'I expect there'll be a rise. Dad, I'm sorry.'

'What about, lad?'

'Well, you know how things are with me and me Mum. She's always wanting every penny I earn. I've been keeping a bit back each week, for me spends. I didn't say as I'd had a rise last time. I know it's wrong of me and everything but I had to. She doesn't give me enough back for anything I want to do. I like going out with me friend. I can't let him pay for me, can I? Specially when it's his Dad who's paying me wages. He must have a pretty good idea of what I take home.'

'There's things the women folk don't have to know about, lad. I let her think she's getting my wage packet unopened but there's ways and means.' There was a twinkle in his father's eye. Archie stared.

'You mean . . . you?'

'Course I do, lad. Always have. I like to have a bit put by for the hard times. You never suffered during the General Strike, even though I didn't get paid for two or three weeks.'

'Yer crafty old bugger,' Archie burst out. 'Sorry, Dad. I didn't mean that.'

'Yes yer did. And you're quite right. Pays to be a crafty old bugger from time to time. Take my advice, son. Get yourself a safe place and put summat by for the rainy days. You'll be wanting to get wed before you're much older. You'll need money for that. Don't let it happen too soon though, before you're ready. It's my one regret that we got wed too soon. But then if it hadn't happened the way it did, you'd never have been born. And that would have been a loss. I'm very proud of me eldest son. You've got where you wanted to be despite everything.'

'Thanks, Dad,' Archie replied, touched by the unaccustomed words from his usually taciturn father. 'What did you mean about things happening before you were ready?'

'I probably shouldn't mention it but well, we jumped the gun a bit. Your Mum and me. Let's say it was best we got married when we did, for your sake. Don't let on to her that I've told you. Proud woman your mother. Wouldn't like

162

to think anyone knew of any weakness.'

'I see. Well, I can't pretend I'm not shocked.' Perhaps the greatest shock was that his Dad had wanted to do it with his Mother in the first place. Let alone before she'd got him safe behind the marriage lines.

'She wasn't always like she is now, you know. Used to enjoy nights out and well, she was a good looker in her younger days. She's had a few problems to put up with. Couple of miscarriages. Makes a woman feel bad. As if there's summat wrong with her. She's never been the same since.'

'I see. I never knew. I have wondered sometimes, though. How you stand it, I mean?'

'You just do. So, have you got a young lady then, son?'

'I've got one in me sights. Haven't exactly been courting her but I intend to put that right. Very soon.'

'Just mark my words. Don't let yourself get caught out. It i'n't worth it. If you can't be good be careful. That's what they say and it's true. You understand what I mean, don't you, lad?'

'I guess so. Thanks, Dad. For talking to me straight. And you don't mind if I keep a bit of my wages back from now on?'

'Be fair with your mother. That's all I ask. Give her what's fair for your keep and get yourself some savings behind you. Maybe we should go out to the pub one evening soon.

163

How d'ya feel about drinking with an old man?'

'I'd be proud to, Dad. And the first drinks are on me.'

'Course they are. Wouldn't have asked otherwise. Now, where's that brother of yours? Time we were off home.'

To Archie it was the first acknowledgement that he was now accepted as a man.

## CHAPTER NINE

When 1930 dawned, Archie and Dora were invited to a New Year's Eve party at Ernie's house. They kissed at midnight and were still kissing when it was five minutes after midnight.

'Break it up you two. You have to come up for breath sometime, you know.' Ernie had his arm round his girlfriend, Mab Pearce. There were several couples, all contemporaries of each other. The parents had gone for a *more civilised* evening, as they put it. Dinner and dance at a local hotel.

'Put some more music on, Ernie, Darling,' Mab urged. 'Everyone's necking all over the place. What would your *Ancients* think if they came home suddenly? Come on everyone, let's dance.'

Mabel Pearce and Dora were good friends,

both working together at Stanway's. It was lucky Ernie had taken to her the way he had as they shared pleasant times together as a foursome. Ernie went to the gramophone and selected a noisy number and soon everyone was jumping around and singing at the tops of their voices.

'Dora,' Archie said quietly. 'Come out here with me a minute. There's something I want to ask you.' This was it. This was the moment he'd been waiting for, for almost two years.

'What is it, love?' she asked.

'I want you to marry me. Will you?'

'What, now?' she teased.

'I'm serious, Dora. I've wanted to marry you ever since I first saw you at that dance. I told Ernie right there and then. He thought I was mad. But I've never wanted anyone else.'

'Oh Archie, I don't know. I'm not even twenty yet. And how can you afford to get married? You don't earn enough, do you?'

'I don't mean right away. I've got a bit of money put by. We'd have to save for a bit. But at least we can get engaged. Shall I ask your Dad?'

'I don't think they'd let me, get engaged I mean. Not till I'm twenty at least.'

'But they like me, don't they?' Archie had been invited home to her parents for Sunday tea on a number of occasions. He always felt comfortable there, even though their home seemed very much more up-market than his

165

own. For once, he didn't care. His own home was little more than somewhere to sleep now. He was waiting to move out at the first chance.

'Course they like you. You're not me first boyfriend you know. I've taken other lads home. My parents like to know who my friends are.'

'You don't mean there's someone else, do you?' Archie asked in alarm.

'There might be,' Dora said with a grin.

'Oh heck. Have I made a fool of myself?'

'No course you haven't. My Mum said that you were the right one for me. "You should marry that young artist boy, if he asks you." That's what she said. Happen she's right. But don't say anything for now. I'll have to talk to them. They can be a bit funny. So, you think you can afford to keep me in the style I know, do you?'

'I shall be able to, give me a few months. Besides, you go to work as well. P'raps you wouldn't want to give that up. Not right away.'

'Me Dad doesn't hold with women working after marriage. Says it reflects on the man. He thinks it looks like a husband can't support his wife.'

'I see. Well . . .'

'But I don't think I would like to give up work though. Not really. I'm going to be made up to manageress soon. Mr Stanway's going to open another shop. I shall be in charge of the one I work in now and Mabel's going to go to the new one. How about that for a bit of news?'

'Well done, love. I'm proud of you.'

'What's going on out here,' boomed Ernie's voice from the doorway. 'You keep disappearing. If I didn't know you better, I'd say you were trying to avoid me. Us. Everyone.'

'Just coming. We had a few things to sort out. This is going to be a great year, I can feel it in me waters.'

'I hope so,' Ernie said. 'About time we had something good happen. After the last two years, we need something to turn us round. But I don't have to tell you how things are. Sales have been right down in the dumps. At least the government are still trying to help a bit. The tax on imported china saved us a lot of competition.'

'I'll never understand how they make china so cheap in them other countries. Still, as you say, it saves the competition from cheap copies. Nothing like the quality of our stuff. And I think once the new lines are coming into production properly, we stand as good a chance as anyone.'

'This is supposed to be a party, you boring old things. Not a board meeting. You can talk pottery tomorrow.'

'One more dance then, Dora. I think after that, we should be getting home. I've got work in the morning. Not blessed with a day off, like some I could mention.'

'Isn't your Dad off tomorrow? . . . today?'

'Miners don't ever work on New Year's Day. They always say it's unlucky. I reckon it could be summat to do with the ale they've supped to welcome the New Year.'

'I'd like to meet your Mum and Dad sometime. D'ya think I could?'

'Might put you off me for good and all. Now, are we having this dance or not?'

During the next few months, there was an air of expectancy throughout the factory. The last year of the twenties had proved disastrous for many companies and several of the smaller ones had considered closing. Once the worst of the slump was over, everyone tried to be optimistic that the bright new designs would sell. Clarice Cliff and Suzie Cooper were the innovators and Draper's planned to be somewhere close behind. Though some of Archie's designs had been taken up and were going into production, he felt less than content with the results. Bright and bold they may be, but to him, they were certainly not beautiful. They were somehow clumsy and lacking in delicacy. But, he set to work with a will and watched proudly as his very own first designs were packed up and sent to the shops all over the country and even to places abroad. Mr Draper took a personal interest in everything that went on, just as his father had done. Ernie was in charge of the sales department now and continued to go on trips to the business fairs that were beginning to be the most popular way of selling.

There were still the more traditional lines being made, though with less enthusiasm by the workers. The paintresses enjoyed the easier task of spreading the bright colours in simple, geometric patterns. If the lines were too thick or a bit uneven, it mattered even less.

Archie was disturbed by the almost careless attitude that was growing among the workers with the newer styes of china. When he was feeling irritated, he would go and watch Tom, as he painted his works of art, exactly as he always had done. They had a timeless quality and there was always a demand for his work.

'I'm doing a full set of plates and dishes for a special order,' he told Archie. The young man nodded. Though his jurisdiction did not extend to the master painters, he was usually aware of what they were doing.

'Fruit mainly, isn't it?' Tom nodded.

'Lots of gold as well. Someone has plenty of money to spend.'

'Seems a shame to use them. Too much washing can't improve them much.'

'Not too bad if it's done properly. No scrubbing at them or using water that's too hot. Always amazes me that the china can break if the water is too hot, when you consider they've been heated to such great temperatures on the kilns.'

'It's cause they're done slowly, with the heat building up gradually,' Archie explained.

'Is that right now,' Tom said, a twinkle in his eye. 'They've been teaching you properly have they?'

'Sorry. I'm being daft. Of course you know all about it. Will you teach me something about colours and the chemistry of them?'

'Now y'are asking summat,' Tom replied. 'I don't have any education you know. All I know is what's what. What works. I know how they'll turn out in the kiln and after all my years, I'm rarely wrong.'

All the same, Archie studied the old man's techniques and stored away hundreds of useful tips in his mind. The artist knew instinctively how much of this powder or that to put into his mix and how much linseed oil he needed to bind it together. He collected adverts from pottery magazines and papers and stored them in a folder he had made out of some scrap card. He began to take them home and spent hours poring over them in the dingy living room of his parents' house. He no longer thought of it as home, exactly.

Dora had finally agreed to become engaged and nervously, Archie went to speak to her father. Henry Marsh was a gentle man. He was a manager in a grocery chain and worked long hours in the shop. One of eleven children, he had long since left the family farm and found his way into retailing. Fresh farm produce was always on sale so he didn't feel that he had betrayed the family's heritage. He'd fought in the Great War, spending agonising hours in the misery of the trenches. He'd picked up a piece of shrapnel in one leg and it had become badly ulcerated, in any case, precluding him from working on the land. Luckily for him, the end of the war had come before he was forced to return to France. He had adored his two little girls to distraction ever since, trying to make up for missing the vital years of their childhood. His wife Mary had always managed to cope with whatever life had thrown at her. She was a wonderful cook and now, with the good food he was able to provide, she happily baked, cleaned and kept the house immaculate.

When Archie had begun to call, he instinctively knew this was the right man for his Dora. There had been several others but none of them had come up to his high standards. He hoped Dora would see him for what he was and show the good sense to make the right choice. He took Archie into the parlour, a stiff uncomfortable room which rarely saw a fire.

'I reckon I know what's coming,' he said to the nervous young man.

'You do? Has Dora said something?'

'She didn't need to, lad. We've all seen it coming. It was a matter of time. Well, I expect you've prepared a speech. You'd best get on with it so we can get back in the warm.'

'The fact is, well, I'm getting, that is we . . . will be getting . . .'

'You want to marry my daughter?' Archie nodded miserably at his sudden inability to express himself. He'd tried to plan what he'd say but he'd made a right mess of it. 'Can you afford to keep a wife? And probably a child or two?'

'I shall, in time. We don't expect to get married for a bit, yet. We want to save up some more. I've been putting a bit by every week in a savings account at the bank. I'd like to buy a ring soon and then start to look for a house. Nothing fancy yet awhile but one day, I'm going to have a proper big house with me own bathroom and hot water and everything.'

'I'm delighted to hear it. I'm proud to welcome you to our family. We're not well off but I think we can help out a bit. My Mary's a very careful shopper and keeps a good home for us. I expect it's rubbed off on Dora.'

'Does that mean you agree? I can marry Dora?'

'If that's what she wants.'

'Oh she does.'

'Do you mean to say you've already discussed it with her?'

'Oh. I'm sorry. Shouldn't I have done? It didn't seem worth bothering you if she didn't want to marry me.' Archie looked crestfallen.

Henry grinned.

'Only teasing, lad. Course you'd have asked her first. I'm not royalty you know. Let's get back to the women folk and give 'em the news.' They went into the other room. Archie's grin was wrapping itself from ear to ear. 'Mary, love, this young man believes he can make our girl happy. What do you think?'

'I'm very pleased, love. I've always said you're the right one for her. Congratulations both of you.' Dora's mother put her arms round her daughter's new fiancé and hugged him. He gasped in surprise and felt his eyes beginning to fill with tears. Never, ever had his own mother hugged him like that. He held onto her for as long as it was decent, drawing the warmth of her very being into his own. Henry thumped him on the back and Dora stood watching this first real welcome from her parents. She too felt moved to tears and knew deep inside she had made the right choice.

'I did think of getting you a ring before I came over today,' Archie told her later. 'But I thought you'd like to help choose it for yourself.'

'Thanks, love. Yes, I'd like that. You did the right thing.'

'We'll go next Saturday afternoon, after work, if you like.'

'What about your precious match? Ernie won't be too happy if you don't go with him.'

'I think this is a bit more important than some old football match, don't you?' Dora was impressed. She nodded. 'Besides,' continued Archie, 'it's an away match next week.'

'You rotten thing,' she said as she punched him on the arm.

'Only joking,' he laughed. Nothing was going to quell his spirits today. He was well and truly on his way. 'I love you,' he said, his voice cracking with the emotion of it all.

Archie kept his news to himself. His own parents seemed to be disinterested in what he did with his life, though he had grown closer to his father since they'd taken to sharing a few drinks together. The china industry was still proving a difficult business, with customers less ready to part with their cash. Superficially, everyone seemed full of optimism but there was always the constant dread of another slump. He had bought Dora the engagement ring she had wanted. He had taken the precaution of visiting the jewellers before he met Dora and getting the owner of the shop to put a selection of rings out, all within the amount he could afford to spend. It was a clever move. When Dora was faced with the tray of rings, all set out on black velvet, she had pounced straight away on a solitaire diamond, set in platinum.

'Oh, Archie, it's just what I always dreamed of. It's lovely. Are you sure you can afford it?'

'Course I can. For you, only the ring you really want is good enough.' He winked at the jeweller and he put the tray beneath the counter, bringing out a tiny box for the precious ring. Dora was grinning happily, as he placed it in her hands.

'Oh, Archie, I'm so happy. Can I put it on now?'

'Course you can, love. It's yours now and always.'

They walked along the road, holding each other's hands when they thought no-one was looking. Dora kept glancing down at her hand as if she couldn't believe it.

'I'm sorry it wasn't a bigger diamond, Dora love. I know you deserve much better. I promise you, one day I'll buy you the biggest diamond that'll fit on your finger.'

'I'm happy with this. It's perfect, Archie. Anything else you buy will never mean any more than this ring does.'

'I'm glad to hear you say that,' Archie said huskily. For once in his life, he felt the urge to let the tears flow. He swallowed hard. He wasn't some soft lad who cried at nothing. 'Well, we'd better go home to your place, see if your Mum approves.'

'Oh she will, I'm sure of it. Speaking of Mum. When am I going to meet your family? You do know I haven't even seen them, let alone met them?'

Archie blushed. He didn't want Dora seeing where he came from. The poverty of his area and his own home were something that constantly embarrassed him. It was wrong of him, he knew. But he also knew well that his mother would never give a proper welcome to anyone he brought home.

'Eh, you're not ashamed of them are you?' Dora asked. He reddened even more. 'That's it, isn't it? For heaven's sakes, Archie. I'm nothing so special that I don't realise how folks struggle around these parts. And you've no business being ashamed of your family. You've turned out well, so they must have done some things right.'

'It's not that I'm ashamed,' he fibbed. 'But you don't know my Mum. She's difficult. She doesn't ever approve of anything I do.' He looked away. How could Dora ever understand? Her family were wonderful. Warm and caring people who took an interest in everything their daughter said or did.

'Right, Well, you'd better tell your Mum that I'm planning to visit them very soon. I have to know what my future in-laws make of their daughter-in-law to be. What will they think if I never come round?' She paused, looking hard at Archie. 'They do know about me, don't they?' Archie looked away. 'You haven't told them, have you?' she said, her voice rising slightly in anger.

'No. They don't approve of anything, like I said. Well, me Dad's all right. He knew I was courting. But he doesn't know I've actually asked you to marry me.'

'I think it's high time they did know. You're

176

not ashamed of me, are you?'

'Ashamed of you? How could I be? You're lovely, kind and thoughtful and you've probably got the best parents in the world.'

'Aye, well it's me you're weddin', not my parents. But I love *you*, Archie. That's enough for me. It doesn't matter what your parents are like. Not really. I mean to say . . . look at the way you've got on. From what I can make out, you fought very hard to get where you wanted to be.'

'And I'm not done yet. I'm going to have a big house with a bathroom and hot water. Then I want at least two cars parked outside.'

'And you'll get it all, Archie. I know you will. But for now, how about letting me meet my future in-laws?'

'Oh heck. I know this is going to be a very big mistake but I'll ask me Mum if you can come for your tea. Next Sunday suit?'

'Yes pleasc. And don't worry. I love you, Archie. How could I not love your parents?'

'Quite easily,' he replied grimly.

His worst fears were realised when Archie broached the subject of bringing his young lady home to meet his parents.

'Typical,' his mother snapped. 'Just when you're starting to earn good money so's your Dad can take it a bit easier, you get the notion to try courtin' some girl. Where's she from?'

'She lives out Normacot way. Near Longton.'

'And what does her Dad do?'

'He's the manager of one of the Maypole grocery stores. Dora's a hairdresser. She's about to be made up to manageress. Doing really well for herself. So, is it all right if I tell her she can come for her tea on Sunday?'

'If you have to. I'm not putting myself out though. She'll take us as she finds us.'

'Is she good-looking?' asked William.

'I dunno. Yes. I think so anyhow. I don't bother too much about looks. She's just a lovely person. I'm sure you're going to like her, Mum. I'll give you a bit extra from me wages this week. Then you can get something a bit special in. I expect Mrs Machin will have some of that ham in at the weekend.'

'Are you trying to tell me how to set out a decent tea?'

'Course not, Mum. But I want it all to be just right. I want you to like her and for her to like you.'

'Don't know what all the fuss is about. She's just a girl isn't she?'

'She's the girl I'm marrying.' He bit his lip. He hadn't mentioned the engagement before and now he'd let it slip without making the proper preparations.

'You haven't gone and got yourself engaged to this . . . this piece. Tell me you haven't.'

'Well, yes. I have as it happens. Got the ring last week.'

'Where did you get the money to go buying

some ring?'

'I've earned it, Mum. Every penny. I didn't see that I had to give you everything I earned. It isn't right.'

Frances's face hardened. Her mouth disappeared into its little tight line.

'We'll see what your father has to say about this. You're an ungrateful sod. All we did to send you to that posh school. We had to do without, for you. This is the way you thank us. Holding back on your wages. I've never heard the likes. How could you, Archie? I've never been so ashamed of anything in my life. You're a liar and a cheat.'

'I'm sorry, Mum, but I think I deserve to be able to have a life of my own. I've always worked very hard. As for the so-called posh school, which, you'll remember, I had to leave early to earn a living. If it hadn't been for meeting Ernie Draper there, I'd have been down the pit with me Dad. I'd never have got on like I have.'

His mother left the room and started banging pots round in the scullery. Archie knew there was nothing to be gained by saying anything more and went up to his room. He had always felt slightly guilty about putting his money away each week but he still felt it was justified. He was twenty-two, after all. Time he started out on his own. His mother shouldn't even be thinking she could control him any more. All the same, he wondered how on earth he and Dora would ever manage to afford somewhere half decent to live.

On Sunday afternoon, Archie stood outside the house, waiting for Dora's little car to appear round the corner of his road. She'd saved hard and bought it a couple of years earlier, helped by her parents. They were glad to be spared the anxiety of having their daughter out and relying on public transport either for her social life or work. Archie smiled to himself, despite the rain that was beginning to pour down steadily. It washed along the street, making tiny rivulets between the cobbles and forming grimy, dark grey topped streams in the gutters. It was never enough to wash anywhere clean. He glanced along the depressing street. No doubt the neighbours would have their curtains twitching within a few minutes, nosing out to see who was visiting. It would be something of a novelty to have a car parked outside. He'd have liked to be able to collect Dora from her home but it was impossible. He held the car door open for her as she stepped outside and took her hand as they went into the terraced house that was his home. He'd helped clean the living room during the morning and organised William to help with the washing up after Sunday dinner. He wanted everything to be just right, to make up for the miserable reception he expected from his mother. He'd tried to see what she'd got in for tea but she'd sent him packing before he could even open the meat safe. He really hoped there'd be some ham and a bit of cake. He couldn't remember his mother ever baking a cake, so it would have to be something like a piece of slab cake from the shop.

'I hope you're not expecting too much,' he said to Dora as he pushed the door open.

'Course not. You've told me a bit about what they're like. I'm not making any judgements till I've met them all.'

'Here we go then.' He gripped her arm tightly as he pushed open the door. 'We're here Mum, Dad.' He went into the living room and held Dora's hand as he introduced her. 'This is Dora. My fiancée.' He said the word proudly, using it for the first time. His mother's mouth was held in its customary tight line and she held out a grudging hand to the girl. Dora took it and smiled one of her most radiant smiles.

'I'm very pleased to meet you, Mrs Barnett. Archie's told me a lot about you.'

'Has he now. Don't s'pose he had anything to say that was good.' Dora hesitated, smiled and turned to Ralph.

'Hallo, love,' he said gently. 'I'm very pleased to meet you. This is our William. He's not half as bad as he looks, I promise you.' They all smiled nervously and William stepped forward to shake her hand.

'She's a bit of a looker, Archie. Can't think

181

what she sees in you though. In fact, I reckon she should wait a bit till I've grown up. I'd have been as big as he is you know, 'cept I was bad a bit, when I was little.'

Dora laughed nervously. She glanced at Archie and smiled at him.

'I reckon you could be right. Still, I've promised him now and I never break a promise if I can help it.'

'Then promise me you'll marry me if ever he lets you down?'

'All right,' she replied. 'But I reckon you've got a long wait ahead.'

'Come and sit yourself near the fire,' Ralph urged. 'Then you can tell us all about yourself. Hairdresser, Archie says you are. Now what does that entail, exactly?'

She talked hesitatingly at first but soon warmed to the gentle man who seemed to be genuinely interested in what she was saying. Frances sat tight lipped, saying little and looking disapproving at her words.

'I could do your hair one day if you like,' she offered, trying to unbend the steely gaze of Archie's mother. 'At home, like.'

'Don't have time for all that nonsense,' she said. 'Besides, who's going to look at me? This lot scarcely notice I'm even in the house.' Dora bit her lip. 'As long as food's on the table and there's a fire going.'

'P'raps a new hair do is exactly what you need then,' Dora said bravely. 'Then they might notice you.'

'Time I started getting the tea. You'll get nothing fancy here, I warn you. You have to take us as you find us.'

'Can I help at all?' Dora offered.

'No thanks. Our William will set the table. You'd best sit and talk. That's what you're here for.'

All the time, Archie was perched uncomfortably on the edge of the table. He was at a total loss as to how to manage the occasion. Dora didn't look too uncomfortable but as usual, his mother was not showing herself up to the best advantage. Still, it was no more than he'd expected. They talked awkwardly as the clatter of tins in the kitchen indicated that some sort of tea was on the way. William appeared from time to time with various plates and cups. One of the purchases Archie had organised was some cream table ware, all seconds of course and so hadn't cost too much. There was even a tablecloth covering the coarse scrubbed pine. It wasn't new but he'd certainly never seen it before. Maybe his mother had borrowed it from one of the neighbours. Give her her due, she'd certainly made some sort of effort and he felt grateful.

Whether Dora was impressed or not, it was difficult to tell. She smiled a lot and politely joined in with the conversation. He couldn't help but compare his own home to that of

Dora's. He found his own sadly lacking in all things, primarily in the warmth of the love that her parents showed.

'Is that a real diamond?' William asked suddenly, when there was a slight pause in the conversation. Dora glanced down at her finger and proudly extended it so they all could see her engagement ring.

'Yes. Isn't it lovely?' She smiled warmly at Archie who blushed and looked down at his hands, embarrassed at what he guessed was coming next.

Frances stared incredulously.

'How could you afford to go buying real diamonds? You could have furnished half a house for what that cost. I s'pose you think you'll come and live here with us do you? Well, you've got another think coming. There isn't room. So don't go expecting it.'

'My Mum and Dad have said we can live with them,' Dora said quickly and very firmly. 'Just for a while. We wouldn't dream of imposing on you, Mrs Barnett. There's plenty of room at our house, especially now my sister's left home.'

'I see,' sniffed Frances, her face implacable. 'And when do you intend to get wed?'

'We haven't decided just yet. There's a lot to sort out.'

'Can I have another cuppa?' Ralph asked to fill the sudden silence that had fallen. 'And perhaps Dora would like one as well. And how about another slice of this cake?'

'I'd love some more tea but nothing else to eat, thanks,' Dora replied politely. 'Then I must be getting back. I'm not keen on driving in the dark.'

'I'm sorry I haven't got me own transport,' Archie said shyly.

'Just hark at him,' Frances snapped. 'Who does he think he is? Own transport indeed. The likes of us never have anything like that. So you've got your own car 'ave you?'

'Mum and Dad helped me buy it. I needed to get to work and there isn't a bus where I have to go.' Frances clamped her mouth together again and looked away.

'I shall have me own car before long. Just you wait and see,' Archie replied through clenched teeth.

'Will you teach me to drive?' William asked to anyone who was listening.

'You'll have to wait and see. It'll be a long time before you're old enough.'

'It'll be a bloody long time before you have a car,' Frances told him. 'I don't know where you get your grand ideas from. That Ernie Draper, I don't doubt. Always knew he'd be a bad influence on you.'

Archie bit his lip to stop himself starting a row in front of Dora.

'I'll walk you to your car. I'll get your coat.' He went into the tiny hallway and unhooked her coat from the peg. He was shaking inside.

How could his mother show him up like that? Always talking about what they hadn't got or didn't do. At least she'd managed to put on a passable spread. Some of Mrs Machin's ham and a few bits of pickle. There was even a chunk of slab cake, as he'd hoped. But it wasn't half as good as Mrs Marsh's home made cakes.

'I'm sorry about my Mum,' Archie said. 'But I did warn you.'

'She wasn't too bad. She has to get used to the idea of her son leaving home and getting himself a wife. It's tough for anyone.'

'You know you said your parents wanted us to go and live with them? Did you mean it?'

'Course I did. Me Dad said it only last week, right after you'd gone home. I haven't had a chance to tell you before.'

'I see. And would you like that?'

'It may not be ideal but it would mean we could get married a bit sooner. Think about it.'

'I don't have to, love. I can't think of anything better than being with all of you. Say thanks to them, will you? And next week, we'll start planning our wedding.' He leaned over to kiss her and pulled her into his arms for a proper hug. 'I do love you, Dora.'

'And I love you. And I think your parents are all right. Your Dad's lovely and that little brother of yours, well he's quite a character.'

'I'm glad they haven't put you off me.'

'Hang on. Like I've said, it's you I'm

186

marrying you know, not your family.'

'Well, I can see I've got myself a pretty good deal.'

## CHAPTER TEN

The wedding was arranged for early August. As Dora's Mother was a staunch Methodist, it was her local chapel that was selected for the ceremony. It was to be a quiet family affair, the only non-family member being Ernie, who was Best Man. Dora's sister was unable to attend as she was heavily pregnant with her second child.

Dora wore a smart cream felt hat with a black trim, pulled down over one side, as was the current fashion. She had a cream wool suit, trimmed with black braid. Archie thought she looked wonderful and told her so.

'It will come in useful afterwards as well. I didn't want something that would only be worn once and then have to be kept in mothballs.'

The newly weds went to Bournemouth for their honeymoon, the train fare paid by Dora's Mum and Dad as part of their wedding gift to the couple. Archie's parents attended the ceremony, though neither of them said very much. His father noticed the obvious affection between his son and his new family and felt saddened. He would have loved to show similar affection but knew that his bad-tempered wife would only mock.

'Enjoy your life, son and make the most of it,' he said quietly, as the guests were waving off the happy pair. 'Take care of her. I reckon you've got yourself a good 'un there.'

'I know I have, Dad. Thanks for everything. Bye our William. Mind you behave yourself now I'm not there to keep you in line. Bye, Mum.'

Ralph remarked that it seemed the end of an era.

Together they signed in the register at the boarding house, Dora smiling shyly at her new husband.

'Mrs Archie Barnett,' she whispered as they followed the landlady up the stairs. 'Do you reckon she believed us?' Archie grinned and put a finger to his lips to silence her. The room was rather small and dark but held a huge double bed.

'Hope you'll be comfortable here,' she said with a slight sniff. 'May I offer you my congratulations?'

'Thank you very much,' Dora blushed. 'How did you know we're newly weds?'

'You're trailing confetti everywhere. Dinner's six-thirty to seven-thirty and breakfast seven-thirty to eight-thirty.' She turned and went out of the room, shutting it carefully behind her.

'I reckon we've got just over the hour before

188

we need present ourselves at the dining room door. What do you want to do?'

'First off, I want to kiss my new husband. Properly, I mean. I haven't had a chance before today. There's always been people around.'

When they finally went to bed after a short walk along the prom in the dark, they lay shyly side by side for a few minutes.

'I never thought I could be so lucky,' Archie whispered. 'I always promised myself I'd be successful and get away from those back streets and the mines. I promise you, Dora Marsh . . . Barnett, I'm going to make you really proud of me.'

'I am proud of you already. Now stop talking and make love to me.'

'You do know this is the first time for me, don't you? I never went with anyone else, ever.'

'Nor me.'

'I hope I don't let you down.'

'You won't love. We'll find out together.'

They came together joyously, gently, satisfyingly.

'I don't care if we're doing it all wrong,' Archie laughed happily the following morning. 'I like it just this way. How about you?'

'Oh, I'm sure we'll get even better with plenty of practice. We've got our lives ahead to try. Let's go and take a look at the sea.'

'If we must.'

'Yes, we must,' chided Dora. 'You've never even seen it properly yet. We can't waste the whole holiday. You've no idea how lovely it can be. I've been lots of times, with Mum and Dad and those two maiden aunts of ours. You know, the ones who gave us that lovely Royal Doulton figurine. She's beautiful, isn't she?'

'Certainly is. You know, that's exactly the sort of thing I'm planning to make one day. All sorts of figurines. Mine'll be just as good as the Doulton ones. Better in fact. I've been reading books to see how they make them. You see . . .'

'Archie. This is our honeymoon and while I love all your ideas and ambitions, I want it to be a very special time for us. Now, no more talk of china, painting, figurines or anything to do with them until at least supper time.'

The week flew by. For Archie, it was the best week he had ever known. Regular meals in the boarding house; long comfortable nights with his beloved Dora and days spent walking or sitting in the sun. Best of all, they talked about everything important in the world.

'You know the big house you're always talking about?' Dora asked.

'I'm having it, for definite.'

'I know. Well, could we call it Branksome? After this place?' They were walking along the area of Branksome Chine, near their honeymoon town.

'Course we can. Anything for you, love. It won't be for some time though. I've got a long way to go before we can afford something really special.'

Though the two generations got on well together, living in one house was far from ideal. Archie and Dora had little time to be on their own and always spent their evenings in the company of the parents. They played cards and sometimes, Dora's cousin Barry came round to visit. Occasionally, he gave them tickets to one of his performances. Archie felt slightly jealous of the closeness of the cousins but he said nothing. He was simply not used to having members of the family who actually got on well. He saw little of his own parents and for some months, not a great deal of his best friend, Ernie. He ran in to him occasionally at work but now he was a designer as well as manager, there was precious little spare time for socialising within the working day.

Archie and Dora walked up to the local park during what remained of the summer evenings. It was some distance away but once they had reached the park gates, they could enjoy a stroll among the flower beds. Sometimes, they hired a boat for a row on the lake to make a pleasant change.

'Let's go back down the hill out of the front gates, just for a change,' Dora suggested one evening.

'OK. Sure you're not too tired? You must have been on your feet all day.'

'No. It's such a lovely evening.' They walked

slowly, looking over the fields beyond the houses. 'Nice up here, isn't it?'

'I don't know why this is always called Longton Park. I mean, this is Dresden, isn't it?' Archie said.

'It's still a part of Longton I suppose. Still, it doesn't matter does it? It's a lovely spot. You could really think you were out in the country here.'

'Haven't ever had much to do with the country I s'pose. Hallo. Someone's got a nice spot to build a house.' Three modern houses were being built on a corner plot. 'Art deco aren't they? Wonder how that'll hold up?'

'I like them,' Dora said, studying the white buildings through half closed eyes. 'Bet they cost a packet.'

'More than we'll ever afford.'

Dora said nothing more but mentioned them to her parents when they got back.

'Have you heard how much they'll fetch?' she asked her Dad.

'I'll make a few inquiries. Why? Do you think you might be interested?'

'Eh, hang on a minute. They'll be far more than I can ever afford. Don't get carried away. We've only just seen them being built. They're miles away from being finished.' Archie suddenly felt afraid. For all his assertions of buying his own big house one day, things were moving a little too fast.

'No harm in finding out,' Henry said to him.

'We all seem to get along pretty well, don't you think? S'pose we were to all buy a bigger house between us? It'd make a lot of sense wouldn't it? We'd have space to spare and not get on top of each other like we do here. Mary can carry on cooking for all of us, until our Dora gives up work and wants to do her own cooking.'

'I don't know. I've never given that angle much thought. It might work. I'd have to ask at the bank of course. But if you were to put in some capital, heck, we might just do it.'

Dora's smile of pleasure was enough for him. Somehow, they'd be getting that house and much sooner than he'd planned. The asking price seemed very reasonable and they chose the house at the end of the three, the one overlooking the road, with the garden wrapping round it on three sides.

'Are you sure you want something this modern?' Archie asked her doubtfully one day.

'Course I do. It's just beautiful, don't you think? I love that stained glass window on the lower landing. Makes everywhere look sunny. And fancy having a balcony leading off the bedroom. It'll be like living in a posh hotel somewhere on the coast. And that terrace on the roof. We can have parties up there. Sit out there in the summer.'

When the building was finally finished and the keys were finally handed over, Dora, her parents and the proud Archie stood in the hall. The parquet floor gleamed as the sunlight fell on it through the coloured glass window.

'What d'you think then?' he asked.

'I really love it,' Dora said happily. 'How about you, Mum? Dad?'

'It's very modern,' Mary replied. 'Takes a bit of getting used to.'

'Handy for work though. I'll be able to drop you off on the way to my job,' Dora offered.

'I should get a car of me own as soon as I can. I don't like being driven everywhere by my wife. Doesn't seem right somehow.'

'You can drive the car any time you want. You know you can. Anyway, a Standard Eight is hardly a posh car. Maybe you could drive over to your parents one Sunday. Bring them back here for their teas.'

'Let's not get carried away. We have to move in first. That's going to be a lot of work for all of us.'

'You haven't been to see your Mum and Dad since the wedding. It's weeks ago now,' Dora chided. 'You ought to go before we start packing up for the move.'

'I know. But I know what they'll be like. Especially now we're moving up here. Let's get the move over and done with and then we'll think about socialising. We'll have to have a house warming won't we?'

'Great. We can ask Barry and his lads to play for us. Have a proper do. It'll be nearly

Christmas by the time we're straight. I've always wanted to have a great big tree. Let's make our party for Christmas as well.'

'I've never had a Christmas tree before,' Archie said. How he'd moved up in the world, he thought. The big house. The job in management and now a proper party with him as one of the hosts.

Once the move was over, the coming party filled the minds of all the family. Dora wanted to invite everyone who hadn't been able to go to the wedding, including her sister who now had two children under two years old.

'Have you thought when you're going to start a family?' Mary asked Dora nearly every week.

'We haven't talked about it much. What with the move and everything, we haven't considered much past that. Maybe now we're settled, we might think about it.' She realised that neither of them had really talked it through. She'd always assumed they'd have a family, when it was right. There was no real reason why they shouldn't start one any time now. If she did decide to go back to work, she knew her Mum would be delighted to look after the baby.

The party was the highlight of the season for all of them. Their friends oohed and aahed over the house, exclaiming over the ultra modern fixtures and fittings. Everything that could be built-in, was. Wardrobes in the bedrooms and cupboards in the kitchen were all purpose built, with shiny chrome handles and geometric lines.

Ernie turned up with one of his many lady friends in tow. He still looked for the perfect woman and seemed to be enjoying the prolonged search. Mabel Pearce had long since been cast aside, much to Dora's disappointment. She would have liked both of their best friends to make a go of things.

'Well, lad,' he said, clapping Archie on the back, 'you're really settled now aren't you? You'll be having the patter of little feet any time now, I expect. No more nights out for you.'

'A family? No way. I don't think so. It's just too much for any woman to cope with.'

'Don't talk rubbish. If it was too much, there'd be a real shortage of people in this world. I bet your little wife is just dying for a baby. Mark my words. I've seen that look in a woman's eyes before.'

Archie was silent. The memory of his mother's huge size during pregnancy and the pain she suffered at the birth of his brother had put him right off the idea. He'd always assumed things might be easier by the time he was grown-up but nothing seemed to have changed much. He often saw the girls at work trying to pretend everything was normal when they were well past six months gone. He gave a shudder.

'You're a fine one to talk, Ernie. You haven't even managed to persuade a girl to stick with you for more than five minutes, let alone walk up the aisle with you.'

'I'm biding my time. What do you think of this one?'

'She's all right. Probably far too good for the likes of you,' he laughed.

'You may be right. But she's lasted a few months and we're still speaking. She's getting on all right with your good lady.' Dora and the girl, Barbara, seemed to be giggling happily together in a corner.

'How are you finding work these days?'

'All right,' Archie replied cautiously. 'Why do you ask?'

'I sensed a spot of dissatisfaction among the workers. There doesn't seem to be quite the usual atmosphere around the place.'

'I think maybe some of them are sick of always doing the deco stuff. They want to go back to more traditional stuff. I must say, I can sympathise. I'd like to see a bit more fancy ware. More style and elegance about what we're producing.'

'We have to go with what's selling. Come on, Archie. Think about it. You were keen enough to try out the new stuff once.'

'Maybe. But it's no longer new is it? We should be looking forward to the next fashion. I reckon that we're going to need to go back and look at what was there before and build on that.'

'Have you heard that Leslie Barker's thinking of starting up on his own?'

'The odd rumour. But I thought nothing much of it. He's head manager of the decorating shop. Why would he want to leave?'

'Happen he's been thinking on the same lines as you. Let me know if you hear anything definite. I think we'd better go and see our ladies, before they fall out with us completely.' Ernie went across the room and began talking and joking with the women. Archie watched him thoughtfully. He'd heard about the coming changes. Leslie was a go ahead chap. Talented and with plenty of drive. If he left, there would be a vacancy up at the top. He knew he was still too young to get the top job but maybe some sort of promotion was in the offing. He moved towards his wife and friends but was stopped in his tracks by the sound of raised voices in the kitchen. He went to investigate.

'She always was your favourite,' Dora's sister Margaret, was yelling.

'Don't be daft, love. It was just more convenient for us to move here together.'

'You haven't even seen our house. Couldn't be bothered to come over, I suppose.' Margaret had drunk a sherry or two over her limit and was letting her jealousy rise to the surface.

'It isn't easy to get away. We've been so busy with the wedding and everything and then the move.' Mary was trying hard to appease her eldest daughter. She did have a point but she'd always been so difficult. So headstrong. Her husband, Derek, seemed a steady enough bloke, but Mary suspected things were not ideal between them. For now, she needed to quieten her daughter before she ruined the whole evening. 'Look, love. I think it'd be a good idea if you had a breath of fresh air. I'll come outside with you and we'll talk about things. Maybe I could come over and stay for a few days. Now Dora's settled, she can look after your Dad and Archie.'

With very bad grace, Margaret allowed herself to be led outside into the chill night air. As the cold struck her, she gave a gulp and began to cry. They sat down on the back step.

'Oh, Mum. Life's so awful. Me and Derek seem to be rowing all the time. He doesn't earn enough to keep us all. The kids get upset by the atmosphere and I just don't know how to cope. Our Dora seems to have it made. Posh house and everything going exactly her own way. And whatever you say, her parents always did favour her,' she added slyly.

'I don't know why you say that. We've always tried to treat you both the same. We helped you get started just the same as Dora. You've got two lovely kids. Derek's a good man really. I'm not sure we can help you out

199

with more money though. Everything we had's gone into this place. Archie's paying the bank loan out of his wages and we manage most of the other expenses. It's team work, Margaret. We all pull together. That's what you two have got to learn to do.'

Archie listened to the exchanges. He felt uncomfortable about the situation at times and felt that Margaret maybe had a point. It seemed that it was not only his own family that had problems. If he was completely honest, he didn't like Margaret much, especially after Ernie's comments on their first meeting. He had often wondered how two such lovely people as Henry and Mary could have produced two such different daughters.

'Didn't have quite the same start, now did we?'

'Well now, Margaret. We all know whose fault that is. You made your own bed and all that. You jumped the gun and have to pay for the consequences.'

'Oh you'd have to bring that up, wouldn't you?'

'This is going nowhere,' Mary told her. 'Come on in again. It's perishing out here.'

'I think I might be carrying again,' Margaret moaned.

'Oh, love. Not already. Don't you take any precautions? You know what I mean.'

'We try but sometimes, Derek just can't or won't stop himself. I wish you lived nearer.

You could help me such a lot. Won't you think about coming our way? I don't see why Dora should have everything.'

Archie could bear it no longer. He marched into the kitchen, asking in a loud voice as he went, 'Who's for a top up?' He went over to the barrel of ale on the side bench and filled another jug. 'Some for you, Margaret? Or do you fancy summat else?' His sister-in-law gave him a withering look and stomped out of the room. 'I'm sorry, Mary. I couldn't help overhearing. I hope we haven't made everything too difficult for you.'

'She's a silly girl. Don't let it bother you. She's just flummoxed about something and nothing. She'll get over it. Now, do you think I should warm up this lot of sausage rolls yet?'

Apart from this upset, the evening was deemed a success by all. Barry and his boys had played their hearts out from a position on the landing, halfway up the stairs. Several couples danced in the hall and those wanting a quieter chat had been in the lounge.

'Great place for a party,' Ernie had told Archie, as he was leaving. The host beamed with pleasure. 'Let me know if you hear anything at work, won't you?'

'Sure. I can always use a leg up myself. Got a lot to pay for these days,' he said with a grin.

'We'll bear you in mind if there's a vacancy. Now, we'd best be off before we get locked out. Thanks all of you. Great party. Great house. Sets me thinking it's about time I got myself sorted. I'm much too old still to be living with me parents.'

'Give them my best,' Archie shouted behind the retreating pair.

Soon, everyone started to leave and it was just the family left. They began to clear up and wash glasses. Margaret had disappeared to bed and Archie felt a sense of relief. At least they had a space before the next inevitable confrontation in the morning.

'I think everyone enjoyed themselves, don't you?' Dora said happily.

'I reckon so,' Harry replied. 'Though I did hear summat going off in the kitchen. What was that all about, Molly?' He used this affectionate name for his wife.

'Oh nothing much. Just our Margaret doing her usual thing. Poor little sister who nobody loves. She'll get over it.'

'I see,' Harry said grimly. 'Well, she's only got herself to blame. I did help a bit when they got wed but she was the one who threw it back in my face.'

'Let's not talk about it now. Don't spoil the evening. I think it's been lovely. Well done, you two. Best party I've ever been to,' Mary said. 'Now I'm going to bed before I drop with tiredness. Are you coming up, Harry?'

He nodded and the two of them disappeared. Archie put his arms round his wife and kissed the back of her neck as she stood at the sink.

'Come on, love. We'll finish off in the morning.'

'What were you and Ernie talking about? I saw you having a serious looking conversation.'

'Oh just a bit about work. Nothing much. He wants me to listen out for any bits of gossip about Leslie. You know, the head manager. Thinks he may have plans to go out on his own.'

'That'd leave a gap wouldn't it? Maybe there'll be summat in it for you.'

'Could be but don't hold your breath. I'm still a bit young for that job. Besides, I might consider going with him.'

'Oh, Archie, no. You couldn't. That would really be a big risk. You don't even know if he could make a go of it.'

'True, but it would be interesting finding out. I'm getting a bit sick of the same old thing day after day. I'd like to widen my field a bit. Try some experiments. I'd like to have a go at some fancy goods.'

'But is the time right? You're only just getting going on the new decorated ware. I must say, I really love the tea-set you gave me for Christmas. Really pretty that.'

'One of my own designs, like I said. I think we have to look at combining the transfer patterns with more hand painting.'

'I liked the way you signed your own initials

on the back. Really makes it special.'

'I've been practising that for years,' he said shyly. 'I always wanted to sign my name with a fancy look to it.'

'Time we went to bed. I bet Margaret's two will be up at the crack of dawn. They were very good at the party, weren't they?'

'I s'pose so. I don't now much about kids. I remember William crying himself silly every night when he was a baby.'

'Maybe we can think about having one of our own. Me Mum was asking me the other day.'

'If you must know, Ernie was talking about it as well. Do you really want to go through all that?' Archie asked, afraid of her answer.

'Course I do. I can't imagine not having kids, can you? I want two. A boy and a girl.'

'Well, if you're really set on it, we'll have to get the order booked. I'm frightened though, Dora. You're much too precious to take any risks. I love you.'

'I know. Come on, love. It's natural to be worried about the responsibility of being a parent.'

He said nothing. It wasn't parenthood that concerned him. It was the whole process of pregnancy and birth that bothered him. He shivered at the memory of his mother crying out and all the blood. Nobody had found a better way of having babies, not as far as he knew. But he loved his Dora much too much to deny her anything.

## CHAPTER ELEVEN

It wasn't until the August of 1936 that Dora knew for certain that she was pregnant. She was overjoyed and on their wedding anniversary, the two of them went out for a special dinner. She broke the news to Archie, tears of joy filling her eyes. A flicker of alarm crossed his face but he managed to smile.

'You are pleased aren't you?' Dora asked anxiously.

'Course I am. If it makes you happy, then I'm delighted. My, my. A Dad. Fancy me being a Dad.'

'I'd like to go and see your parents. Tell them the news. They'll want to know they're going to be grandparents, don't you think? It's their right to know.'

'I s'pose so.' Over the years Archie had grown so accustomed to his parents', or rather his mother's, lack of interest in anything that he'd almost given up including them in any news. 'We'll go over at the weekend.'

'You'd better send a card to say we're coming or they might be out.'

'I suppose so.' He had never admitted his mother's difficulty with reading but went along with her suggestion. Always better to give a warning than to drop in unannounced. At least his Dad and William would be pleased to see them. Archie's brother was now eighteen and had got himself a job at the pithead. It was a bit of a dead end but it earned him some money and he knew he could always look for something else when the time was right.

Mary and Harry were delighted with the news, though Mary claimed she had known for some weeks.

'I could tell. Something about a woman when she's pregnant. Besides, I thought she was looking a bit on the plump side.'

'I never am,' Dora protested. 'Am I?'

'You look wonderful to me,' Archie told her. 'But hadn't you better think about giving up work? You don't want to be on your feet all day, do you? You'll have to take care of yourself.'

'Don't fuss. I'm not ill. Just expecting.' Her smile of delight was enough to settle his fears, at least for the time being.

The visit to see Archie's parents was planned for the following Sunday. They drove over after lunch, thinking that their reception might be slightly better if a meal wasn't involved. The street looked as dingy as ever. Archie gazed round at the cobbles and the grey gutters, dirty houses, so stained that the bricks could scarcely be seen. He couldn't help comparing it with their own tree-lined road. They were high up and far enough away from the grime of the factory chimneys and the pit head fires to feel as if the air was clean. Here in his parents' own locality the black was so ingrained into the fabric of the buildings that nothing could ever make them clean. He knocked at the door and waited. It seemed strange to be knocking on the front door of his old home. Somehow, it didn't feel right to walk round the back and push their way in through the gate. After a wait, William came to open the door.

'Hallo there. How're you? You'd better come in.'

'Hallo, William,' Dora said. 'How's life treating you?'

'Not so bad. Not now you've come to see us. Had enough of my brother yet? I can offer you a decent home, if you fancy a change.'

'Go on with you. You never alter do you?'

'Not where you're concerned.'

'I'm very flattered but you'll soon be finding yourself a young lady and you won't even have the time of day for me.'

'I shan't, Dora. I'll never find anyone else that'd do for me. There's no-one else like you but until you realise your mistake, I s'pose I'll just have to bide my time. Anyhow, me Mum and Dad are waiting in the living room.'

'Hallo Mrs Barnett. Mr Barnett.' She leaned forwards to kiss them both. Frances held herself rigid and almost allowed Dora to contact her cheek. Ralph held her arms and gave her the merest suggestion of a hug.

'Hallo, Dora, love. Son. So, how's that new house of yours?'

'It's lovely. You'll have to come over and see for yourself. How about it?'

'I'm not sure I can be bothered,' snapped Frances. 'Long way to go and I'll only make myself discontented with what I've got.'

'What's it like, Archie?' asked William.

'Come and see for yourself,' Archie said wearily. He was already wondering how soon they could make their escape. He felt overwhelmed by this house. Oppressed by this family. Nothing had really changed here for as long as he could remember. The room looked as dingy as ever, the table cover looked the same as it always had. Probably never even been washed, he thought. After his own bright, cheerful home, always spotlessly clean and with good furniture, this seemed like a bad dream. He watched Dora chatting to his parents as if she really liked them. She was such a wonderful woman. He knew just how lucky he was. His Dad was beginning to look quite old. How old could he be? Nearly fifty he supposed. He looked like an old man. He broke out of his dream to find Dora nudging him.

'Go on. Tell them our news,' she was urging.

'What?' he said stupidly.

'Go on, Archie. I was saying we've got some news for them.'

208

'Oh, yes. Right. Well, it's like this . . . we, Dora that is . . .'

'When's it due?' asked William bluntly.

'What?'

'The baby. When's it due? I s'pose that is what you're blatherin' about?'

'Er yes. We're having a baby.'

'Bloody daft. You should know better. You with your posh schooling and all.' Typical Frances reply, Archie thought.

'I thought you'd be pleased,' Dora said softly, as if she was about to cry.

'We are. love. Pleased as punch,' Ralph chimed in, putting his arm round her shoulders. 'I reckon this is really something to celebrate. Now I think we've got a drop of port in the cupboard. Left over from Christmas.'

'I never knew you had port at Christmas,' Archie said in disbelief.

'Things have changed round here since your day. You're not the only one who's gone up in the world.' Frances gave a sniff as she produced the bottle and even some tiny glasses. When he saw the size of them, Archie realised how the bottle had managed to last from Christmas till August. One mouthful and it was empty. He said nothing and lifted his glass as his father made a small toast.

'Here's to our new grandchild. Did you want a boy or a girl?'

'I want a girl but Archie really wants a boy first.'

'One'll be enough. Mark my words,' Frances announced grimly. 'Once you've been through having it, you'll not want him near you ever again.'

'I'm sure I'll cope,' Dora said firmly.

'That's enough, Mum. I won't have you upsetting poor Dora like that.'

'Suit yourself. Just trying to put her in the picture. I wish someone had told me what it was like before I'd had either of you.'

'I think Dora's going to be a wonderful mother,' Archie said defiantly. His own fears were already quite bad enough to keep him awake at nights.

Ralph asked after his work and the conversation got onto safer ground. He told them of the possible promotion once his boss had left. It had become official now and once he'd worked out his notice, Leslie was leaving. Archie had heard nothing more yet but he guessed he was in line for something at least.

'I'm proud of you, lad,' Ralph told him. 'You've done right well for yourself. We'd never have made a proper miner out of you but despite that, you've got on. Better than some I could mention.'

'Oh, who're you talking about?'

'That Billy Machin for one. Right bad one he's turned out to be. Got arrested for thieving. Blamed it on anything but himself. You know his Mam died?'

'No I didn't. Used to keep the corner shop

210

they did,' he explained to Dora. 'I used to do his sums for him in exchange for the odd smokes. Poor old Billy. Thicker than two short planks he always was. So, is he in the clink?'

'Just out. I couldn't believe he'd go pinching stuff from his own kind.'

'It was him as killed his mother. The worry of it all was too much for her. Little rat.' Frances's eyes narrowed and her mouth compressed into a hard line. 'Mind you she always was a bit above herself.'

Ralph leaned forward to the fire and lit a spill, taking the tiny flame to his pipe.

'She was a decent enough soul. Did her best to help them as needed it.'

'How do you mean, Billy killed his mother?'

'The worry of what he did. She mayn't have been a pillar of the church or anything but she couldn't cope with the shame.' Frances couldn't keep the gleam of delight from her eyes. Having a scandal so close to her door had filled her mind. 'They still haven't got anyone to take over the shop.'

Ralph glared at his wife and turned to his son and daughter-in-law.

'Now, when are you fetching us over to see this new house of yours?'

'When do you want to come?' Nobody answered him. By the time they were leaving, the subject had been dropped. He could not bear the idea of his mother picking faults with everything, as he knew she would. She'd hate

211

everything, if only to spite herself. He'd never forgotten or forgiven her for selling the plate he'd so lovingly painted. That had been a major milestone in his life and she'd parted with it for the sake of buying a new pair of shoes. His brother may have needed shoes but he'd always had to manage himself. The memory of the holes padded with paper came back to him. Life was never going to be that bad again. Nobody should have to put up with such deprivations. There must never be a war again, not like that last one.

For the next few weeks, Dora continued with her job at the hairdressers. She grew large quite quickly and soon everyone was noticing. She was finally persuaded to give up working when the boss suggested that she did not present the right image to a beauty salon. She felt sad when she left, knowing she would miss the other girls and the friendly customers. All the same, she was excited about the baby and knew that she could well do with a bit of a rest.

'Are you sure you got the dates right?' Mary asked her daughter one morning in November. 'Only you look so big, I can't think you're only six months gone.'

'I think so,' she said biting her lip. 'Yes I'm sure it is.'

'P'raps you're expecting twins.'

'Oh, Mum, do you think so?'

'You could be. There's twins on both sides of our family. Your Dad had twin brothers.

Your Uncle Billy was one of twins. Uncle Reg was lost in the war. And your Aunties Lizzie and Annie are twins from my side. And we've got some cousins with twins.'

'I never realised. I'd better ask the midwife when I go to see her again. Twins. Just imagine it.'

When she mentioned the possibility to Archie that evening, he looked more than a little shaken.

'Isn't that dangerous?' he asked. 'I mean, having one's bad enough but two together.'

'Don't be soft. You don't mind do you? I mean, well Mum's here and she'll help out. It's like getting two for the price of one. One pregnancy instead of two. I must say, I certainly won't mind that. I feel so huge and fat already. And there's still nearly three months to go.'

'I know. That's partly why I'm worried. Doesn't the midwife say anything to you?'

'I haven't asked her yet. I'm seeing her next week.'

It turned out to be another month before anyone knew for certain that it really was twins. Dora was so thrilled that she could talk of nothing else. She wrote to her sister and even told her cousin Barry. He was delighted for her and shook hands with Archie.

'Well done, my man. I couldn't be more pleased if it was my own.'

'You have to find a woman first,' Dora said

acidly.

'You're right. Now you're taken . . . Actually, there is someone I'd like you to meet. I've been seeing her for a while now. Can I bring her round soon?'

'Oh Barry, that's really great. I'm so pleased. So, is this the one? You going to ask her to marry you?'

'Hang on. I've only just met her. But she is different to the usual hangers on at the gigs. Most of them are hoping you're someone famous.'

'There's time for you yet. You'll get there one day.'

'I reckon we'll both be famous some day,' Archie told him. 'Bring this girl of yours over to see us.'

At work, things really were coming to a head for Archie. As he'd suspected, someone else had been brought in to supervise the decorating shop. Mr Draper had spoken to him personally, taking the trouble to explain why he had not seen fit to promote the young man.

'Give it a few more years, lad, and you'll get to the top. Bit more experience handling the workers is what you need.'

He was naturally disappointed, especially as he'd need every penny he could earn once the twins arrived. When he got an offer from Leslie Sansom to take over the design and management of the decorating shop at his new factory, he was in a great dilemma. He felt he owed loyalty to the Draper family. They'd always been such good friends to him and had given him a job, even when he was little more than a kid with ambition. They'd always treated him as a friend of the family, despite his background. All the same, Leslie's offer was too good to miss. There was a good salary and plenty of room for him to expand and do some of the stuff he'd been wanting to do.

He explained it all to Dora, who told him it was up to him to make the decision but naturally, she'd support him in anything he wanted to do.

'Talk it over with my Dad if you like. He's always one for giving sound advice.'

Archie and his father-in-law sat up till late, weighing the pros and cons. He was trying to look at the situation in an unbiased way.

'You have to think of the best future for you, lad,' he said thoughtfully. 'I mean to say, you'll never be in line for the top job at Draper's. Young Ernie will always be there. On the other hand, you wouldn't want to be just management would you? Waste of good talent. But would you ever be able to do what you really want to do there? From all as you've said, they're a bit *stick in the mud*. Take a long time to make any changes.'

'You're right. I've got a better future with Leslie. I still feel a bit bad about letting down the Drapers though. I'd hate to fall out with

Ernie. He's been my best mate since we were at school together.'

Archie spent a sleepless night, tossing and turning as his brain tried to cope with how to tell Ernie and Mr Draper what he wanted to do. He knew he'd have to front up with his boss but he'd no idea what he was going to say. He knew he was keeping Dora awake as he'd been tossing and turning. Poor girl needed her sleep more than he did, She was now growing so big, she wasn't able to do anything much without getting out of breath.

'I'm sorry, love. My brain won't stop churning round. I'll go down and make a cuppa. You want one?'

'No ta. I'd like one but it'd mean I'd have to get up and pee again. I really can't face it.'

'Right, love. You get back to sleep. I'll have a lie down on the couch in the front room. Then I won't disturb you.' He sipped his tea in the kitchen, looking at his reflection in the windows. He knew he had to move and somehow, he had to make Mr Draper understand. In the event, it was much easier than he'd expected.

'I thought you might want to leave us. It was a gamble I took when I didn't make you manager. I knew I'd be risking losing you. I wish you well, lad. You've done us proud here but I think you're right. Leslie's new venture will give you more scope in areas we can't tackle. He's a new company with new ideas.

We have a reputation for the sort of stuff we can't easily change. I think Ernie will miss you. He thinks a lot of you, does my son.'

'Thanks, sir. I reckon I feel the same. I didn't want to you think I was ungrateful. You gave me a chance when most others wouldn't have done.'

'You've more than repaid my confidence. I don't bear any grudges though I'll not deny, we'll miss you. I wish you luck. I really mean that. I think you've got a natural creative talent. Wouldn't surprise me to see you going out on your own one day.'

'Oh I doubt that. I'd never have the money to get started.' Archie found himself blushing at the very suggestion. Hadn't he always dreamed of being famous on his own one day? Signing his own china with his own name?

'Anyone can always do anything if they've a mind to it. Now, I'm about to have my afternoon cup of tea. Will you have one with me? I think Miss Baines will oblige.'

Archie grinned. It was perfect. She'd made him a drink on his first day in the factory. Now she was being asked to make one, on what was nearly his last day. She came in and placed the tray in front of Mr Draper.

'Seems to be something of a habit, drinking tea with certain of the workers,' she said with a sniff. Archie could hardly keep his face straight.

'It was coffee last time, Miss Baines. On me

217

very first day here. It was a very long time ago.'

When his final day at Draper's arrived, Archie was feeling distinctly odd. He found himself wandering round the other departments, places he'd hardly ever been since his earliest days. He found excuses to go to ask various things, just so he could look for the last time. Ten minutes before knocking off time, Mr Draper and Ernie arrived in the decorating shop. Everyone had stopped work and he hadn't liked to say anything, as it was his last day. To his amazement, Mr Draper called for silence.

'You all know that Archie here is leaving us today,' he began. There were murmurs from the girls. 'He'll be sorely missed. We all know how well he's got on during the years he's been with us. Very different from the scared little lad who came into work that first day. Talented man he is now, designing a number of our best lines all by himself. But the time has come for him to move on. I'm sure you all join with me in wishing Archie Barnett here the very best of luck.' There was a ripple of applause from the room and Ernie stepped forward holding out a small package.

'For you, Archie. Something to remember us all by.'

Archie blushed furiously. He felt a lump growing in his throat that was practically choking him. He took the parcel with trembling hands and pulled the string off.

Inside was a gold wristwatch.

'Blimey,' he murmured. 'Thank you ever so much, Mr Draper.'

'It's from everyone. They all chipped in to get you something really nice. It's engraved on the back.'

Archie turned it over.

*From all your friends at Draper's China. November 1936.*

'It's wonderful. Thank you. I've enjoyed working with you all and I'm really sorry to be going.'

'You can always change your mind. They'll take th'watch back,' called out one of the girls.

'Not with writing on, they won't,' called another.

'I'll never forget you. Thanks again.' Suddenly, Archie knew he had to leave. But someone was calling for three cheers. He had to stand and listen, his eyes desperately wanting to release their watery burden and get rid of the lump in his throat threatening to choke him. Men didn't cry. But it was the end of an important era, after all.

At last he was free to go. As he turned away from the factory gates for the last time, he remembered his very first day. He remembered the parcel that contained his working overalls. Mr Draper had been good to him all right, but now it was truly time to move on. He took a breath and walked away.

'Hang on, Archie,' he heard and turned to

see Ernie rushing after him. 'I insist on buying you a pint before you go home.'

'Oh heck. Why not? It isn't every day you get a gold watch, is it?' They went into a nearby pub and sat with a pint of best bitter each. They reminisced about their schooldays and the dances they used to go to. Ernie was still seeing his girl and was still planning to get engaged.

'Funny old business growing up, isn't it? I still feel like a kid inside.'

'Aye, well once you get a wife and a baby or two on the way, growing up hits you fast.'

'How is the lovely Dora?'

'She'll be glad when it's all over. Another six weeks or thereabouts. It's harder to tell with twins, apparently. Speaking of which, I'd better get home. She's getting very tired and a bit emotional to tell the truth.'

'Give her my best,' Ernie said, draining his glass.

'Ernie . . . well I just wanted to say thanks, like. For everything. I don't know where I'd be if it wasn't for you and your family giving me a chance.'

'Shut up, lad or you'll have me in tears. Just don't forget me. I expect you to stay my mate for the rest of our lives. Understood?'

By the time he arrived home, Archie felt exhausted. The house was un-naturally quiet as he let himself in.

'Hallo!' he called. 'I'm home.' A worried

looking Mary came out of the kitchen. 'What's up? Where's Dora?'

'She's all right. At least, we think she is. There's been a bit of an accident.'

'Oh no. What's happened? Where is she?'

'She's in bed, resting. She had a bit of a fall. Silly girl insisted on hanging the curtains in the nursery. I didn't know what she was doing and she fell off the chair.'

'Why couldn't she have waited? Stupid girl. Is she all right? What about the babies?'

'We don't know yet. Now just calm down. You'll get nowhere by panicking. The doctor's been and he says she's to rest.'

'I'll go up and see her. Oh heck. Why did I let Ernie persuade me to have that drink?'

'I thought you were a bit late. How was it then? Your last day at Draper's?'

'All right. They gave me a gold watch.' He was halfway up the stairs as he spoke. 'Dora? You all right?' he called as he went into their bedroom. Dora was white as the sheets on her bed, lying back propped up on the pillows.

'I'm so sorry, Archie. I know I was stupid but I wanted to get things ready. Don't tell me off. I feel so rotten.'

'Oh, love. I'm so sorry. And I was late as well.'

'You couldn't have done anything. How did it go?'

'OK. They gave me a gold watch.' He held his wrist out for her to see. 'Could have

221

knocked me down with a feather. Even the girls chipped in for it. Mr Draper was really nice. Very complimentary. I must say, it was a relief to know they didn't hold it against me. You know, after all he'd done.'

'That's good. Just think. My husband with a gold watch.' Her voice was fainter and Archie sat holding her hand, willing her to sleep. It was probably the best thing for her. He could hardly believe it. Practically eight months gone and she went standing on chairs to put up ruddy curtains. He couldn't bear it if he lost his Dora. Of course he wanted the babies, perhaps only because she did, but it was her he really cared about. She dozed off and he sat staring at her.

'Come and have a bite to eat,' Mary called softly to him.

'I couldn't eat a thing. I'll stay here with her for a bit.'

'Leave her to sleep. The doctor says it's best.' She took his hand away and led him downstairs. He toyed with the food on his plate and tried to eat, for Mary's sake. It was a tense weekend. Dora was in terrible pain but could take no relief because of the babies. The midwife came to inspect her and listened with a trumpet device pressed against Dora's belly. She had an expression on her face that made him question her further. She took him out of the room before speaking.

'I think you need to prepare yourself. I'm

not sure yet but I can't hear any heartbeat from the infants. It may not mean anything at present but you must be prepared. It might be that the fall has moved things round and I just can't get close enough to hear anything. I'll be back in the morning but just make sure she stays in bed.'

'What happens if they're not . . . not still living?' His voice croaked with emotion as he spoke the unspeakable words.

'They'll still have to come out naturally. I can't do anything at present. Not till we know for sure one way or the other.'

Archie found he was shaking. He couldn't stop shaking. He couldn't even face going back into the bedroom. He'd give this dreadful news away, he just knew it. The midwife went back in to her patient and instructed her to stay in bed. He saw the little wiry lady out, and went into the kitchen to Mary.

'It's bad news, isn't it?'

'I think it could be. I don't know how she'll cope. After all this time. All the waiting. All the wanting.' Suddenly, he could no longer hold back the tears. He knew men shouldn't cry but this time, he simply couldn't stop it. Mary put her arms round him and held him close. She was such a comfort. Her fine hair tickled him under the chin and her ample bosom was soft and comforting against him.

'I love her so much,' he sobbed.

'Course you do, love. But it's the babies you

might lose, not her.'

'How do I know? Maybe she's damaged herself too much.'

'She'll pull through. Got a lot of strength, that one. You'll see. Now, how about a nice cuppa?'

'I s'pose so.'

'You can take one up to Dora. She'll be needing something to perk her up.'

'It'll take more than tea this time.'

Because Archie was starting his new job, he felt obliged to leave his wife in her mother's care. There was no alternative but he felt terrible about it.

'I'm so sorry to be leaving you, love,' he said, emotion practically choking his words. 'Your Mum's promised to get word to me somehow, if you need me.'

'It's all right, love. You go on. Show 'em what you're made of. Good luck.' He kissed her forehead and left her, certain it could only be a matter of time before she realised her precious babies were no longer moving inside her womb.

'I think the babies are dead,' she whispered to Archie, a couple of days later. 'I haven't felt them kick or even move at all for ages.'

'I know, love,' he replied sadly. 'The midwife said she thought so. But you're going to be all right. That's the main thing.'

'But I so wanted these babies. Or even just one of them. What did I do that was so wrong?' There was nothing to do but wait.

In early December, rumours were beginning to circulate that things were not right in royal circles. The new king, Edward the Eighth, was planning to marry the divorcee, Mrs Simpson. When the news finally broke that he was to abdicate in favour of his brother, Mary's indignation knew no bounds.

'How can he do it? Give up everything just like that? What about his duty? To all of us? It simply doesn't seem right to me. I reckon he should just keep seeing her in private. I mean, all the kings have always done it haven't they?'

From the mild mannered, rather straight-laced Mary, it came as a shock to all of them.

'I think it's rather brave of him, and so terribly romantic,' Dora announced. 'Fancy loving someone so much that you'd give up being king for her.'

'I've never taken much interest in royalty,' Archie said. 'Except of course, it means we shall have to bring out a new range of commemoration ware. In fact, we've already got a few plates ready for the coronation next year. Maybe they'll become collector's items.'

'Dumped in the dustbin, more likely,' Dora suggested.

'All the same, we should get in first with the changes. Won't hurt to get a few ideas on paper.' The women continued to speculate while Archie was busily planning new designs for the rest of the evening.

'At least the Duke of York's decently married. Elizabeth is quite good-looking enough to be a queen, I suppose.'

'Mum, you're such a snob at heart,' smiled Dora. Archie saw the flicker of light on her face and felt better. Poor Dora. Nothing seemed to interest her much these days.

'She's the snob. Pretty but very sort of condescending. Still, if you've got money like that and look like being a queen, I suppose you've got a right to be a bit snobbish. Wonder if she ever does the dishes? You sit still, love. Keep your feet up. I'll do the dishes on my own. Won't take long. I did the pots before we sat down.'

'At least the new king smokes, so they say. Like a chimney.'

'Shows it can't be all bad, then doesn't it?' Archie said, lighting another cigarette. 'Want one, love?' Dora nodded and he passed one to her.

'I may be losing my taste for smoking,' she said rather miserably. 'I seem to be feeling sick such a lot of the time.'

The days dragged on, Dora remained in her bed most days, still feeling extremely ill. It was two days before she went into hospital. The midwife had decided that there really was no hope for the babies and it was beyond her abilities to do anything in the home. She was given a dose of castor oil, making her retch and feel even worse. When Dora felt the first grinding spasms that heralded the labour pains, she was in a ward with a number of other women who were either giving birth, awaiting a birth or who had already delivered. Knowing there would be no baby to love at the end of it all made the pains so much worse to the point of being unbearable. The tiny boy and girl were delivered stillborn during the afternoon. By the time Archie visited after work, it was all over. Mercifully, it had been a short labour and Dora was now heavily drugged to give her the rest she badly needed.

'How was work?' she whispered to Archie.

'Sod work. How are you?'

'Tell me about work. I can't bear to think of anything else.'

He tried to talk about the comings and goings of his day but there was a great wedge of cotton wool stuffing the back of his throat, preventing him from speaking. As soon as he saw her sleeping, he went in search of the doctor.

'How is she?' he demanded to know. 'How is she really?'

'She'll survive, all right. Physically that is. I'm not sure how bad mentally she is scarred. The babies obviously meant a great deal to her.'

'We can always have another one though, can't we?'

'I'm sorry but it is not advisable. There was some damage to her womb and possibly the

227

ovaries too. There could be problems with conception and even if that part was successful, I cannot guarantee that she would be able to carry to full-term.'

'I always knew having babies was a bad idea. But she wanted one so much. It's just not fair is it? Her sister's got two already and never had a spot of bother. Didn't even want them much, from what I can make out. And she's expecting again. It isn't fair, is it? I'm sorry doctor. I just don't know how I'm ever going to tell her.' He still held the memory of the way he'd felt the night he'd learned about his scholarship place and his parents had told him it was impossible. Well, he'd managed it, if only for a few months. But he'd done it. P'raps this doctor was wrong. P'raps they might be able to have another child some day. He hoped and prayed that Dora wouldn't want to find out.


# CHAPTER TWELVE

'I can't face going back to that house,' Dora said unexpectedly the next evening when Archie visited the hospital. 'In fact, I don't think I ever want to see it again.'

'But I thought you loved the house,' he protested.

'I did once. But now, I know it's the bad

228

luck that's been haunting us ever since we moved in.'

'You're being silly, love. The house hasn't got anything to do with it.'

'I can't live there. Every time I go into that room I shall remember. That's where our children were conceived and where they died. Please, Archie. Can we make a new start? I'm sure Mum and Dad will understand.'

How could he refuse her? All their hopes and dreams. His precious big house he'd always wanted. What was any of that compared to Dora?

'I'll see what they have to say.'

'This won't make a difference to us, Archie, will it? We will try for another baby, won't we? Just as soon as I'm better.'

It was with a heavy heart that Archie went back to his beloved house that night. He didn't know what he was going to say to the wonderfully kind couple who had done everything they could to help them get the place. He broke the news to them.

'I think it'll be for the best,' Mary said surprisingly. 'We hadn't told you, what with everything going on, but Henry's being transferred to another branch. He's got to work in Newcastle after next month. It's a heck of a journey from here. I think it would be sensible to try and move nearer there for him.'

'Really?' Archie was confused. 'But I thought you enjoyed this place as much as we do?'

'Oh, it isn't really us, all this fancy stuff, is it, love?' she said to her husband.

'Bit too modern for us. I think we might like to move to something a bit less grand. Something a bit more traditional. There's always a place for you, though. Whatever happens, you won't be short of a place to stay.'

'Thanks, both of you. You're the best parents anyone ever had. I can't pretend it's not a set back but we'll all come through it won't we? Trouble is, I'm not sure how Dora's going to take the news that she might not have another chance to have a kid. I can cope easy enough, but I don't think she will.'

'She always has wanted children. Used to love playing with her dolls when she was little. Now our Margaret, she couldn't be bothered with them at all. All she wanted to do was play at dressing up. She's got two kids already and we think there's probably another in the pipeline, if you get my meaning. Even said she was expecting at that party but it turned out to be a false alarm. Ironic really, isn't it?'

'That's pretty much what I said to the doctor. You know, you've made me feel much better. Thanks again. How do you think we set about finding somewhere else to live?'

'I'm going into town tomorrow. And I'll see if there's anything in the paper. And you'd better organise a "for sale" sign for here, Harry. Sooner it's on the market, sooner it can be settled.'

Archie climbed the two sets of stairs to the flat roof terrace. The wind was blowing and he shivered. When they'd held their house-warming party, some of the guests had come up here. There had been other occasions when they'd entertained up here, high above the six towns. There was a view right over the Potteries. He could see the fat kilns dotted round the landscape, looking like huge bottles dumped as leftovers from a giant's party. The pall of smoke hung over everywhere, looking as if the same giants had over-indulged in smoking their pipes. It was no place to bring up a child down there at the bottom of the hill. No clean fresh air anywhere. But his dream was solid. Smoke or no, pottery and the Potteries was the only place his future could be satisfied. He punched his hands together. He promised himself he would get an even better house one day and that one would really be in the country, away from the smoke. He sighed gently and went to their room. He lay in the big double bed with his hand over the place where Dora should be. What did anything matter as long as she came back where she belonged? Their life together would be everything it should be, no matter where they were.

When Dora was ready to leave hospital, they arranged for her to go and stay with her two maiden Aunts for awhile. They were both nurses of sorts, health visitors in a different part of the Potteries, and would take care of her while the family arranged the move. As Archie was now driving the car, it was decided to favour Henry's place of work for finding a house. They looked at a semi-detached house in Hartshill. It was still one of the slightly posher ends of the Potteries, high above the smoke that bellowed from the chimneys and kilns. Several of the managers from the larger companies had homes built in the area. It was an easy bike ride for Harry to reach his work and if Dora ever felt like going back to work, within easy reach for her, too. It was slightly further for Archie but having the car made that of little consequence.

The house, named Branksome after their honeymoon place, received several offers, all well above what they'd paid for it. All the same, the price they had to pay for the new house left them with very little spare cash. Because they were in rather a hurry, they didn't wait for the best offer and accepted a cash deal. For Archie none of this mattered compared to getting his Dora back home. Christmas never really existed that year, but they managed a token celebration when they had moved.

'Thanks, love. Thank you all of you,' she said with heartfelt gratitude when they all sat down for their first meal together in the new home. 'I don't quite know how you managed it so quickly but I'm very grateful.' She burst into tears and sobbed against Archie's shoulder.

'Do you good to get it out of your system,' Mary said comfortingly.

'But I so wanted my babies. Poor little things. They never had a chance. And a boy and a girl. Just what I always wanted. We can try for another, can't we, Archie?'

Mary and Harry looked embarrassed. It wasn't the sort of thing any married couple talked about at the meal table. Archie saw their faces and gave his wife another hug.

'Come on now, love. You have to get your strength back. We can talk about the future later.'

'But . . . Oh all right. I haven't asked about you. You haven't told me what the new job's like. How're you getting on?'

'It's going well enough. It's much cleaner than Draper's. We've got one of these new electric kilns. Makes so much difference. Just for the decorated ware, you know. They're considering a tunnel kiln for the rest. Amazing really. The ware goes on stacking trolleys and gets fed through the tunnel in a continuous motion, firing the ware the whole time. And Leslie's invested in a heck of a lot of machinery. Some of the lines are made completely by the machine. All the operator has to do is to put the clay in the right place. The machine presses it out into the shape and drops it down onto the belt. Then someone waits at the other end for the pots to come off. Amazing it is.' They were all smiling at his enthusiasm. He stopped and looked embarrassed. 'Sorry. I am going on a bit aren't I?'

'I'm interested. But tell me, all this automation, doesn't that mean a lot less jobs?' asked Harry.

'I suppose so. There are still the women to put handles on cups and so on. But they still have to be fired and decorated. That's the really time consuming work. Where the skill is.'

'You would say that. That's your end of the job.'

'I know, but I still think it's the way to go for the future. Keep the actual straightforward lines mechanised and let the skill show in making the more decorative stuff.'

'I hope it works out for you, lad.'

'Thanks. All of you.'

'I like your enthusiasm, Archie,' Harry said, touching his shoulder.

'Do you think Dora's got over the idea of having another baby?' he asked later when Dora had gone up to bed.

'I doubt it, lad. She's always wanted one of her own. You'll just have to accept that it's still her biggest ambition.'

'Oh dear. I see more trouble ahead.'

'Have you let your parents know about all the changes? You know, in the situation at

234

home?'

Archie reddened. He'd never given his own family a thought.

'I s'pose I'd better go over and see them. They haven't even got the new address. I'd better go over tomorrow night, after work. If that's all right with you. I s'pose I should have let them know.'

'Always knew she wouldn't be much good to you,' Frances told Archie the following night when he broke the sad news. 'If you'd let us know you were coming I'd have got summat in for your tea.' He glared at her words but held his tongue. He didn't want to antagonise his mother any further.' Frances still managed to ask any number of difficult questions about Dora and their future plans. Archie still dreaded the prospect of his wife having another baby. He tried to fob his mother off by saying they were waiting to see the doctor before they knew if it was possible to have another child.

'There's plenty of kids around looking for a good home,' Frances said. 'Saves all the nastiness with trying to have your own. Specially if . . . well you know. That Mrs Savage in the next street for a start. She's just had her ninth and they haven't got two halfpennies to rub together. Funny how some folks can drop them like hens laying eggs and others can't even manage one.'

'Yes, well we'll have to wait and see.' Her

words dug deep into Archie's heart.

'I could have a word with Mrs Savage. Dare say she'd be grateful if someone took their latest off their hands'. Archie shook his head in disbelief. He could just imagine what it would do to Dora to offer her a ready made baby at this stage.

After an hour, Archie was longing to get away. His mother made him feel almost guilty for having proved her wrong about his future. He may have taken a step backwards in his personal plans but he knew he was still determined he was going to succeed in his life as a producer of quality china.

He arrived home weary and hungry. Dora was resting in her bed. Mary had kept something hot for him, guessing that his own mother would never have food to give him. She knew the type. Selfish and always discontented with her lot. He told his mother-in-law about the visit and the difficult task of breaking the sad news. He also remembered, at the last minute, to tell her that he'd invited his brother over, the following Sunday. She seemed pleased and rested her hand on his shoulder as she spoke. Never had he experienced anyone outside this family having such gentle, physical, contact with another human.

William's visit was a great success. Archie realised it was one of the few times he'd seen his brother away from their home and parents.

236

They found themselves laughing and joking together for probably the first time in their lives. They even did a bit of gardening, under the strict eye of Harry. When they went in for tea, William flirted shamelessly with Dora, asking if she was sick of his brother yet. When she was, he told her, he would be more than happy to take over. Mary smiled at the lad.

'I reckon you'd have a bit of a wait. Maybe you should start looking for some nice girl of your own.' William frowned. That was what everyone kept saying. They all saw him as a stupid kid, but he wasn't. He'd grown up a lot lately. Whenever he looked at Dora, he felt exactly the same. A roaring jealousy rushed through his body. They could all laugh and joke about it but his light-hearted comments covered a reality that none of them could see. He loved Dora. Ludicrous as it was, he knew she was the only woman he would ever truly want. He could never tell anyone about it, not the true depth of feeling he was storing away inside. His own brother's wife. It was forbidden in any case. Didn't it say something about it in the Bible? The boy grinned, agreeing that he would start looking but he knew there was little point. Dora would always be the only woman for him, whatever the impossibility of the situation.

'How're you getting on with your job?' Archie asked. William had started work in the office at the colliery.

'S'all right I s'pose. Shanna stay there for long. Too boring.' The boy hated every minute of the so-called safe job. He was not as clever as his brother and found the lists of numbers confusing. He wanted to do something more physical but no-one, least of all himself, wanted him to go down the pit to the coal face. 'You got anything going at your place?' he asked his brother.

'Not at the moment. But I'll keep my ears open. They'll be taking more men on down the clay end, once we get up and running properly.'

'Right. Just make sure you keep me in mind. Ta.' For William, it was as if he'd got the job already. He planned to give in his notice at the pit at the first chance.

Once tea was over, Dora and Mary went through to the scullery to wash the pots. The three males settled in front of the fire. Harry passed a pack of cigarettes to his son-in-law. William reached over and took one himself. Despite the angry glare from his brother, he lit one of the paper spills in the pot by the fire and passed it round. He'd been smoking for as long as he could scrounge a Woodbine from anyone. He was not above sneaking one from his Dad's pack, if ever it was left lying around.

'No good for your chest,' Archie muttered. He felt irritated, after all those years of having to give way to William and watching him having the best bit of meat or special care

238

because he'd been ill. He even thought resentfully about his precious plate that had been sold to provide new shoes for the boy. In all honesty, it wasn't his brother's fault. It was his mother. She had never provided the sort of love that Mary could give. Warm, motherly tenderness came naturally to her. To Frances, such feelings would be seen as weakness. Once more he sent up a private prayer of thanks for the change in his life, his beloved Dora had been spared, this time at least. He didn't want her to have another baby. He couldn't bear the chance that she may not survive.

'You coming in to see them?' William asked when Archie drove him home.

'I'd better get back. Early start tomorrow.' Any excuse, he thought.

'You won't forget to sort out my job, will you? Thanks for bringing me home. My posh brother eh? Who'd have thought he'd be living at the nobs' end of th' Potteries and driving his own car? You've gone up in the world, lad. Don't you forget them as you've left behind, will you?'

As he drove home, Archie pondered his brother's words. He'd worked very hard to leave his past behind him. He knew that he felt no deep affection for any of his own family, well, maybe his Dad was an exception and perhaps he could grow fonder of his brother, once he got over the resentment. He recognised that it was only an abiding sense of duty that made him keep in touch.

At work, Archie felt happy organising groups of talented painters to produce patterns that he drew out for them. He often wondered if they might have done a better job if they were left to their own devices. But they needed to produce consistent patterns and he and Leslie met regularly to discuss any changes. Their aim was to become well-known for affordable, quality, fine bone china with a range of hand-painted designs that could be guaranteed for several years. The idea of customers being able to replace individual breakages in a range was relatively new, with the growth in availability to a wider market. Some of the women still tried to tease him a little, though with a degree of respect to temper their words. After all, he was younger than many of them and though he now wore a suit to work all the time, he was still Archie, the apprentice who'd made good. One or two of them remembered him from their previous work places. If one of their number ever complained about being fed up or not liking something, the older women would turn on them and give them a tongue lashing that quelled everything for some days. Mr Archie had a loyal following and most of his 'girls' would do anything for him, given half a chance.

'Always behaves like such a gentleman, even when he's telling you off. Not many around like him.'

'I'd like to get him on his own in a dark alley some night,' one of them laughed.

'Don't even think about it. He's got a wife. Never looks at anyone else. Never has.'

'I heard he's a right little jumped up snob. I knew this girl called Ada went out with him. Had his hands all over 'er till his mate stopped him.' The pottery workers were a close knit community who always knew someone who knew someone else.

'I conna believe that. He's had plenty of chances with any one of us girls and turned away like he was some sort of monk.'

Nobody wanted to believe the bad words they were hearing. Archie was respected by most of them and they well knew, there could be plenty of worse bosses.

'Well, maybe he was young then. I suggest you shut up and keep your nastiness to yourself, Flossie Jenkins. I bet you're no better than you ought to be.'

He loved the smell of the paints, the turps, the linseed oil that filled the air of the long workshop. Two lines of benches with plenty of natural light gave the feeling of uncluttered space and the hum of the hand operated wheels as the gilders put the gold lines on the edges of plates, gave a sense of dynamic activity. If he could only manage to introduce some new lines: fancy goods as they were called, his purpose would be complete. Archie

wanted to make figurines, china flower bowls
. . . lots of things he'd begun to see in the
shops. In some ways, he hadn't really moved
on to the things he wanted to do. He was
getting there, but there were still a number of
hurdles to get over. Draper's had always made
quality china but they had been stuck in a rut
like Leslie's enterprise. But Archie was still
young enough to fulfil his ambitions, he told
himself after a particularly difficult session
with Leslie.

Dora returned to her job in hairdressing
and life settled into a routine. There had been
no more talk of babies over the past couple of
years and Archie hoped it had been forgotten.
He concentrated on his work and managed to
put by a few pounds each week, hoping one
day that his dreams of their own business and
own home were growing closer.

As 1939 progressed, there was a degree of
tension in the air. Many people were talking of
an imminent war. After the First World War,
everyone had said it could never happen again.
But there was unrest in Europe. Archie and his
family paid little attention to it, never believing
it was going to happen. Harry became
withdrawn and silent for a time. He had been
in the hell of the trenches in the first war and
knew he'd never survive anything like that
again. He hoped he was too old to be called up
this time around, but he feared for Archie and
what it might do to his beloved daughter, if her

husband did have to fight.

'I think we should all have a holiday. Go to Blackpool or somewhere. North Wales. Rhyl's nice, so I'm told. What do you think?' Archie suggested one evening in April. 'We could do with a bit of a break.'

'Can we afford it?' Dora asked excitedly.

'Bit of the calm before the storm,' Harry said wryly.

'You really think there's going to be another war, don't you?' Mary whispered in horror.

'I can't bear to think of it,' Dora said with a shudder. 'When we knew you were in France last time, we dreaded every knock at the door. Mum nearly had a heart attack if the telegraph boy came into the street.'

'I know, love,' her father said. 'But if it happens, it'll never be as bad.' Archie listened to the exchange and made no comment. He dreaded all thoughts of having to take part in a war. People should never be forced to fight against their will but there was no way he would be called a coward. He'd do his bit if he really had to. He just hoped it never came to the test. It couldn't ever happen again, he told himself.

'So, how about this little holiday? Just a weekend, I was thinking. Give us a break while we can.'

'I think you two should go on your own. You have precious little enough time together. Do you both good. Bring the colour back to your

243

cheeks.' Mary was adamant. She had been worried about Dora ever since the loss of the twin babies, even though it was over two years ago. She had been back at her beloved hairdressing shop but she was still pale and listless and had lost much of her sparkle.

'OK. If you're sure. We'll have us a weekend somewhere nice. What do you fancy, Dora?'

'Let's go to Blackpool. It'll be fun.'

They were full of plans for the next few days. They planned to make their trip as soon as it could be arranged, before the Season began. Though she normally worked on Saturdays, as did Archie, they managed to arrange for the time off. On the Friday evening, they set off in the little car, luggage piled on the back seat. It was dark by the time they reached the end of their journey. Blackpool itself was brightly lit and the trams bustled along the promenade, loaded with laughing people. Once they had settled in their hotel they could hardly wait to get out into the midst of the happy throngs swarming about the town.

They sat in a shelter overlooking the sea and munched hot fish and chips from newspaper wrappers.

'Why is there never enough vinegar?' asked Dora. 'I shook loads over my chips and it's all disappeared.'

They laughed together, held hands as they ran over the wet sand and shivered in the cold

244

winds that blew round the iron struts of the pier.

'I do love you, Dora,' Archie yelled to the wind.

'Let's go back to the hotel. We can have a night cap in the bar and get a good night's sleep. Then we can make the most of tomorrow.' Dora felt happier than she had for many months. Maybe, just maybe, this was the time she could move on to make new plans for their family. It should be just about the right time of the month, she thought. She wasn't going to say anything to Archie. He was far too worried about her health but she knew this had to be the right moment. It might even be her last chance to have her own baby. Though she wasn't really religious in any way, she sent up a prayer to anyone who might have been listening. While Archie was at the bar, buying them both a drink, she added, 'A girl, with blond hair and blue eyes, if there's a choice.' She smiled at her own gullibility but all the same, she felt content with her decision.

'You look happy,' Archie remarked, setting a half of bitter before her.

'I'm just excited. We're going to have fun this weekend. You know, I've been thinking, we should try to get a place of our own soon. Stand on our own two feet. It's all very well relying on Mum and Dad but we don't really get enough time together, do we?'

'I know what you mean but there's no way I

can buy anything for us. Not yet awhile.'

'I wasn't thinking of buying necessarily. We could always rent somewhere. There must be plenty of places available.'

'Let's see what happens. None of us know what the future holds. It really looks as if this war's going to take off. We just can't tell what it's going to mean for us all. I doubt too many folks will be wanting fine pots if they can't get food to put on them. It might not be the best business to be in. But let's stop going on about it. We're here to enjoy ourselves not to mope around. Drink up, now. I'm beginning to feel very tired. It's been quite a day.'

They made love that night, on the deep feather mattress that had rolled them both into the middle of the bed. It was obviously used to its occupants sleeping in the middle, it was so deeply indented. Dora felt warm and contented and knew it had been the right time. From the start, she simply knew she was pregnant, gloating over her news and hugging it to herself. The following day was busy. They visited all the piers, ate spun sugar candy, flung wooden balls at the coconut shy and carried their hairy brown prize with them for the rest of the day. Archie took pot shots at a target with a rifle and won a stupid looking cloth doll. They took the tram for a ride along the Front, as far as it went. After a walk along the beach, they returned and went back to the hotel to change. They went to see a show at the pier during the evening and when they finally sunk into their bed at nearly midnight Dora felt quite exhausted.

'It feels as if we've been away for ages,' she said as she snuggled against her husband.

'And we've still got most of tomorrow as well. You'll have to decide what you want to do before we set off back home.' But she was already asleep.

'I think this must have been one of the very nicest times we've had,' she said several times during the following day. 'We shall have to do it again sometime.'

'You're right. And if the war doesn't come to anything or if it's soon over as they say, we will think seriously about finding ourselves somewhere to live. We scarcely know what it's like to manage on our own. Be quite a change though. You'd have to do all the shopping and cooking. Don't suppose you'd have time to go to work.'

She smiled to herself, certain that her private prayers had already been answered.


## CHAPTER THIRTEEN

For the next few weeks, Archie was totally wrapped up in his work. War or no war, they were beginning to make their mark in the showrooms of the bigger stores. They were producing good quality china and by keeping the costs at a minimum, it represented good value. Dora was happily settled at her own work, providing Marcel waves for the fashionable ladies who frequented the shop. She had known instinctively that she was pregnant, right from their first night in Blackpool. She knew it would be a girl but all the same, she continued to send up her superstitious prayers for the safe delivery of her blue-eyed, blond girl-child. Her mother was aware of her daughter's contented air and felt suspicious, especially as she hadn't noticed any of the usual monthly disposals. Wisely, she kept quiet, knowing that she would be told when the time was right.

When the end of July came, Dora knew that she could hide her secret no longer. She had been surprised that Archie seemed not to have noticed either that she'd missed her monthly periods or that she was evidently putting on weight.

'I've got something to tell you,' she said when they were in bed one night. 'I think, well I know, I'm having our baby.' She felt Archie stiffen and he turned over to her.

'What?' His voice was hard and angry sounding. She bit her lip in the darkness.

'I . . . I thought you'd be pleased.'

'Oh, Dora. Dearest Dora. How can I be pleased at something that could kill you? Oh heck. How did it happen? I mean when? I thought we'd been careful.'

'I think it was that first night in Blackpool. Oh, Archie, don't be angry. I'm so happy. It'll be all right this time. I'm sure of it. I'm going to be very careful all the way through.'

'Well, I wish I was sure. What do your Mum and Dad think about it?'

'I haven't told them. Course I haven't. I had to tell you first. Though I expect Mum's guessed. You can't keep much hidden from her.'

Archie lay still. His mind was racing. He'd been so involved in his precious work, he had scarcely noticed anything outside the damned building. How could he have missed seeing his own wife's condition?

'I want you to hand in your notice at work. Immediately. I'm not having you wear yourself out standing all day. I mean it, Dora. No arguments.'

'It isn't necessary, Archie. I'm fine. So fine in fact that you haven't even noticed I've missed my periods for the last couple of times.'

'I don't care. I do know now and you are going to take it easy. Don't you realise you silly girl, your life is in danger? The doctor said you'd be taking a great risk if you should ever conceive again.'

'You never said. He never said anything to me.' Her voice was small and accusing.

'We didn't think it was sensible to tell you. Not given the state you were in. Then I sort of

249

pushed it away to the back of my mind.'

'And that was why you'd never talk about us trying for a baby again?'

'I s'pose so. I couldn't bear to lose you, Dora. If the question ever arose about you or the baby surviving, it would be an open and shut case.'

'But that would be denying the child a right to life.'

'I don't care. You're my life. You're the one person who drives me to do everything I have to do. One day, we'll have the big house again, the cars and I'll be someone. I shall have my own factory and my chain will be known all over the world. But it'll all be for you. Everything's just for you. You hand in your notice tomorrow and then we'll get you the best doctor we can find.'

Neither of them slept much that night. Archie was terrified at the implications of Dora's news and she tossed and turned, unable to get comfortable. When Mary greeted them at breakfast time, she took one look at them and turned to concentrate on her cooking. Her pursed lips were clamped tight and she waited to hear confirmation of what she already knew.

'So, when's it due?' she asked at last, when nothing had been said.

'By my reckoning, around the middle of February.'

'At least it's approaching the spring time. Can still be treacherous in February. Won't be easy.'

Once the ice was broken they began to plan in earnest. Dora reluctantly agreed to give up work and to make an appointment with her doctor as soon as she could.

'As long as I don't die of boredom,' she moaned. 'Maybe I can see a few friends. I seem to have neglected them for a long time. There's Myrtle and Joan Jarvis, my old school friends. And Barry. We haven't seen him for ages. He's still planning to marry that Nadine. She's nice and very good for him. Maybe we could ask them over some time?'

'OK, but I don't want you replacing work with spending hours in the kitchen, cooking or walking miles to see people.'

'I'm not an invalid,' Dora protested. 'I'm only pregnant.' The very words gave her a flood of pleasure. She sat down suddenly and blushed with even greater pleasure.

'What is it? What's the matter?'

'It moved. The baby moved. She's letting us know she's a part of our lives.'

'Did *she* indeed? You're so sure it's a girl?'

'Course she is. Blond hair and blue eyes. I put in the order myself.'

Everything was going well for them and Archie began to relax a little. Work had settled into a routine and he loved his role as manager of the decorating shop. Once the 'girls' were trained to his satisfaction, he began to work on some new designs and often lost himself in the sheer pleasure of creating something new. Leslie left him to decide on the new designs and always encouraged any changes he wanted to make. Dora truly seemed to be thriving and Mary and Harry supported them in every way possible. The main uncertainty in their lives was in the growing threat of the war in Europe. It seemed inevitable. To Dora, it seemed that events in Poland had very little to do with them. Her world, her thoughts were all centred around the baby growing inside her. But as Harry pointed out, the affairs of the world continued to press in on them all. There was an obligation for Britain to help the Poles following a pact made some years earlier.

'Who does this Hitler think he is? How can he demand to *take* the city of Danzig, wherever that is?'

'How can anyone demand that we all go to war again. You'd think we'd have learned our lesson the first time,' Mary said bitterly. 'I can't bear to think of all our young men being sent away again. After that last lot . . .' She closed her eyes, remembering the horrors she had lived through when Harry was fighting in France. He wouldn't ever talk about the dreadful weeks in the trenches and then his poor leg . . . That had never been the same again after the shrapnel. She swallowed, regaining control. 'And this poor baby. What sort of world is it to bring a new life into?'

Gloom settled over all of them as they

listened to daily news and scoured the newspapers for every hint of how it was going to affect each member of their family and community. By autumn, a sense of inevitability had settled over all of them. Speculation about call-up was the main topic of conversation in every pub and round most tables in most homes.

'Have you heard that City lost half its players?' was the devastating news brought home by Archie. 'The call-up spares nobody, it seems.'

To Dora, the loss of a few football matches for Stoke City seemed very trivial compared with losing her own Archie or even her Dad, should they begin to recruit men of his age. She took to shielding her growing stomach with both arms whenever she walked outside the home. It was as if she could somehow protect her precious child by the simple action. Each day, the news seemed to get worse. September 3rd dawned and expecting the worst, everyone found a radio set to listen to. At eleven o'clock, the words spoken by Neville Chamberlain sealed the fate of the country.

'I bet nobody ever forgets those words,' Dora said, tears starting in her eyes. 'The country is now at war with Germany. Oh God. How could it happen again?' She sat miserably, protecting her bulge and feeling guilty that she was thinking only of herself, her baby and her family. All around Europe, people were going to lose their homes, their jobs and even their lives. There would be shortages of even the most basic things. All the same, one had to make everyday life a part of the reality. It would be very easy to do nothing. However trivial, it was the washing, the cooking and doing all the usual things that helped one to get through the shocking daily events that came to them.

For Archie, it seemed as if a blow had been struck to his very core. How could he justify spending all his time drawing patterns to use on china teacups. It was wrong. He couldn't bear the thought of having to sign up for the army and leave his wife and the child they were so anxiously awaiting. He spoke at length to Leslie about their future. As many of their workers were women, it was unlikely they would lose them to the war effort but if the men had to go to war, the women would have to take over their roles in every sort of industry in the country. There was nothing for it but to acknowledge that everything they held precious in their world was about to change. The factory in its present form would probably have to close. Some china manufacturing would have to take place but the highly decorative ware would have to cease. It was all at the wrong time for the relatively new factory that was only just beginning to make a name for itself. The stuff they produced was for the luxury end of the market. All that would be wanted for the foreseeable future would be utilitarian ware. Plain white or cream.

'It could all be over by Christmas,' Leslie said. 'I've heard several people on the radio saying just that. It's all temporary, I'm sure.' It was with a heavy heart that Archie broke the news to his workers. Production would halve, as from the start of next month. After that, nobody could tell. Everyone was so shocked that they scarcely argued. It was as if the very life blood had been sucked out of them all.

'We'll be back to normal before long,' Archie tried to cheer them all. 'You'll all have your jobs back when it ends,' he promised.

'Them as survive, maybe,' said Nellie, one of the younger 'girls'. 'I reckon nothin'll ever be normal again. It's the end of life as we know it.'

'We're not done for yet. We shall keep going a while longer. But I have to say, if any of you want to go off to other jobs, I won't blame you in the least. Take whatever you can get, I'd say.'

'Is that what you'll be doing?' another of them asked.

'I dunno yet. We shall have to wait and see. Now, come on. There's still a couple of hours to go. Let's get back to it, make the most of the work while it's still here.'

At the end of the day, Archie went home with a heavy heart. After all his struggles, his battles to escape from his old life, it seemed so

255

unfair that success should be snatched away from him at this time. He mustn't let Dora see how worried he was. It would be particularly bad for the child if she knew how much he was worrying. All the same, he was carrying a deep feeling of futility and failure inside.

The next weeks were clouded with the feelings of uncertainty in most homes in the country. Men were leaving every day and setting off to join the army, navy and air-forces. Gradually, the occupations that were considered essential were being designated and Archie heard that mining was among them. Even if his age wasn't against him, his own father wouldn't have to go to war. Instead he would continue to fight the constant war of life down the pit. Archie shuddered, knowing that particular life would have seemed just as bad to him as any war.

During October, Dora began to feel ill. She admitted that she was feeling rotten and this time made no fuss about staying in bed. Archie felt his heart sinking once more. It was almost the same time in the pregnancy that things had started to go wrong before. Would anything ever go right for them? He began to think they were jinxed.

'Must be all the worry of the war and everything,' he tried to comfort his wife. But she continued to lie listless and in obvious pain. 'Does it feel like you're having contractions?' Archie asked, feeling stupid.

Why did he know so little about the process of childbirth? He'd never forgotten the terrifying screams he'd heard from his own mother when his brother was born. It sounded so dreadful he'd wondered how the process of child birth could possibly continue. Somehow, it always did. He'd tried to ask Mary to tell him but she had been embarrassed saying *it was woman's stuff* and men had no business knowing what was going on. She had mentioned contractions, when he asked how he'd know if it was starting. But he had little idea of what it really involved.

'Should I get the midwife to come? Or should I get the doctor?'

'I don't know, Archie. I really don't know. It's much too soon for it to be labour pains. I've still got nearly three months to go.'

'I'm going for the doctor then. Don't worry love. We'll do everything we can to make sure it's all right.' He left her and stifled the rising panic that was choking his throat. He didn't know how she'd cope if she lost the baby. Worse still, he didn't know how he would cope if he lost Dora. He rushed round to the doctor's and made him promise to come as soon as he could. Mary fussed round her daughter and did her best to keep her cheerful.

'Thanks, Mum,' she whispered after Mary had sponged her face for the umpteenth time. Her voice sounded weak and suddenly she gave a small scream. 'Oh . . . oh it hurts, Mum. What's happening to me?'

'Archie'll be back in a minute, with the doctor. Just try to lie still.' With a worried frown, Mary went to look through the window to see if there was any sign of the doctor and her son-in-law. 'Do you want a nice cup of tea, love?' she offered.

'I feel too sick. I daren't let go, in case it gives trouble with the babe. Oh, Mum, I can't bear it. I can't lose this one. You won't let them take it away, will you? Promise me you won't.'

'They'll have to do what's best for you. Now, stop your mitherin' and lie back and rest.'

Two hours later, Archie was pacing the corridors at the local hospital. It was very close by and once the doctor had taken a glance at his wife, he'd rushed her straight into the surgical ward. He'd suspected appendicitis but with the advanced state of the pregnancy, especially given Dora's history, he'd been unable to give any sort of accurate prognosis. Archie knew he'd never forget the stricken look in Dora's eyes as she was laid out on the trolley.

'Don't let them harm the baby,' she'd begged. 'Promise me you won't.'

The doctor had already told him that the chances of keeping the child were virtually nil. If they tried to save the child, it was more than likely that Dora could die.

258

'What the heck's the use of such a premature baby without a mother?' he'd demanded. 'Save my Dora. She's the important one.' How could any man choose differently? He didn't know his child and in any case, it was far too small to survive if it was born now. He glanced at his watch for the fourth time that minute. It seemed to be going on forever. He half wished he'd let Mary or Harry come with him. He'd insisted on them staying at home as there seemed little point in all of them cluttering up the hospital corridor. At each click of a door or sound of footsteps, he started forward. How long did it take to perform an operation? It seemed like every minute was three hours long. He continued his pacing. He'd never forget that smell. The oddly disinfectant smell that pervaded everything. A soft footfall behind him made him swing round nervously.

'Harry! What are you doing here?'

'Same as you, lad. Waiting to hear the news. Mary insisted I come. I left her turning out the kitchen cupboards. Said she couldn't stand the waiting. Needed something to do.' He laid his hand on the young man's shoulder and nodded, comfortingly.

'By, but I'm glad you're here. I was driving myself barmy, imagining all sorts. I er . . . I had to say that Dora should be saved instead of the baby, should there be any choice in the matter. She didn't want me to but it was all I could

259

say.'

'Course it was, lad. Absolutely right.'

'God, how much longer?' he said desperately.

'It isn't the right time to say anything but our Margaret has given birth to another daughter. We got a telegram this afternoon. I'm sorry, lad. It's tough on you both to see her having them so easily.'

'For heaven's sake don't tell Dora. I think it would just about finish her off.'

At last the door of the theatre opened and the surgeon came out. He wiped his brow.

'Mr Barnett?'

'Yes. That's me. This is my father-in-law. Harry Marsh. Dora's Dad. How is she? Dora?'

'As well as can be expected.'

'What's that s'posed to mean?'

'She's come through the operation quite well, considering. She's had an appendectomy, greatly complicated by her advanced state of pregnancy. A most interesting case.'

'Oh, interesting is it? I'm glad to hear it. And is she still pregnant?' The sarcasm was lost on the surgeon.

'Well, as far as we can tell, she should keep the baby. It's not by any means certain of course and she may still lose it. Nor can we guarantee that there might not be any damage to the foetus. We've done all we can.'

'And Dora's going to be all right? Can I see her?'

'She's still rather sleepy after the anaesthetic. We had to monitor everything very carefully. You must realise that we actually had to lift the entire baby out to perform the operation. Complications, you understand. We've taken every possible precaution and hopefully, she should manage to complete her term and give birth normally. She will of course have to take a great deal of rest, most of it in bed until the birth. There are a great many more stitches than usual and with the distension caused by her pregnancy, we have to take great care that they don't give way. Nothing strenuous at all. For several weeks, she'll probably have some degree of pain. The incision had to be unusually long because of the child. And the healing may be slow with the extra pressure. You can see her briefly but she needs plenty of rest.'

'Thank you so much, doctor. This will mean a lot to her, knowing she hasn't lost the baby.'

'Yes, well it's early days to give an accurate prognosis.'

The two men went into the ward and looked at the woman they both loved so dearly. She was pale and exhausted and lay back on her pillow looking so white they neither of them knew what to say. Her eyes flickered open.

'Am I all right? Is the baby still there?'

'Yes and yes. Don't try to move and don't say anything, love. It's going to be all right. Now, get some sleep and we'll be in first thing tomorrow morning.'

'Don't make yourself late for work,' she murmured feebly.

'Sod work,' Archie hissed. 'You come first, in every way.' He stood beside her, holding tightly to her frail hand. She always had such soft hands. Took great care of them. There was even now, pale pink nail varnish on her nails. He smiled fondly. It was part of his wife. His Dora. 'Try to sleep. You'll soon be feeling better.' He kissed her head and he and her father slipped away quietly.

Dora's determination to keep her baby gave her strength. The doctors and nurses had told her to expect the worst. Even if she went to full term, there was still the possibility that the baby may not be quite normal. But that would never matter to her. Whatever the child needed in the way of extra care, she would give it. Willingly. Once back at home, she gritted her teeth and did everything she could to rest, eat healthily and avoid stress. The latter was not so easy, in view of the growing pace of the war. Archie did his best to keep work running smoothly so that she was not worried about him but it grew more difficult each week as orders were cancelled and workers were being laid off.

One bright spot was the announcement from her cousin Barry that he and Nadine had become engaged. Marriage was some distance off, however, as he was working away from home. Dora was delighted to receive a letter from Nadine and wrote back with enthusiasm.

'*My stomach looks like a patchwork quilt. I had twenty-six stitches instead of the proverbial seven or eight. Maybe if I wear a high enough collar, it won't show! But at least they saved the infant.*'

Her light words held a depth of emotion that no-one could ever realise.

They spent a quiet Christmas. Barry and Nadine came over for Boxing Day and they enjoyed a quiet day together. Barry had lost none of his enthusiasm for his band and was convinced it was only a matter of time before he hit the big time.

'I'm certain that even if the war does go on, people will need a bit of lively music to enjoy and take their minds off their troubles,' he said. All the same, it seemed that everyone's plans were on hold until they knew what was going to happen. Though in some ways, events had never quite got going the way everyone was expecting, the war was certainly nowhere near being over by Christmas, as the politicians had so optimistically predicted. They'd heard that William was signing up and Mary shook her head sadly.

'He's so very young isn't he?'

'They're not fussy who they send in to get shot. He's old enough.'

January seemed even more depressing than usual and the weather turned bitterly cold.

'What a time of year for a baby to come into the world,' Dora wailed. The snow began to fall in February and people were outside shovelling snow from their paths. The roads were largely impassable and both men of the family spent many hours struggling to work. Both parents went down with heavy colds and Archie completely gave up trying to get to work. Dora knew it was almost time for the baby and began worrying herself that it would stand no chance if it came into a household filled with germs, especially with the weather so cold. One morning, she struggled along to the corner shop and bought bottles of disinfectant, cotton wool and various other bits she would need for the birth. Despite all her previous problems, there was no question of her confinement taking place in hospital. Hospitals were for people with serious illnesses. She would have to rely on the midwife, a few prayers and plenty of disinfectant. Mary was beginning to get over her own cold and, feeling better, had got up for the afternoon when Dora started her labour. During the first contractions, she said nothing. She went upstairs and made her preparations. When she was certain, she asked Archie to fetch the midwife.

'Why?' he asked foolishly. He was quickly galvanised into action when she sagged, as another contraction hit her. Making sure she was as comfortable as possible, he set out on

Henry's bicycle to fetch the midwife. He floundered through the deep snow, spurred on by the urgency of the situation. It was his first meeting with the woman and he felt a sense of shock, seeing the tiny woman who was supposed to be the solution to his problem. They floundered their way through the snow. Drifts were several feet high and on one occasion, he quite expected his companion would be buried. He sat her on the cycle and pushed her to the house. Once she arrived, she took complete charge. Mary appeared, still full of cold and was quickly dispatched back to bed.

'Can't do with any extra patients at the moment. Now, Archie, get the kettle on and make everyone cups of hot sweet tea. And back up that fire. We'll need the warmth later.' She scuttled off upstairs to Dora and apart from the occasional bumps, he heard nothing of the trauma he believed was going on in the room above. Dora did not scream the way his mother had and he was afraid that things were going wrong. Using the offer of more cups of tea as an excuse, he went up to see how things were progressing.

'What's the time?' the little midwife demanded, as she heard him approaching the bedroom door.

'About four, I think. How are things going?' He heard a tiny cry and pushed the door open. Dora was lying back, covered in perspiration and laughing with delight.

'Your daughter was born at four o'clock. Well, near enough. Here she is. Say hello to the little thing.' Archie stood motionless, looking at the bundle the woman was holding. 'Come on then. Take hold of her. Poor little mite. She'll think no-one wants her if you don't brace up.' Tears filling his eyes, he stepped forward and took the towel-like bundle. In the middle lay the reddest most wizened face he'd ever seen.

'Isn't she beautiful?' Dora said feebly.

'Er . . . well yes. I s'pose she is.' He stared at the tiny creature and at once fell in love, felt a sense of total panic, followed by concern for his wife. 'Are you all right, love? I mean, you've been very quiet.'

'She's fine,' the midwife chirped as she worked on cleaning and clearing his wife. 'Good girl. Made no fuss and delivered perfectly. Wish they were all like her. The way some of them yell, you'd think they were the first ever to give birth. But your missus was a real good'un.'

'She's one of a kind,' Archie said proudly. 'But the baby. Is she all right? They said there might be some damage. You know, after the operation and everything.'

'She's got a bit of a blob on her arm but everything else looks fine. We won't know till much later of course. When she starts to grow a bit.'

'She's going to be just fine, I know it. And she'll be a blond and have blue eyes.' As her mother was speaking, the child opened its clear blue eyes and stared at her father with all the wisdom of the world held in her gaze.

'You're right, she's got blue eyes,' Archie breathed, his own green eyes glowing with pride. The midwife didn't bother to tell him that all babies have blue eyes to begin with. The colour came later. 'Can't say if she'll be a blond. She's completely bald.'

'Right now. We'll get Mother settled and then sort out the little one. You have got someone to help you, haven't you?'

Archie explained that the rest of the household was down with flu or at least, with heavy colds. Dora interrupted and said she'd made disinfectant cotton balls to hang round the crib. Nobody was going to risk infecting her precious baby. There was a small fire burning in the bedroom grate and the light was warm and cheerful. Despite feeling as if she'd been kicked hard in the stomach, Dora was ecstatic. She never once considered the possibility of there being anything wrong with the baby. The red mark on her arm was noticeable but never enough to worry about during those early months. They decided to call her Carole Mary. Dora's parents could hardly wait to get over their colds and come to make a fuss of the baby. The fact that they already had three grandchildren from their other daughter seemed to mean little in comparison. Mary occasionally felt guilty but she had never got on particularly well with Margaret.

It was the spring of 1941 when Leslie announced that he was forced to close down the factory for the duration. *The duration* was the term springing up all over the country, as if trying to give an air of continuity ready for when things got back to normal. Archie felt the call of duty and without saying anything to his family, went to sign up. He hoped his education and experience of management might give him the chance of some rank. He failed the medical. Though it was unexpected, he felt a sense of overwhelming relief. He was however, expected to do war work, whatever that might turn out to be. He did not have to wait for long. There was a munitions factory opened in the middle of unspoilt countryside, some way out of the heart of the Potteries. They said the skills used in the manufacturing of china were evidently suitable for those expected to work on munitions. It was the steady hands and ability to paint that were the main reason for this, or so they said. Many of the former workers were forced to board the fleet of buses that collected the workers each day and travel the miles to the Royal Ordnance Factory at Swynnerton. Archie joined them and soon found himself working in the research and development department.

Some of his own former workers were working there, packing gunpowder into shell cases. It was dreadful work, dangerous in every way. After a few months, the girls all took on the tinge of yellow to their skin and were offered cheap make-up as compensation. The sight of them all wearing turbans wrapped round their heads was imprinted on his mind for ever. Occasional curlers peeped out from the swathes of fabric and he wondered if they ever took them out to let their hair flow free. Despite their cheerful attitudes, it broke his heart to see such talent being wasted but it was work that was urgently needed.

A large estate of partly prefabricated houses was built much closer to the factory and many of the workers were offered homes there. Archie broke the news to the family and it was agreed that it would be for the best for him and his little family to accept one of them. Mary was distraught at the thought of losing the close contact with her daughter and grandchild and begged them to stay. Their minds were made up quite dramatically, when a bomb fell near the end of their road one night. Though they had dutifully built their Anderson shelter, a row of curved pieces of corrugated iron, buried well into the garden, it was too cold to take the baby out to the shelter. Instead, Harry crawled under the large heavy old kitchen table and made himself and the baby a safe nest there. The rest of them went out to the shelter but once the noise had stopped and the all-clear siren sounded, they came gladly back into the house. Harry and the baby were fast asleep and the racket of his snoring resonated through the house.

'I think this does it for me. The houses at Walton are all reinforced and have built-in air raid shelters,' Archie told them.

'When would we move in?' Dora asked. She felt torn between leaving her parents' home and having their own space. It was truly time for them to stand on their own feet, she decided.

'Well, not for a while. Looks like being next spring at the earliest. Some of them are finished but we've missed out on the first wave. We already have a home, so we're not a priority case.'

'This is the start of the next part our lives, isn't it?' Dora said, feeling a mixture of pleasure and trepidation. She had never before lived away from her parents.

## CHAPTER FOURTEEN

Over the next months, they continued to try and live as normally as possible. Dora began to cut and set various friends' hair in the kitchen. War or not, many of the local women wanted to look their best and the few shillings she had managed to earn were all carefully saved towards buying their own furniture. Mary and Harry gave them the bedroom suite they were currently using and they sorted out curtains and bedding ready for the possible move. Some of the furniture they had bought for Branksome was stored in the garage. It gave them a good start. As restrictions began to hit hard, everything was used and recycled. Harry brought home all the wood he could scrounge from tea-chests and delivery crates from the shop. He had always enjoyed working with wood and was most ingenious in making odd bits of furniture, tables and shelves.

Dora and her mother were busily doing the washing one morning, when there was a knock at the door. Through the coloured glass panel, Dora could see a tall figure waiting. She opened the door and gasped in amazement.

'William? Is that really you?' Her brother-in-law seemed to have grown beyond all recognition since she had last seen him. He was wearing the khaki uniform of a soldier.

'I've joined up at last, as you can see. Guess what? They've made me a P.T. instructor. Bet that'll get Archie going. He was always on about me being the runt of the family.'

'Come on in. I can't believe it. We've heard nothing from you in months and now this.' They made tea and sat in the kitchen chatting, catching up with each other's news.

'And where's my niece?'

'Oh good heavens,' Dora exclaimed. 'Poor little thing. She's out in her playpen on the lawn. I'd forgotten all about her.'

William went outside. Lying fast asleep on her rug, lay the baby. He leaned over and spoke softly.

'Wake up, little one. Your uncle's come to see you.' As she opened her eyes, she grinned a toothy grin and sat up. 'Watch me,' he called as he stood on his hands and walked round the playpen, his face on the same level as the child's.

'Show off,' Dora called, impressed by his fitness. The baby gurgled with pleasure and shouted Dad-Dad-Dad, her latest word.

'I'm not your Dad, worst luck,' William said as he righted himself. 'Might have been if I hadn't been bad when I was a lad. Held me back, that did. That brother of mine wouldn't have stood a chance if I'd caught up with him.'

'Go on with you, you're always coming out with that old line. Bring her in now and we'll see if we can find something to feed you on. I dare say you've got an appetite to match your size, these days.'

'I've got some bits from the NAAFI for you. Tea and sugar. I'd better keep a bit back for Mum and Dad.'

'Take it all to them, love,' Mary said. 'Harry looks after us well enough. Not that he gets us extra of course but at least we always know we're getting get our fair share. Your Mum may not be so lucky.'

He stayed with them for the night, so he had the chance to see his brother and talk about their new lives. They all felt a sense of closeness, possibly for the first time in their lives.

'If nothing else, the war certainly unites people, doesn't it?' Dora said as he was leaving the next day. 'Say hello to your Mum and Dad from us.'

When the next Christmas arrived, Harry made a small chest of drawers for Carole, using an old tea-chest. She pulled herself up against it and made several tottering attempts to walk before she fell down on to her well padded backside. She chortled at her new trick and made them all smile. Carole was such a happy little girl and gave them all plenty to think about apart from the dreadful war. Her blond curls and blue eyes won all their hearts.

'Are we going to see your Mum and Dad this New Year?' Dora asked.

'I'd much rather stay here.'

'I think we should. We didn't see them over Christmas. It's been ages.'

'Won't be any buses New Year's Day. But then, I'm working anyhow.'

'We could go after you finish work on the Tuesday. We're seeing Barry and Nadine for New Year's Eve. It's the thirtieth on Tuesday, so it's near enough. We'll have to go on the bus this year.'

It was a much more difficult journey on the bus than when they'd had the use of the car. They'd sold their little car the previous year when petrol was difficult to get. Dora had watched it go with a great deal of sadness. It had represented her first bit of independence.

'Hallo, Mum.' Archie forced a smile as his mother opened the door.

'What a surprise. Thought you'd forgotten where we live. Come in. By, she's grown. I bet she doesn't even know who I am. Hallo, little Carole.' The child smiled up at the stranger and grinned. She muttered words that passed as *hello*. His mother looked older, he realised but then, he hadn't seen her for a very long time. Maybe she'd mellowed a bit he thought hopefully.

There was a fire burning in the grate and a kettle almost boiling on one side of the fire. Ralph was sitting with his feet up, looking very weary. He stood up and gave them his usual warm welcome. He took the child and sat her on his knee, bouncing her gently. She lay against him happily and after a short while, she was dozing in front of the warm fire.

'She's a champion little lass,' he said proudly. 'Something about a little girl that's different. You don't feel as if cuddling her, you're making her soft like you would a lad.' Archie stared at his father. He never remembered being cuddled by either of his parents. He decided it was because he was a lad and they hadn't wanted to make him *soft*.

'You're not working tomorrow, are you?' he asked Ralph.

'Yes. And we've been asked to go in on New Year's Day, this time round. They're not insisting of course, 'cos of the tradition. It's purely voluntary.'

'But you've never worked New Year's. None of the miners have.'

'No. But I shall go. Our shift decided unanimously that we'd support the war effort. Seems they still can't get enough coal, even after we've worked all the hours God sends.'

'And for no extra pay, I'll bet. You've all gone soft if you ask me. I don't like it. You working New Year's. Not right. It's bad luck.' Frances was as sharp tongued as ever.

'Aye, well I reckon we're all suffering a fair amount of bad luck at the moment. Maybe this next year will see an end to it.'

'I can't imagine what it's like down the pit,' Dora began. 'How do you stand it, Dad?'

'You never really get used to it. Going down in the cage every day, seems like you just have to survive long enough to come up again. It's dirty, dusty and bloody hard graft. You work with your pick until you've prised out a load of pieces of coal and then shovel it into trucks when there's enough. Some days, the dust's so thick you feel as if you have to try and drag air into your lungs, just to stay alive. You made the right choice, Archie lad. I'd never truly

275

want anyone of mine to have to work down there among the stench and dirt. I don't even blame young William choosing to fight the war as an alternative.'

They were all silent for a moment or two. Dora shuddered and sipped her drink feeling slightly guilty for her own comfortable life. She'd never fully realised just how much Archie had to fight to get away from that fate.

'Nearly 1942. I keep wondering when this war will all be over and done with,' Ralph said glumly.

'We all keep hoping. We're moving house, in the spring,' Dora told them. 'Archie's workplace has got a new lot of houses being built. We've put down for one. It's a big estate. Quite near the country. And they say there'll be plenty of open spaces for the kids to play in.'

'All right for some,' was Frances's only comment.

'You can never be pleased for us about anything, can you?' Archie said bitterly.

'Leave it, Archie,' Dora told him. She couldn't bear them to quarrel on the one visit they'd made in months.

'I'll make us some more tea,' Frances announced.

'We'd better be off soon,' Archie said almost as soon as tea was finished. 'We don't want to have the baby out too late in the cold.'

As they were leaving, Ralph seemed to cling

to the baby and his daughter-in-law for longer than ever before. It was as if he couldn't bear to let them go. Dora was touched.

'Thanks so much for making the effort to come and see us. You've got a proper little charmer there. Look after her, won't you?'

'She's the most precious gift I've ever had. Nobody's going to harm her in any way, I can promise you that. She won't have any brothers or sisters, you see. I'm not much of a woman, am I? Could only just about hold on to this one.' Dora felt tears pricking the back of her eyes.

'I disagree. I think you're one very special woman. My son's a lucky man.'

'Oh I am,' Archie said. 'And I know it. Bye Dad. And thanks for the tea, Mum.'

'Don't leave it so long before you come again, son.' Ralph shook hands with his son and unexpectedly, suddenly pulled him into a hug. Archie was nonplussed. It was the first time he could remember such a thing.

'Happy New Year to you both,' he stammered as they walked away down the street. He turned to wave and saw his Dad was still standing outside, watching them leave. He raised a hand as they turned the corner. 'Crikey. Whatever came over me Dad?' he asked

'Maybe he's realised what a clever son he's got. And he was very pleased to see our little Carole. I s'pose New Year's always a bit of a new start. We all keep hoping this blinkin' war's going to end soon.'

They arrived home late. Their baby daughter had long since fallen asleep and Archie carried her half slung over his shoulder. It was a clear, cold night. Mary and Harry were waiting for them to come, a kettle boiling on the side of the fire.

'We thought you'd got lost. Come on up the fire and get warm. The tea won't be long. Should be having summat a bit stronger to celebrate.'

'Can't see there's much to celebrate,' Archie said gloomily.

"I'll just put Carole down and then I'll be back for that cuppa. She's sound asleep. I won't wake her now to change her. She'll be all right.'

'And how were your parents?' Mary asked.

'All right. In fact, me Dad seemed better than I've seen him for some time. He seemed sort of, I don't know . . . more affectionate.'

'That'll be the baby,' Harry said, nodding wisely. 'They always bring out the best in people.'

They celebrated New Year's Eve quietly with Barry and his wife. They now had a baby son, who was put to bed upstairs for the evening. They solemnly drank a toast 'to better times', in draught beer that Barry and Archie had fetched home from the pub in lemonade bottles.

'Not quite like some of the parties we've had in the past, is it?' Barry said to his cousin. 'Remember those nights at the Castle?'

'Can I forget them? You were doing so well with your band Barry. I hope you haven't given up on it.'

'Certainly not. When the lads come back, we shall soon get going again.'

'I'm just glad he hasn't had to go away,' Nadine told them all. 'There's something to be said for having one of these essential occupations. Good job you weren't still trying to run your band. You'd never have been able to use that as an excuse.' Nadine was still slightly jealous of the close relationship between the two cousins.

'Always did say that it was a good idea to get a qualification. Who'd have thought a mere draftsman could be considered as a vital part of the war effort on the home front?' Barry grinned.

'Talking of war efforts at home, did you hear about this home guard they're setting up?' Archie asked.

'Why, are you going to volunteer?' Barry asked.

'I think it's expected. When we move to Walton, on this new estate they're building, every able bloke will be expected to join. Make up for not being sent off to fight, I s'pose. Might even be a laugh.'

'Typical blokes,' Dora grimaced. 'If you

don't join up for real, you have to play at being soldiers.'

'You won't be saying that if wc end up saving all our lives.' The debate went on for some hours. Clearly the women didn't take the idea seriously but the men enjoyed the prospect of doing their bit. Harry and Mary went off to their beds, while the others sat discussing, wondering what the coming year would bring.

'Damned war. When shall we ever get back to doing what we all want to do?'

'Some folk never will again,' Dora said softly. It was a sombre moment as the young people gave thought to the uncertainty of their lives. Soon after midnight, Nadine, Barry and their baby left.

'Happy New Year, love,' Archie said to his wife as they settled down. 'Early start tomorrow. Today. Wake me up, won't you?'

Life at the Swynnerton Ordnance Factory had quickly settled into a dull routine. There were constant bangs as the minor accidents became a part of the routine. Occasionally more scrious explosions rocked the buildings and made everyone's ears ring. Even though it was a new year, most people went about their work just as they had the previous day. Archie was working in something of a no-man's-land, stuck between managing a group of workers and helping to develop some new processes. His skills at management and knowledge of the chemicals in the pottery industry meant that he was capable of much more than simple production line work. He had felt strangely edgy all morning, as if he was waiting for something to happen. He put it down to the late night celebrating New Year. He ate his lunchtime sandwiches with a group of the others. Some of the office workers joined the group, sitting at one side of the workshop.

'They were talking of some pit explosion,' one of the secretaries was saying. 'Someone who drove down with some supplies told us.. It was up Burslem way somewhere. That's your neck of the woods, isn't it, Archie?'

'Yes, me Dad works at Sneyd.' The cold chill was running down his back and he felt himself breaking out in a sweat. He thought about the miners at his Dad's pit who were, unusually, working this New Year. But then, he tried to tell himself, so were dozens of others. There were loads of pits all over the Burslem area. All the same, the feeling of dread didn't leave him. He thought of the sweltering heat below ground. The dry dusty air, if air it could be called. His Dad had told him what it was like at the coal face. As his son got older, Ralph had been more honest about the horrors of life below the ground. 'Sweat runs off you and leaves paler tracks down your face. Every time they blast a new bit of the seam, there's dust filling the air. We move in almost before it settles and start picking at the rubble.

You don't bother waitin' 'cos it doesn't ever get much better. You keep going. Keep digging. Ripping out the next bit of the face. If you once stop, you realise how dirty and dusty it is and how knackered you're feeling. There's good seams under Sneyd. Not too much waste among the rock. You think another couple of truckloads and it'll be over for another day. But it's not till that moment when the cage comes up top again, you can relax. You drag the cleaner air into your lungs with gratitude for another shift over and done.'

Archie shuddered, thinking the chances were that the cage had not come up to the surface, this one last time. He couldn't imagine the horror of suffocating under the ground. It brought home every reason why he'd refused to follow his father deep in that terrible dark place. Many sons did follow the family tradition. Many families worked side by side down there. The chances were that several members of the same family would have perished, side by side in this tragedy. He went into the office and asked one of the girls to make a phone call for him. The offices of the local paper were the only place he could think of. He had to know for sure though secretly, he already guessed. The look on the secretary's face was enough. It was indeed his Dad's pit that had suffered the explosion. Some men had got out and some were still trapped below ground. Others, it was reported, had been killed instantly. There was no means of his getting home until the end of the afternoon, when the transport arrived. He walked round in a daze, pale faced and sick with dread. He stumbled onto the coach and sat staring out of the window. He tried to plan what he should do but nothing seemed clear or possible. As the bus stopped, he dashed into a shop and put three halfpence on the counter for the evening paper. He scanned the headlines.

### SNEYD COLLIERY EXPLOSION.
Rescue Teams Continuing Investigation.
### 48 MEN STILL IN THE PIT.

He felt physically sick as he read down the page.

*Two men dead. Two gravely injured. One suffering secondary shock. Forty-eight still in the accident area.*

The explosion had happened at seven-fifty in the morning just as all the men were starting work. He shook his head. He'd been starting work at the same time himself, unaware of anything. He remembered his feeling of unrest during the morning and wondered about the powers of telepathy. The details were still confused when this edition had gone to press and he scanned down the page for more details. He knew his own father was among the missing men. He felt tears burning the back of

283

his eyes, thinking that his father could be lying waiting for the faint sounds of rescue. Were his friends lying dead around him? Was he still fighting to get air into his damaged lungs? Was it all over? Maybe someone had got through in the time that had passed since the paper came out. He turned and walked slowly down the pleasant tree-lined avenue that was his home. He had made his break from the dirty, dusty life he'd lived and was beginning to achieve his ambitions. Before the damned war had started. If it hadn't been for the damned war, his Dad would never have been working New Year's Day. It was just as bad, if not worse, as being killed in action in some foreign part of the world. He looked up. Dora was waiting outside the house, wearing her coat over her overall.

'You've heard then,' she said simply. It was not a question. He held out the paper to her. 'I know. We fetched one earlier. It is your Dad's pit, isn't it?' He nodded, unable to speak. 'It might not have been his area though. We don't know.' Dora put her arms around him, trying to bring comfort.

'He's there all right. I've known summat was up, all day.'

'Do you want to go over to be with your Mum?'

'I dunno. There's nowt I can do. But I s'pose someone should be with her.'

'There may be something on the news. We'll

284

put the radio on while you have your tea. And you must have something to eat. You need to keep up your energy.'

'I couldn't, love. It'd choke me. Just thinking of him down there,' he shuddered. 'And last night, we were sitting here, laughing and joking. Makes me feel so guilty.'

'You or William might have been down there with him, if your Mum had her way. Doesn't bear thinking of. Look here, it'd be better if you went over tomorrow. By the time you'd get there tonight, it'd be nearly midnight.'

'I reckon you're right. Makes more sense to go in the morning.'

The following hours were a mixture of hope and despondency. The mine chiefs made constant statements. The rescue teams came up with stories of hearing noises. The second day, everyone knew that there was no longer any hope for the missing men. The air was too bad and there were too many rock falls for speedy recovery. The death toll was estimated at fifty-eight. The group of wives and families waiting at the pit-head made a pathetic sight. Archie had expected his mother to be among the group but she was still at her home, looking pale but pretty much the same as always.

'No point standing out there with all them miserable faces for company,' was all she would say.

'There's women that have lost everything.

285

One of them had two lads, only sixteen and seventeen and her husband. There's talk of setting up a relief fund.' He was trying to say anything to break the hard, glassy expression on his mother's face. 'They . . . they haven't found all of them yet. They haven't found me Dad.' He felt the tears at the back of his eyes but he couldn't let his mother see. He felt as far away from her as ever. Even this tragedy failed to bring real, deep emotion to his mother's eyes. The knock at the door made her move.

'You'd better come in, Mavis Cartwright. Though I know what you've come to say.'

The little woman came into the room and saw Archie standing close to the meagre fire.

'Terrible business, lad. You'll know why I'm here.'

'They've found him, have they?' Frances said sharply.

'Aye. I'm so sorry. He was a hero. He was sheltering the last young lad. Trying to stop the blast from hitting him. They're saying all the men in that section died right away. No-one suffered injuries. It was as if the air was sucked right out of the place. I'm sorry. What can I do? Make a cuppa or something?'

Frances sat down and shook her head. She remained silent and Archie watched to see if she was going to cry.

'It's all right, Mavis. Thanks very much for coming round. I'll see to her now. Thanks.

And I'm sorry for your loss, too.' The woman pulled a grubby scarf over her head and went back into the grey streets.

'I can stay over if you like, Mum,' he offered. In his heart, he wanted only to leave this dreadful place and get back to the warm, cheerful home his wife and her parents had made for him. But he knew he was being more selfish than ever and sat down again.

'You best get back to that posh wife of yourn. I'm used to being on my own. I expect the funeral will be at the end of the week. I'll let you know.'

'But I can't leave you like this. Not on your own.'

'Bugger off can't you? I want to be on my own.'

Torn between his own grief and duty to his mother, he put the kettle on the fire and picked up the familiar brown teapot. He added more tea leaves to the pile already in the pot and poured boiling water in. He poured the dark, treacly liquid into a mug and stirred in the sterilised milk favoured by his parents. The tea took on its unnatural, orange-gold hue. He'd forgotten just how much he hated it. It was a symbol of something from the past. He left it untouched on the table.

'Well, if you're sure. I'll get back. Carole hasn't been too well. I should see if she needs anything.' His voice tailed off. He knew he was making excuses. Justifying his need to escape.

'I'll be in touch. You can always get a phone message to me at work.'

'They'll have to get him out first,' Frances said without expression.

'And don't worry about anything, Mum. We'll help out where we can. Funeral and that.'

'I'd expect the pit bosses to pay for that. Their fault wasn't it?'

'I shouldn't think so. Accident, they all say.'

'They'd have to say that. Go on with you. Get to your own home. I'm all right.'

'I'd better let our William know. I expect they'll give him leave.'

Leaving the gloomy, sad home behind, Archie made the long journey back to Dora. He felt tears burning behind his eyes. His father had been such a special person; always standing up for him if his mother disagreed with his plans. Thank heavens Dora had insisted they made that visit, what was it? Just a couple of nights back. He'd never have forgiven himself if he hadn't seen his Dad that one last time. The fondness he'd shown to them and that hug as they'd left. Almost as if he'd known something was going to happen. He'd worked hard for all of them for his entire life. He'd seen little in the way of pleasure . . . or fun. What a waste, Archie decided, and made up his mind that whatever happened over the next months, war or no war, he was going to get the most pleasure possible out of life and he would make sure his wife and baby daughter had the best of everything he could manage. Perhaps the planned move would be the start of the next phase of his life.

The funeral took place the following Saturday. The small group of family and a representative from the colliery watched the simple coffin as it was lowered into the ground. Little Carole whimpered at the cold, oblivious to the tragedy being enacted around her. Her parents tried to keep her head covered with her pink and blue blanket, as if this could somehow protect her from more than the cold. It seemed right that she attended the grim proceedings. She was too young to have any lasting memories. They believed it might have given small comfort to her grandmother and it was the last connection she would have with her paternal grandfather.

There was a sense of unreality about the whole proceedings. It'd been in the paper and several people he didn't know were standing around in the gloomy light. Every detail of the disaster and lists of the men lost had been in the *Evening Sentinel* and everyone shared the pain of loss. His mother looked somehow diminished and he felt the first stirrings of sympathy for the woman. William stood tall in his soldier's uniform, looking grim and very grown up. He had a forty-eight hour pass so at least his mother wouldn't be alone that night.

Archie felt relieved to think he didn't have to stay with her and the relief was swiftly followed by guilt. He was glad nobody could read his mind.

Dora's father had accompanied the family and was a strength to them all. He also provided some ham to make sandwiches for the small group returning to the house after the funeral. A glass of sherry each and the obligatory sliced, buttered fruit loaf were handed out and everyone but the close family escaped as soon as was considered decent.

'I got the letter from the bosses,' Frances announced in her usual expressionless voice. 'William read it for me. They say how sorry they are and that they know words mean little. They're quite right. A few bob wouldn't come amiss.'

Archie told her about the growing fund that had been set up by many of the local leaders. Everyone who had been bereaved would have a share, when the time came. She remained unimpressed.

'There was even a message of sympathy from the King and Queen,' Dora tried to comfort her. 'I thought that was nice of them.'

'Royalty never did owt for me,' Frances said ungraciously.

'You know, I don't think anything would ever cheer your mother up. I know she's had a lot to bear in the last few days, but she's always been the same,' Dora remarked as they finally made the journey home. 'She's very hard work, isn't she?'

'You don't know the half of it.'

## CHAPTER FIFTEEN

It was May when Dora and Archie finally moved to the Walton estate. Their new home had a flat, reinforced concrete roof and was brick built, in a row of six identical houses. There were rows more of identical houses, all set in identical roads. There were open spaces and wide grass borders along the roadside. The planners had done their best to provide safe houses that were comfortable to live in. The whole estate was growing fast, simple, partly prefabricated units that could be assembled quickly. Each ground floor had an air-raid shelter incorporated, windowless but with a ventilation opening high in the outside wall. There were three bedrooms and two living rooms. The back door opened into a long, narrow garden.

'So much space,' marvelled Dora.

'It's a start. And we'll be able to grow our own vegetables, once we get the ground dug over. Somewhere for little Carole to play as well. I reckon we'll be happy here. What do you think?'

Dora felt happier than she could remember.

Despite the shortages, at last she had a home of her own. She could arrange everything just as she wanted and didn't have to ask anyone's approval, apart from Archie of course, but they always agreed about everything. Proudly, she hung the painting Archie had done for her, for last Christmas. It was his first attempt, unframed and painted in oils with a scene of a Scottish lake. She began to get to know the neighbours, many of them with small children of their own. She wheeled the pram down to the welfare clinic and met several of the other mothers. They compared notes about the weights of their babies and collected supplies of orange juice and jars of cod-liver oil and malt, designed to supplement the diminishing rations they were able to find in the shops. There was a camaraderie among the women, unknown in times of peace and built on the need to manage and share the privations.

The war droned on, news bulletins becoming a major part of the daily interest. Despite the all too frequent booms from the factory, she at least felt insulated from the worst of things. They heard from William occasionally. He had continued to instruct and train the men in his division and rose to sergeant. He had become almost obsessed with fitness but at least he had remained in England and was relatively safe. Dora wrote dutiful letters to her mother-in-law but never received a reply. She had no reason to suspect that it was largely because Frances could not read or write properly and didn't have anyone to help her and assumed it was through lack of interest.

When the following winter arrived, Carole developed a cough that wouldn't seem to leave her. They called the doctor and to their horror, he diagnosed pneumonia. For several dark days, the parents anxiously watched their precious child fighting for breath and burning with fever. Dora slept hardly at all and Archie was near to dropping with fatigue and worry. The doctor visited daily and when he was at his most worried, he suggested a new medicine, not yet fully on the market, but one which was proving most effective in the treatment of a number of illnesses. The child was given penicillin and showed a rapid improvement. Dora wept tears of relief as Carole slept peacefully for the first night in weeks. Though the worst was over, both young parents knew that this could herald many future problems for their precious daughter . . . the only child they would ever have. The doctors had finally forbidden any further pregnancies. For Archie it was a relief to have the issue finally closed. For Dora, it was a huge disappointment but it made her all the more determined to take the greatest care of her little girl.

Everyone had become used to the restrictions imposed by the war but the friendships between the most unlikely people was growing. The men set off for the Home Guard meetings with a bravado that came from knowing they were unlikely to be tested. Sparsely equipped, they were practising various routines so they could play their part should the invasion happen. Wearing their caps and tunics, a gesture towards uniform, they practised marching with broom handles to replace rifles.

'You know, if anyone had ever told me I'd go crawling across the Downs Banks on me belly, five nights a week, I'd've told them they were off their rockers.' Archie stood up, brushing leaves and grass out of his jacket top.

'Get down, yer daft bugger,' yelled the sergeant. 'That's not only you wiped out but it's given away our position.'

'Oh yes? Who to? Nobody around as I can see.'

'That's not the point.' The sergeant was getting more frustrated with a company who refused to take things as seriously as he did. 'Oh bugger it. We'll call it a night. You're right, lad. What self-respecting Gerry's going to come round these parts?'

The weary men rose to their feet and dusted themselves down. They broke up into small groups as they tramped back to their homes. They mostly all lived on the estate and walked silently through the night, all too aware that they'd be up for work again in a few hours.

While their men were doing their bit for the war effort, several of the women would get together in each other's homes, drinking tea and chatting. They took turns to nip back to their own homes to make sure the children were sleeping. It all helped make the long evenings pass. They too found something to laugh about, a bonhomie found through their deprivations. There was union in knowing they were all equals in a world once used to a strong class system.

Once a week, Dora and Archie organised a baby-sitter and went to the local pub, a new building put up at the same time as the housing estate, where the locals and many of the Americans billeted in the area could share a drink and a bit of social life. They became pally with a couple about the same age as themselves and invited them to come round to their home when they had time off. They were delighted with the chance to share a proper home and spent many evenings with their new friends.

'Are Uncle Bud and Auntie Mary a Mister and Mrs?' Carole asked. The adults looked slightly uncomfortable.

'Not exactly, honey, but we both come from the same town back home, so we're very good friends. Say, how's about I send you a new dolly to play with when we get back home?'

'Thank you very much,' the child said, her eyes alight with pleasure. 'But what will she be called?'

'We'll have to think of a nice American name, won't we?' The distraction from the awkward questions had worked. It would be many months before Carole received her doll, Jackie-Lou, they had decided it should be called.

'First thing I'll do when we get back home is to visit the toy store and find a doll that looks like a Jackie-Lou,' promised Mary. She hugged the child and gazed wistfully over her head towards the man she had fallen in love with. Unfortunately, his wife back home would be waiting so theirs was a brief interlude, as were so many other wartime romances.

In every home on the estate, there was a determined effort to prove they could overcome anything. Large groups of mothers and children set out for the lanes to gather blackberries during late August. The allowance of extra sugar for jam was a great incentive and happy groups of purple stained children played around together and competed to fill their jars. They took picnic meals with them and experimented with bread and marg filled with the gritty fruit in its uncooked state. Never had food tasted so good. The mothers chatted while the children recognised that this was what life should be like. The last bits of crust were fed to the ducks as the weary trail dragged themselves home. The distant booms from the factory, so much a part of their lives now, were largely ignored. The final blackberrying triumph came the following day when each home in the road put out pots of freshly made jam, served on huge wedges of new bread. No need to waste any of the precious margarine ration with such delights.

The children usually went to the end of the road to wait for the works' bus to come back and greet their fathers as they returned home. Carole ran to her father and slipped her hand in his, walking along, trying to hear and understand what the men were talking about. She desperately wanted to tell him about her day, the jam and the new bread, but he was grim faced and didn't seem to be listening to anything other than his workmate.

'Dreadful business,' Jack was saying.

'Certainly makes you think. Never expect anything like that, not here.'

'What's the matter, Daddy?' Carole persisted as she tugged his hand.

'Nothing for you to worry over, love. See you tomorrow, Jack. Bye.' They went inside and the little girl pointed at the table.

'See what we've made, Daddy? I helped, didn't I, Mummy?'

'What's wrong, love?' Dora asked, seeing the expression on her husband's face. He shook his head, indicating the presence of the child. 'Was it something to do with that great bang this afternoon? I did wonder. Louder than usual.'

'What are the big bangs, Daddy?'

'They're testing paintbrushes, love,' he replied absentmindedly. It satisfied the child and she went off to play with her dolls.

'Testing paintbrushes?' spluttered Dora. 'That the best you can come up with?' Her laughter died quickly, as he began to speak.

'Some detonators went off when they were packing the shells. Terrible accident. Oh, love, I couldn't bear to look. One poor woman . . . pregnant she is . . . lost both her hands. Blown right away. Several of the others were really badly burned.'

'Oh God. How awful. Will she lose her baby as well?' She shuddered at the thought.

'Nobody knows. She was lying there screaming, "How can I look after my baby without hands? How can I hold it? I won't be able to stroke its hair." Just kept on and on about it. I doubt I'll ever forget today. I'll tell you one thing. I'm going to look round the whole workshop. See if I can't come up with a few ideas to make some of it a bit safer. There has to be a way of making some improvements.'

'When's it all going to end? Year after year. Such terrible loss and injuries. How many more people have to suffer? They said it would never be like the last war. Not even the people staying at home are safe in this one. They said it would end in a few weeks. What is it now? Five years? Do you realise Carole will be going to school in a few months? I can't believe it.' The horror stayed with him for many months.

After Easter the next year, Carole started school. It was a total change in the lives of mother and daughter. They both had to get used to the changes and some days, Carole begged to stay at home. It was very tempting but Dora would not listen to her pleas and sent her off on the school bus. The school was dark and old-fashioned and suffering badly from lack of resources. They mostly learned to write on pieces of board, painted black. The older children used slates but even these were getting to be in short supply as breakages could not be replaced. Carole was a bright child and was soon moving up the school to the older classes. She discovered the pleasures of reading for herself and was always lost in one book or another. War time was simply a way of life, the only life the child had ever known.

When May arrived, the news was better. The end of the dreadful war seemed to be imminent. Rumours flew round the world that Hitler was dead but it took a few more days for the final announcement of peace to be made. Celebrations in the streets of London filled the news broadcasts and finally, May 8th was to be V.E. day. Victory in Europe. Schools were to be given a holiday and every town in the country was set to celebrate It seemed that things were going to return to whatever counted for normal. Despite the announcements, some people were holding back, unable to believe it was finally over. That night, there were to be fireworks in the town square and everyone was going. Hastily gathered flags and bunting were put up on every available post and even some coloured lights were found from the depths of the cellars at the council offices. Carole and some of her younger friends were put to bed early, promised that they would be woken later and taken to the town. Sleepily, she rode on her father's shoulders, wondering what on earth was happening. Everyone was cheering and the excitement soon filled her and she joined in with great glee, mainly because it was the latest time she had ever stayed up. She saw her friends from their road and they ran wildly around, weaving between the adults' legs. Whatever the end of the war meant, it was good to see everyone laughing and singing together. It was the first time she had ever seen lights shining out at night. There were no blackout curtains covering any windows. It was beginning to dawn on everyone that the war years were finally over.

'What are you going to do now?' Dora asked her husband. 'You'll be out of a job at Swynnerton, thank God.'

'What else but go back to the pot banks?

I'm sure Leslie will have me back. The decorating will be starting up again soon.' Throughout the war years, plain white pottery had been the only manufacturing that had taken place, except for special orders for the export market. It was considered a waste of resources, when the talents of the largely women painters could be used in the war effort. Apart from the manpower issues, the cost of materials for a non-essential commodity was possibly a greater saving.

'I can't believe we shall get back to running our lives again, instead of being told what we should do. Oh, Archie, isn't it wonderful?' They clung to each other, relieved they had come through it all, relatively unscathed. For a moment, they remembered Ralph. Though he had not been fighting abroad, he was nonetheless a victim of the war.

'Can I be in this hug please?' said Carole, clinging to their legs.

It was amazing how quickly everyone settled back into a normal life. In many ways, the camaraderie was fast disappearing, as people fell back to their old jobs and some degree of a class structure crept back into society. Many of the men stayed on at the munitions factory, making things safe and closing down the work sheds. Speculation was rife about the possible future of the place and rumours of factories and new jobs ran round the estate. Air-raid shelters were quickly turned into spare rooms or general dumping grounds for junk.

Food rationing continued but there were many things coming back into the shops. Mary began a weekly routine of visits and brought some of her own and Harry's sweet ration for their grandchild.

'You shouldn't, Mum,' Dora told her. Her mother had always had a sweet tooth and she knew what it meant for her to give them up. 'You don't send sweets to Margaret's kids, do you?'

'I don't see much of them, do I? How are things with Frances, by the way?' Mary asked.

'Haven't seen her to tell the truth. She made it plain I wasn't really welcome. She got her welfare handout after the mine disaster and somehow, she seems to have gone a bit funny. Archie goes to see her a bit but it seems I'm not wanted. Not that I mind. She's a miserable old cow, to say the least.'

'I think Margaret will be coming over to stay with us for Christmas this year. It's months since we saw them. Will you and Archie come for the day, as well? Be nice to be all together again.'

'It's months till Christmas, Mum,' Dora laughed. 'But yes, when the time comes. If that's what you want. I was going to ask you here. Be the first time I've done it myself. William is getting his de-mob by then and I thought he could come over on Boxing Day. Let's see what happens, shall we?'

For Archie, being back at Sansom's was wonderful. He quickly settled back into a routine and met up with many of his old 'girls'. They cheerfully teased him, as they worshipped him for his cheerfulness and good leadership. He never lost his temper, as most of the managers did, and always listened to their problems. They knew they could trust him with their secrets and worked all the harder. Carole and Dora came to visit the factory occasionally, and the 'girls' all made a terrific fuss of the child. She was a serious little girl, always asking questions and wanting to have a go at everything they were doing. One of the 'girls' sat her on her knee and held her little hand as she tried to paint the permitted blue coloured edge on a plate. The plate was ruined but nobody minded.

'I can do it better when I'm bigger,' decided Carole. 'I'll practise with my paints at home.' The massive rows of plates and cups were quite amazing to the child and she wondered where all the people could be to use them.

As the months went by, Archie once more began to get frustrated with always having to follow the same routines. As Christmas approached, he did some painting himself for Christmas presents. He painted a tea set for Mary and Harry, his favourite primroses with a standard print border, even though they were not supposed to take any decorated ware for the home market. Everyone was still having to accept plain white or cream-ware. He also managed to organise a dinner service for Dora, an elegant gold rimmed, bone china set. It was the beginning of having the sort of china on his table that once he'd dreamed of as a child.

'I wish Mum and Dad were coming here now,' Dora said. 'I'd like to show off my new china. It's so beautiful.'

'There'll be other times. It'll be nice to see Margaret again, won't it?'

'I doubt it. We'll no doubt get an ear bashing about how we've spoilt Carole and how we're too snooty for our own good.' Archie looked surprised. He'd never quite realised the depth of feeling held by his wife towards her sister.

'By the way, Mum wants to see Carole,' Archie told her. 'I hope it's OK, but I've said I'll take her over on Christmas Eve. Just for an hour or two.'

'I take it she didn't want to see me?' asked Dora crossly.

'She didn't say but you can come if you want. I didn't think you'd want to.'

'I don't. No, of course I don't mind you going. How will you work it?'

'Can you put her on the bus and I'll meet her off it, at the other end when I come out of work. Then we can go on to Mum's.'

'Do you think she'll be all right? She's only little. I'm not sure. I think I should go with her.

I can always do a bit of shopping after.' In the event, that was what happened. Dora spent a couple of hours shopping in Longton and enjoyed the atmosphere of post-war shops and their bright lights. She bought a large chicken at the market and planned to cook it on Boxing Day when her brother-in-law was to come over. She felt pleased and content with herself. She had a loving husband, a beautiful child and two very dear parents. The only blot on the landscape was the impending day to be spent with her sister and family.

Archie's visit to his mother was reasonably successful. The old lady was mellowing a bit, he decided. She gave her grandchild a parcel to be opened the next morning. Archie was pleased that she'd taken the trouble to produce something and remembered the day he'd first been given a present. The exercise book and pencils. It was probably still upstairs in his old room.

'You'll have a glass of port,' Frances told him, rather than asked. 'There's glasses in the cupboard.' He took out two small glasses and poured from the bottle that was standing on the side.

'Cheers,' he said lifting the glass. He hated port but dared not refuse it. 'I've got a card for you. And I've put a little something inside. I didn't know what you'd like for a present so you can buy yourself something with it. Hope that's all right.'

'Thanks, son. Good of you, I'm sure.'

'When's William due back?'

'Your guess is as good as mine. I'll see him when he decides it's time I s'pose. He's a law to himself these days.'

The stilted conversation went on and Carole sat bored and waiting to go home. She was asked various questions from time to time but apart from that, felt as if she was wasting time. It was never like that when she visited her other grandparents. There was always something to do. The button box to sort out or some paper to fold into something.

'Can I sort out your button box?' she asked timidly, half afraid of the rather dominating woman she hardly knew.

'Button box? I don't have such a thing. Now, Archie, tell me about the factory. How many workers are there?' Carole continued to sit on the edge of the sofa, looking bored.

Archie was amazed at the apparent interest and replied mechanically. He could see the little girl was bored and was trying to think of some way he could make his escape. He downed the last of the revolting port and politely stood up.

'I suppose I should be getting this one home. Be bedtime by the time we've got there. Don't want to miss out on Santa, do we? I'll just go up the yard, if that's OK. Do you want to go, Carole?'

'Yes please,' she said, not sure why they

should want to go up the yard but it certainly sounded better than being left alone with the intimidating old woman. She wondered why they were going to spend a penny outside instead of using the bathroom but accepted the novelty happily. Her Mum would be very surprised when she told her, she thought. Archie left his mother's home with a sense of relief.

'Hallo, Archie,' a voice called out as they turned the corner of the street. The man was a scruffy looking individual, wearing an old army great coat. He was unshaven and had a shifty air about him.

'Er, hallo. Heck. It's Billy isn't it? Billy Machin?'

'That's right. Back from the war. Like hundred of others, no work. After giving my all for my country, this is how they treat you.'

'I'm sorry to hear that. What sort of work are you looking for?'

'Anythin' that inner minin'. I'm not going down the pit, not for nobody.'

Archie shifted his feet uncomfortably. He needed to catch the bus and get his little girl home. He didn't want to be reminded any further of his past, the past he'd worked so hard to escape.

'I'll let you know if I hear of anything,' he said desperately. 'Where are you living now?'

''Ere and there. You can always leave a message with your Mum. I can call in to see if there's anything going down.'

'OK,' he agreed. 'But I don't know of anything much around. You know how it is.' They shook hands and Archie subconsciously wiped his hand down his trousers after the contact as they went to the bus stop.

'Who was that dirty man, Daddy?' Carole piped.

'Hush, love. Don't say things like that. He can't help it if he hasn't got anywhere to get clean.' All the same, he hoped fervently that this contact did not lead to anything.

Christmas Day with Dora's sister and family wasn't too bad after all, especially as they had to return home quite early in the evening to catch the last bus. They decided that it had been just the right amount of time as they hadn't been able to fall out. At first, Carole had been pleased to discover she had three cousins but they had teased her and she felt uncomfortable.

'What's a goodie two shoes?' she asked on the way back home. Her parents looked at each other and smiled.

'Why do you want to know that?'

'Tommy said I'm one. Because Grannie says I'm a good girl and they aren't so good. I'm not sure if I should be one of the goodie shoes things. The way they said it wasn't very nice.'

The following day was more like the Christmas Dora had wanted. William arrived cold and hungry around midday. He'd brought presents and was full of excitement at his coming release from the army.

'How do you fancy a pint?' Archie asked.

'I could knock spots off it,' laughed his brother.

'All right if we go round to the Lamb?' Dora nodded.

'Don't be too long though or the dinner'll spoil.'

'So what are your plans?' he asked, as the two brothers set off for the local pub.

'Not sure yet. I've learned quite a bit of mechanics and stuff. Might go in for something to do with machinery. I'm going to have a bit of a rest first. Get me head together.'

They played card games during the afternoon and much to everyone's surprise, Barry and Nadine arrived later, with their own little boy. They had been staying with Barry's mother in the town nearby. The two children played together and stayed up late to have supper with the grown-ups.

'I'm impressed, Coz,' Barry said to Dora. 'Being able to put on a spread like this, when you didn't even know we were coming. You must have inherited your talent from Mary.'

'I wanted it to be a special Christmas this year. End of the war and everything.'

'Certainly has been. Did I tell you, I've got a booking at the Castle for New Year's? You should come over. Take the little 'un to your

309

Mum's and have yourselves a night out. Be like old times.'

'We might. But New Year's difficult. You know, after the pit disaster. Archie still feels it.'

'I understand but we all have to move on. It's been a few years now. It's going to be quite a celebration, I can tell you. There's plenty of women that have lost their men.'

They did go to the dance and enjoyed themselves hugely. Carole stayed with her grandparents and wondered what it was going to be like when it was a new year. Perhaps it would look different somehow. She tried to stay awake but she heard nothing, even when the church bells rang out and people were singing out in the streets. Nor did anything seem very different the next day when she looked out of the window. She'd been expecting everything to look different somehow. There was a general air of optimism in the family as they all made plans for the next months.

As soon as February arrived, Dora began decorating their house. They provided buckets of distemper at minimal cost at the estate office. It was all boring cream but Archie brought home a few grains of colour to add to the mix and stippling became the vogue. The basic colour was covered with dabs of paint in a contrasting colour, painted on with an old brush which gave the irregular effect they wanted.

'Just in time for your birthday,' she told Carole.

'Can I have party?' she asked. 'Some of the others at school have parties and I'd like one.'

'Why not?' her mother agreed. 'You mustn't invite too many children though. By the time you've asked your friends from the street, that will be quite enough people.'

Archie was happy to see them so excited and promised to try and leave work a bit early on the big day. It was all a great success and they ate jelly and evaporated milk and stuffed jam sandwiches till they nearly burst. The games they played were noisy and simple. Music for musical chairs was supplied by one of Dora's neighbours who hummed tunelessly, stopping every few seconds to eliminate the contestants. Carole was knocked out early and protested loudly that it was her party and she should win something. By the time they all went home, Dora and the other adults were totally exhausted. Carole went to bed eventually, clutching her best present ever, a box of paints. She was overtired and protesting loudly that she wanted to paint *right now*.

'You just want to spoil my happy day,' she wailed as she was dragged upstairs.

'You'd never be considered a goody two shoes now,' Dora laughed.

'Good. I'm glad,' stormed the child as she flopped onto her bed and fell instantly asleep.

'I often wondered what a children's party might be like,' Archie said ruefully. 'Exhausting is all I can say. Not like our Carole to be so ungrateful.'

'She's just tired out.'

'All the same, we need to be careful that we don't spoil her. Just because she's the only one we've got.'

'Oh, Archie. You do say daft things sometimes.'


## CHAPTER SIXTEEN

A year later, Archie confided in Dora that he was feeling frustrated once more at the lack of variety in his work. Though Leslie gave him relative freedom in the designs they used, it was still flatware that was the sole production line. Tea-sets and general tableware and none of the figurines or other more interesting things that he craved. Though he recognised that he was very lucky to have such a good job, it still wasn't enough.

'I'd like to start up on my own. Have my own factory,' he announced.

'Blimey,' Dora burst out. 'That's quite a step. Can we afford it? And how much would it cost to set up? We're hardly rolling in money. We've just bought the car for a start.'

'What I was thinking, was that I could start

in a small way. I can rent quite a decent sized place for not very much. Just a big room really. That way, I can still carry on working for Leslie and bringing in a decent wage.' There was a fire in his eyes that Dora hadn't seen for some time. His enthusiasm was infectious and the words tumbled out. 'Then I'd get one or two women working part time at first. I can get some items made as "out-work" now. There's lots of women who'd jump at the chance of earning a few bob while they stay at home to look after the kids. Now the war's all over, they miss the work and the company. They'd all got used to working again.'

'But what about all the equipment and kilns? How on earth would you fire the stuff? They must cost a packet.'

'I'm going to talk to Leslie. I reckon he'll let me fire some stuff when there's space in the big kilns. I'm thinking of fancies. You know, flowers, small stuff. They wouldn't take up much room. And I can probably buy stuff second hand. Some places are up-grading so they'll be selling off their old equipment.'

'Looks like you've got it all planned. Have you actually done anything about it yet?'

'I've looked round a couple of places. There's one in Longton. Just across from Sansom's. Very handy. It'll mean working all hours to start. I'd stay on with Sansom's until I get something established. Like I said, that way my wage will still be coming in. We won't

313

starve.'

'Seems like you've made up your mind.'

'Course not. Not without your say so. It affects you too. I won't go ahead without your approval. Course I wouldn't.'

'I'll never stand in your way. But don't forget we've got Carole to think of now. I suppose I could always do a few folks' hair again. They'd be pleased to have personal service, and if we need a bit extra, well I'll do what I can to help.'

'I knew you wouldn't let me down. Let's go and look at the new workshop on Saturday. What do you say?'

'All right. Oh, Archie, it's what you've always wanted isn't it?'

He said no more but nodded happily. His mind was already seeing his own stamp on the bottom of the finest bone china he was capable of producing. Silently, he blessed Ernie Draper Senior, the man who'd given him his first chance.

'Wonder what happened to old Ernie? I know he went away to fight but I never heard any more of him. God, I hope he made it. It's terrible how you let people go out of your life.'

'And Mabel. I should write to her. See what happened to her. Isn't it amazing how people come and go? I saw her every day for years of my life and now she's simply disappeared.'

'Is this really what you want?' Dora asked doubtfully the following Saturday as they stood in the large, empty room. Carole was dancing around happily, loving the unaccustomed space. It was bitingly cold with ill-fitting windows and no heating. Archie nodded his head enthusiastically.

'I know it isn't much to start with. But it's only temporary, until we get going properly. Then I can afford bigger premises. But as I don't have much capital, this is the best way to start.' His fervour was catching and Dora was beginning to smile, just a little.

There were several long work benches at the sides which would be a start and with a few bits of specialist equipment, much of which he could beg or borrow, he'd be all set. Dora agreed to back him in what she really saw as rather a hair-brained scheme. She knew that if she didn't agree to it, he would feel forever frustrated. He had to give it his best shot and she should support him.

It was just a few weeks later that Carole and Dora were invited to accompany him to the new workshop, one Saturday afternoon. The first tiny figurine was ready for inspection. The little crinoline lady, less than six inches high, was glazed, painted and ready to be fired in the new electric kiln, his first really significant purchase.

'I felt you should be here for the first piece.'

'What's she called?' asked Carole.

'I thought I'd name her after you. Would you like that?' The child beamed and nodded her approval.

'How do you make her?'

Archie took her across to the casting bench and showed her the mould. It was in three parts and when he took it apart, she could see the hollow inside that was the reverse of the lady. He fitted it back together and secured it with a thick elastic band. Then he poured a greyish looking liquid into the mould and left it to stand. She watched, waiting to see how the lady got out of the mould. Her father tipped the mould upside down over the jug and the liquid clay, the slip he called it, was poured back into the jug, leaving a thin skin of solid clay over the inside of the mould. Some time later, Archie slipped the elastic band off and very carefully removed one of the mould's plaster pieces.

'Wow,' breathed Carole, seeing the partly exposed figure. The other pieces were removed and the tiny lady carefully lifted out. 'It's like magic isn't it? But why is she soft and soggy? And why has she got funny lines all over her?'

Patiently, he showed her how the lines as she called them could be carefully removed with a little knife, once the clay had dried a little. Fettling he called it. Next he took a soft sponge and wiped the marks away, leaving a smooth finish.

'It has to be fired next. Baked in a very hot oven until it becomes hard.'

316

'Can we take it home and cook it tomorrow with our dinner?' asked Carole. 'Please, Daddy?'

'Sorry, love. Needs much hotter ovens than we have. It needs to be fired twice before I can even start painting it.'

'Why is this new one much bigger than the painted one?' Carole asked.

'When it's fired, the water goes out of the clay and then gradually, the clay changes and becomes very hard.'

'Where does the water go?'

'What happens when the kettle boils?'

'Steam,' yelled Carole excitedly. 'So you get steam in the kilns and it comes out of the top?'

'Almost right. After that, the pottery has to be glazed to make it shiny and fired again. When all that's done, we come to the interesting bit when it's painted and begins to look pretty. It's all going across to Uncle Leslie's kilns on Monday. Along with several other things I'm trying.' He showed them some simple brooches in animal shapes.

'Very modern,' Dora said approvingly. 'I'm so proud of you, love. I'm glad you've made this start. It's going to work, isn't it?'

'Of course. Never doubted it. Now, let me show you this.' He picked up a little rubber stamp. He pressed it into a dish of amber coloured liquid and pressed it against the bottom of a piece of fired china. Then he dusted over the sticky mark with grey powder.

'*Staffordshire Fine Bone China, Made in England by Archie Barnett,*' Dora read. She blinked away the tears that sprang into her eyes.

'Does that mean you're famous now, Daddy?' Carole asked.

'Not quite. But one day, maybe,' he replied. 'Just one more task before this lady is finished.' He took a fine brush and wrote *Carole* on the base. 'I shall always write the name of each figurine on the bottom. That way, everyone will know the name of the lady who's standing on their shelves.' He closed his eyes. This was phase one of his ambitions. He had made his first piece of china, designed completely by him, modelled and created by him. Archie Barnett china was on its way.

The following weeks were crazily busy. Having the car meant the family were no longer reliant on public transport to get around. It saved many hours of waiting for buses and driving along indirect routes. Weekends were virtually non-existent as Archie worked constantly, trying to build up his first collection. Leslie Sansom had been a wonderful friend, allowing him to fire his pieces in the various firings . . . biscuit ware first and then the glost ovens for the glazed ware. Finally and the most rewarding, the last firing of decorated ware was done in his own small kiln. When the finished object came out in all its glory, he took it across to show his

318

friend. Leslie was very complimentary about the work and as always, wished him success. Archie was making totally different items to them and would never be a rival to his own company's work, though he recognised that he was about to lose a valued friend and colleague.

Often on Sundays, Archie would drive Dora and Carole to her parents' house, while he worked on his own in his little workshop. There were one or two local women who made flowers for him and he would collect them and use them to make different products. Some were set in bowls to make the traditional flower baskets and bowls while others were used to form lids and decorations on small china boxes. He was in seventh heaven, allowing his creativity to blossom and flourish. He had the idea of making tiny flower sprays to make brooches and even tinier ones to make matching earrings. The clips and fasteners were easy to obtain and already he'd had several salesmen calling to offer him specialist items. He realised that he would soon need someone to be at the workshop full time. The mould maker and caster were probably the most important, especially if he could use one person to do both jobs. There were plenty of people around needing jobs and he knew it was just a matter of finding the right one. The main problem would be his wages. A skilled man did not come cheap and as yet, the small factory, if such it could be called, was not trading. Another week or two and he would have a selection of samples. A thought hit him. If Ernie was back from the forces and still working as a salesman for his father, perhaps he would be willing to take some of Archie's things. Once he had a few orders, he could safely employ someone, even give up working for Sansom's and work on his own full-time. He could hardly contain his excitement. It was also time they put in a telephone and bought a few things for the house. Hugging his plans to himself in delight, he went to collect his family.

Archie knew that his own enthusiasm was enough to make his dreams come true but he also realised that it was necessary to give some time to his marriage. Dora was the most precious thing in his life followed by little Carole. That little girl was going to have all the things he had missed. She was going to get the chance of a good education and go on to University if they could manage it. Every spare moment for the next weeks was spent working on his collection of samples.

He'd followed up his thought of contacting Ernie and they had met up again, after the long gap. They had both changed and their childhood closeness was never re-gained, not least because Ernie had spent time at the front during the war. It was a very different man to the young fun-loving friend Archie remembered. They had little in common any more. Ernie's nerves were shattered and he could no longer manage the travelling. He did however, recommend a good man who was freelance and always willing to take on new clients for a percentage of the order. It was a start. A start that paid off well. Within the first fortnight, Bill, the traveller, came back with orders for several dozen items. This was his chance and Archie took the momentous decision to leave Sansom's and start his own company on a full-time basis. He could do all the processes himself, though it would be very hard work. As long as he could rent proper firing space in the kilns, it would save money elsewhere. Once the orders were coming regularly, he would think about taking on other staff. He blessed the days at Draper's when he had learned all the manufacturing processes the hard way, from the bottom up. Leslie was naturally disappointed to see him leaving and told him there would always be a place for him if he needed it. The girls also made a fuss of him and made him promise to take them on, if his business grew large enough. He knew the best workers and promised gladly.

The most unexpected feature of his new life was the loneliness. Always before he had worked with large groups of people and he missed the companionship. He was also rather inclined to spend rather too long dreaming or planning, as he euphemistically called it. He quickly realised that although he could draw exactly what he wanted the finished object to look like, he was not sufficiently skilled at the three dimensional modelling. But there was no problem with that. Among the closed community of pottery workers, he soon found people who had all the necessary skills. Many of them worked in their own homes as well as in factories and it was easy to find several excellent workers. He bought another second hand smaller kiln for firing more of the decorated ware and this saved many hours and breakages, previously spent when transporting his work to the kilns at Sansom's. The closer it was to being finished, the more costly the breakages. It wasn't long before he was ready to take on one more worker. He decided to engage a caster, a middle aged lady who was very much cheaper to employ than a man. After all, he was still planning to be a very hands-on boss at this stage. It also meant that he was himself working harder to complete the jobs. His paperwork was also beginning to build up. Invoices needing paying were totally mixed up with receipts and even the odd cheque for goods received were buried in the growing pile. Mrs Cade, his caster, sometimes watched as he worked. He was totally absorbed in his pleasure at seeing the intricate china pieces turning from the grey clay into objects of delicacy and beauty. All the same, she was a practical soul and could see at once where he needed help.

'My sister-in-law does some book-keeping for some of the little firms. I'm sure if I had a word, she'd soon get you sorted. A couple of hours a week would do it. At this stage, anyhow. Shall I have a word?'

'Book-keeper? I don't really think I need one at this stage. I was always good at sums at school.'

'Oh I'm sure you were but it's more than just doing a few sums, isn't it? I've watched you over the last couple of weeks. You hate having to do anything that keeps you away from the pots. I noticed you were doing a design on the back of the clay invoice yesterday. Fag packets. Bills. Receipts. You don't care what it is, once you get your hands on a pencil, do you? Now, I'm going to make us a cuppa and then we'll have a look and see if our Marjorie can help out a bit. She doesn't charge much. A few bob. Be well worth it.'

Archie stared in surprise at the little woman. She usually said very little and this speech was one of her longest ever. She did have a point. The thought of doing his books was always pushed to one side. He always persuaded himself he would tackle it later, at the end of the week. There were too many other things, more interesting things to do.

'All right Mrs Cade. Get your Marjorie to call in one evening, after we finish. You're probably right. I do need someone to do the books. I was going to take them home but it doesn't seem the best plan. Dora likes me to spend what bit of time there is, with her and the little 'un.'

He told Dora of his growing empire. She looked troubled but she said nothing. She hoped he wasn't trying to run before he could walk. She did offer to look at the books herself but he smiled gently and said that he wouldn't want to trouble her with such tasks. Besides, she certainly wasn't much good at sums, however efficient a housekeeper she was. So far, the expenditure was still less than the income and the business was growing all the time. Each new line he tried was quickly snapped up. There were already a dozen different pieces he was selling regularly. Brooches were going well and some miniature jugs, the latest addition, also seemed popular. Tiny sprays of hand-painted flowers decorated the sides, complemented by gilded handles and tops. His orders for Christmas were already coming in very well and it was still only September.

'Shouldn't you be concentrating on just making one or two different things?' Dora asked. 'You just get one line going and you're already working on something else.'

'That's the secret. Keep new stuff coming out. If I only have one or two lines, we all get fed up with them and then the buyers think they've seen it all before. We have to keep expanding the range. I want to try some other shapes of vases, the little miniatures, you know. Then I plan to try a proper, large figurine. They're really complicated to make you know. Every little part has to be made so it will come out of the mould and then they're stuck together with slip when they're being fettled.'

'You've lost me, Archie. I don't know what you're talking about.'

Archie picked up the precious Royal Doulton figurine they'd been given as a wedding present and began to show her how it would have been made. If there was any gap on the model, such as a bent elbow or hand, that had to be made in a separate mould and stuck on afterwards. Any joins were smoothed out with the sponge and nobody would ever know it wasn't all made as one piece.

'It's much more complicated than you'd think,' she said. 'Are you sure it's what you want to do?'

'I think it's a good idea. And I can help with that fettle-thinging,' Carole announced. 'Like I did when I came to see the Carole lady being made.'

'I'd certainly be happier if I knew you were being kept on the straight and narrow,' laughed Dora. 'And you will no doubt be taking on more people as you expand the lines.'

'The flower maker is fine working as outworker. Painting's more difficult because of carrying it. I certainly need a couple more part-timers. One of the packers is going to come over after he finishes at Sansom's, just for a couple of hours. I can't tell you what it means to me, love. Just giving work to people means such a lot.'

Dora was somewhat upset when a refrigerator arrived one day. She had no idea it was coming and was waiting with angry words when Archie came home. He looked so pleased with himself that she bit back her words and settled for a mild chastising.

'Why didn't you tell me? I looked such a fool. There wasn't even a space cleared to put it. I had to get the men to help me move stuff in the old air-raid shelter to make room for it. I told them to take it away but they said they wouldn't.'

'It was a surprise. Besides, I knew you'd say no if I told you it was coming, so I thought I'd just get it. And we're having a phone put in next week. We need it for work.'

'Come on. Why do we need to have it at home if it's for work?'

'So I can take orders and phone to tell you when I'm coming home. You always complain you don't know how late I shall be. Besides, it'll be nice for you to phone grocery orders through. To the butcher and the shop. Save you time. And now you've got the fridge, you won't need to go shopping so often.'

'You've got it all worked out, haven't you?'

She gave him a hug and they stood together, for several minutes. It was all a part of getting the things he wanted in life, she knew. Whatever fears she had about falling into debt, she knew this was his way of proving he was worth something. It would have been wrong to spoil his pleasure.

'Car, telephone, refrigerator. What's next? You'll be wanting one of these television things I suppose.'

'Oh no. That will have to wait a bit. I don't think there are enough programmes for us to watch yet. One day soon, maybe.'

'So, you'll just have to make do with going to the pictures,' Carole said happily.


## CHAPTER SEVENTEEN

Life was moving in different ways as many more restrictions of the war years were coming to an end. The lives of the residents on the estate needed something more and as people had a little more money, various recreational groups were forming.

Archie was helping put together a local cricket team and one evening a week, several of the old home guard group met at the centre to discuss tactics. With the aid of a small grant from the council and a lot of hard work, a local farmer was persuaded to allow them to use a field, a little way out of the village and they raised funds to build a proper pavilion. The team proudly joined a league and began to make a small impact. It was a good humoured group and they all became firm friends. Archie was more than proud when he was asked to captain the team and took his duties very seriously. Carole earned pocket money by oiling the cricket bat with linseed oil and putting whitening on her dad's boots. Dora was roped in to making teas and gained a new circle of friends.

By 1949, the order books at the factory were already full. Archie, with Dora's backing, made the big decision to move to a larger factory. There were already several workers crammed into the original room and the need for their own large kiln to fire the biscuit and glost stages was becoming desperate.

'I need to expand properly, very soon,' Archie had said somewhat tentatively one evening. 'For a start, I really need my own kiln for biscuit firing. I can't keep trailing everything over to the other factory and the timing's never right. And if I get a big kiln, I shall need a bigger space to put it in.'

Dora looked even more concerned.

'And so where is this new place to be?'

'There's a building in Fenton. King Street. Once upon a time it was two houses. Been knocked together. I can't move too far or the girls won't be able to travel with me. But I reckon this one will be ideal. On the bus route and everything. I don't think I can afford to turn it down.'

'Funny. I somehow guessed there would be a place you just couldn't turn down.'

'This is it, Dora. I have to have a go. If I don't I'll always think I've missed my chances. I know I can make it work.'

For the next weeks, he was busy moving equipment to the new factory, though Dora felt *factory* was a slightly grandiose name to give the little building. It had been used for manufacturing earthenware, heavy, crude pieces that had helped the war effort supplying plates and cups for government orders. It had lain empty once the war was over, when the company had followed the way of so many of the smaller companies and was unable to continue. Post-war shortages of clay and coal to fire the ovens had been disaster to many of them and the lack of the necessary chemicals for painting meant that the white or cream ware had continued on the home market.

Now, there was a new optimism everywhere. This was the heart of the pottery industry and once things began to pick up, it was going to be a boom time for them all. The King Street premises were ready for the move. A sign was painted to hang across the front of the building. *Archie Barnett, Fine Bone China.* It was written in the same flowing script that Archie had practised for so long. The factory soon filled with workers and carpenters began to put up partitions to make a small showroom at the front of the building. Beside this, Archie had a small office, tucked into a cubby-hole beneath the stairs. He had no intention of spending much time in any office, so it was minimal. He had a secretary who came one morning and the book-keeper for one afternoon. The rest of the time, Archie stuffed the post into cardboard boxes and answered the phone when he had to. The typewriter was balanced on a filing cabinet, to one side of his desk. Dora secretly worried about his lack of office organisation but knew it was beyond her abilities to help in any way. All his workers loved him and it seemed, would do anything for him, staying late and happily working flat out when necessary. He was always an idealist and a dreamer. He continued to use any paper, cardboard, anything to draw out his ideas and create shapes. Sales reps called with new products and equipment for the manufacturers and he was always ready to try something different. There were new lithographs, transfers to decorate china, many of them with rich gold patterns integrated into the designs. He immediately bought them, knowing he could make opulent looking pieces with addition of gold rims. It made them expensive, but the market, especially the growing export market, would lap them up, he felt certain.

Each time there was a new line, he took home a sample for Dora. Soon, the collection was too big for the china cabinet and they put up extra shelves in the lounge. This room was only used for high days and holidays but this meant less cleaning and the china was safer. Friends began to call round, especially after the cricket matches, when there were often impromptu parties. Archie's reputation was growing. People saw his work and wanted to buy pieces for presents. It was especially precious, when they knew the manufacturer personally. There was a constant stream of things brought home from work and often, when someone admired a particular piece, he would hand over one of Dora's collection, promising to replace it when the next batch came out. Often, she had to fight very hard for the replacement and some never arrived.

Once established in his new factory, the product range grew and the orders were even larger. Many pieces were sent abroad for the growing export market and they all felt excited to think of Archie Barnett China finding its way into homes in America, Canada, Australia, New Zealand and many more countries. Some weeks, more goods were sold overseas than to the home market.

'Just think. There are people sitting in their homes all over the world looking at a piece of my china every day. I can't imagine what some of these places are like. And to think, the china came out of our little factory in the middle of Fenton.' Dora smiled at his words and kept her fingers crossed that it continued. Archie always enthused about the various pieces he was designing. One day he came home looking particularly excited.

'We've got a new idea. You're going to be the model for one of our next figures,' he told his daughter. 'We are going to make a set of characters from *Alice in Wonderland* and you are going to be Alice. Well, what do you think?'

'What will I have to do?' she asked.

'Just sit very still for awhile while the model is made. You'll be sitting on a mushroom when we make the figure properly.'

Carole chuckled and said they'd never find a mushroom big enough or strong enough. All the same, she found her copy of *Alice's Adventures in Wonderland* and read it again with extra interest. She could see why they had the idea of using a mushroom but still felt puzzled as to how it would be done. In the event, she had to sit on the edge of a desk for a long time, her bare feet swinging. Mrs Jacobs, the model maker, had to keep asking her to sit still. Carole wanted to have her hair loose for the modelling, and had even insisted on buying a new blue ribbon to make a headband. Alice always had a headband and long hair.

However, the sculptress preferred to have her looking more contemporary and asked the child to keep her hair in pigtails.

'Bit strange, isn't it?' Carole asked her mother when she got home.

'She's a very clever lady. She knows what she's doing. Anyhow, it makes Dad's model a bit different, doesn't it?'

Carole was bursting with excitement to see herself but it took a very long time before there was anything to see. Once the first clay model was finished, there was the long process of making the moulds. The original model was carefully cut apart to make the shapes that would be needed for the mould and each of the legs and arms were made separately. She was cross to think that she would never see the actual sculpture as it had already been cut apart to make the moulds. Finally they were all ready and the first pieces cast. Archie had given in to her badgering and allowed her to come and watch the process. She stared at the face of the model as it came out of the mould and asked if it really looked like her. She was assured that it did and she pulled a face.

'It's a bit weird. I only see myself in the mirror or on a photograph so I don't know what I look like all round me. I s'pect it'll be all right. OK. Thanks, Daddy.'

There were five characters in the set. Carole fell in love with them all as soon as she saw them in the various stages. She was promised the whole set for Christmas and though she was pleased, she hoped that was not all she was to get. After all, they always took home the pieces of china when they were made. When she opened the box on Christmas morning, she sat staring at them and for once, really began to appreciate the beautiful creations her father had made. She had grown up taking Archie's beautiful creations totally for granted. To the child it was simply what her father did, just as her best friend's Dad made shoes at the nearby Lotus factory. But now, as she handled the delicate pieces, she looked at the fine details, realising that she was holding something very special. The March Hare was sitting with his long legs ungainly, and untidily folded together. He was cheerfully spreading butter on his pocket watch. The White Rabbit was standing elegantly by a tree stump, while the Mad Hatter wore his top hat proudly with the 10/6d label clearly showing. The Caterpillar was wonderful. Carole was not keen on real caterpillars, but this one sported a fez and had a lovely smile, as he held his arms out sideways with a devil may care expression. His hookah rested beside him and he was so beautifully shaped she could almost see his many pairs of legs moving. As she held Alice in her hand, she fell silent. In all honesty, she wasn't sure she looked much like this delicate little model, bare legs swinging over the edge of her

334

mushroom. She was so perfect. The whole model stood on a greenish-brown base, painted to look like earth. She fingered the shapes for a long time, thinking what a clever father she had.

'Aren't you going to open your other presents?' her Grannie asked. She nodded but for once, if she'd received nothing else, it wouldn't have mattered so much. For the whole of Christmas that year, she kept looking at her china and even put it on her chest of drawers in her room, wanting to keep it there for at least some time, she told her Mum. It could join the other things later, when she'd got used to it.

Carole passed her eleven plus exam and was offered a place at the local grammar school. Archie was so proud and vowed she would never have to suffer the way he had and leave when she was still too young to have achieved anything. She would never have to wear second-hand uniform. Everything would be the best they could manage, even if it meant they might have to do without something else. Feeling slightly self-conscious, she stood for inspection before leaving that first morning. She put the empty satchel, apart from a pencil box, over her shoulders and took a deep breath before leaving to catch the school bus at the end of the road.

Dora wiped away a tear and Archie gripped her arm, knowing exactly how she must have been feeling.

'Our little girl. All grown up,' he whispered. 'I feel ridiculously proud. She's going to make it, isn't she? Wonder what she'll do with her life.'

'Probably be a dreamer just like her father,' she laughed.

'She'll be a good'un if she turns out like her Mum,' he said, giving her a hug. 'Now, I'd better get off to work and earn some money to pay for our daughter's expensive uniform. Oh and don't forget we've got the theatre this evening. Not the best planning, on Carole's first day. Hope she doesn't get too much homework. I'll be home as soon as I can.' It had become a feature in their lives to go to the theatre in Hanley once a month, for a live variety performance, a play or musical. One more sign of Archie's progress up the social ladder. Carole usually accompanied them, despite the rather late hours.

Archie came home early, anxious to hear about the first day at grammar school. How different from his own welcome home, he thought bitterly. His mother had seen the whole thing as a waste of time and a source of inconvenience whenever he was later home than usual. His family were never going to know of the privations he had suffered. Carole was extremely non-committal about her day.

'Pretty boring really,' she announced. 'Oh and I've got homework. I'll have to take it with me and do it in the interval, I s'pose.' Her parents looked at each other and felt slightly guilty. Their plans had not been well thought through. Carole seemed happy enough with the arrangements but they realised they needed to modify some of their ideas. Archie was torn between wanting all the trappings of success and wanting Carole to achieve success where he had failed. He took a keen interest in everything she was doing, hoping to fill a few of the gaps caused by his own early departure from education.

Nineteen fifty-one saw the culmination of years of planning for the Festival of Britain, to celebrate and encourage more optimism throughout the country. The Great Exhibition of eighteen fifty-one made it an auspicious date to select. Most of the celebrations were to be held in London, with the new South Bank site of the magnificent Festival Hall and Battersea Fun Fair being centre pieces. Bonfires were lit all over the country and smaller exhibitions, especially in the pottery industry, were held to promote everything that was good about Britain. The china industry featured strongly with special commissions taking their place amidst the rest. The optimism was mixed, as shortages were still biting in many areas. Meat rations were still causing a deal of hardship and in the Barnett household, Carole eased things by deciding she didn't like meat any more. By the time the festival was closing, election fever had taken over. The Attlee Government had suffered much criticism of late and to Dora and Archie's delight, Mr Churchill was returned to office. They had shared the guilty feelings of many, when he'd been voted out 'after all he'd done for Britain during the war years'.

For Archie, the growth in his business was everything he had hoped for. He'd become friendly with many other small potters in the area and shared ideas about the actual manufacture. Experiments with new glazes and colours continued to fascinate him and some of them found their way into his work. But always, his first love was for the figurines and he produced fine work that many said rivalled even Royal Doulton in their quality.

Early in nineteen fifty-two, King George the Sixth died. It seemed the entire country mourned the loss of this gentle man and sympathised with his lovely wife. They remembered a visit he had made to Stoke in the early war years and it seemed everyone had a story to tell. The day of his funeral seemed to affect everyone. Many firms held lunchtime services for the workers to pay their respects. Two minutes silence was held at two o'clock that afternoon and many were hiding their tears at the loss of their once unwilling and shy king. They all felt a part of it, with many representatives of the local police forces joining their colleagues to be on duty at

Windsor. The new young Queen Elizabeth was also viewed with a degree of sympathy. In the midst of the shock of losing her father, she was expected to come to terms with the fact that she was now the head of a very large community of people the world over.

'And just when the poor dear was having a bit of a holiday,' one of the girls said. Pictures in the newspapers showed the small sad figure descending the steps of an aeroplane, already holding herself high, as the Queen of England and the Commonwealth.

The news leaked out that the King had died of smoking related illness and many people began to consider the implications. If the King himself could die, what chance was there for the rest of them? Dora and Archie, always heavy smokers, tried to give up. It proved too difficult and they pushed away the idea of the threats to health and resumed the habit, thinking *it would never happen to them.*

The advent of the new queen meant there would be a coronation. This had dramatic implications for the whole of the Potteries. A whole year was to pass before the actual ceremony and the date was arranged for the following June. Whatever the reason for the long gap between the accession and the coronation, it gave ample time for preparing commemoration memorabilia. It seemed that everyone was planning something special, large and small companies alike. For Archie it seemed his moment had finally arrived. He was geared up to make long runs of smaller items and his imagination ran riot. Coronation mugs were his first priority. There would be different sizes and all would carry official badges. It seemed that any crests, badges, whatever were to be approved by 'The Palace'. Hundreds of designs were submitted and only a relative few accepted. Lavish badges were produced and the lithographs sold to a number of manufacturers. Archie was delighted with the ones he had chosen and began to plan how he might best use them. Traditional beaker shapes were the obvious choice and he began production of these but he wanted something more special, something unique. He doodled on even more invoices, pads and even the office wall was not exempt.

'I want to use the royal lion as a handle,' he announced to the mould maker. He showed the sketch of the lion attached to the side of a small mug. 'If we make it the right size for these badges, and gild the whole of the handle, I think it's what we're looking for.' The mould maker lookcd at him sceptically.

'You're talking about a whole lot of gold. Make it a very expensive piece.'

'I think it's worth it,' Archie insisted. 'I bet no-one else's thought of anything like it.'

'It's different all right. Shall I have a go, then?'

'You? Do you think you can model it

yourself?'

'I reckon so. Get me a proper drawing done up. Make it the scale you want, allowing for the shrinkage of course. I'll see what I can do.'

Archie set to work. It was a project he felt strongly about. He took a clean sheet of paper and unusually for him, began to construct lines with proper measurements. The finished result would always be considerably smaller than the clay model as everything shrank during the firing. As water is driven off to harden the clay into biscuit ware, the correct proportion for shrinkage has to be ensured, to prevent spoilage. It needed to be of even thickness to ensure that no cracking or splitting could take place. They all knew how shapes could distort in the immense heat of the ovens. He worked for several hours, not even noticing when the workers left for the evening, calling their good nights. It was when the ringing of the office phone finally brought him back to reality that he saw it was almost nine o'clock. An extremely irate Dora demanded to know exactly when he intended coming home for supper. He barely listened to her words, he was so excited about his project. Frustrated beyond belief, Dora slammed the phone down and threw his tea on the back of the fire. She felt angry with herself and bored with being alone. Carole had of course gone to bed much earlier.

'How do you think it feels?' she demanded

when he finally arrived home almost two hours later. 'I'm on my own all day and then all evening as well. I'm sick of it. I don't ever seem to do anything these days. You're always working.' She knew she was being unfair but with cricket taking up the weekends and now he'd joined the golf club to extend his social group, his spare time was non-existent. She began to hate the trappings of success.

'But you always knew I'd have to work hard. I'm doing my best. For you and Carole.'

'And yourself. Don't forget that. It's your own ambition that's driving you.'

'I have to try it, Dora. You must see that. If I have to work late some nights, well that's just part of the price to pay.'

'I bet you managed to find time for a pint somewhere on your way home.'

'I didn't, love. Not this evening. Oh I know I have done occasionally but I've had this marvellous idea. I've been working on the drawings and John's going to have a go at making it tomorrow. I needed to get it finished. There isn't much time. Look here. This is it. I've brought it home to show you. This is what I've been working on. I think this is going to be really big, Dora. What do you think?'

He held out his drawing for her to see and enthused well into the night about the prospects. She couldn't be angry any longer. Seeing his absolute pleasure in his work made her realise exactly why she had married him.

'Come here you daft thing,' she said, pulling him into a hug. 'It's wonderful and you're right, it is going to be big. But all the same, I was worried half to death not knowing where you were. I thought you might have fallen down those awful stairs after everyone had left. I kept trying to ring, several times I tried. That was what worried me most. Then I thought you'd had some sort of accident on the way home.'

'I suppose you tried ringing the pub as well. Make it obvious to everyone what a terrible husband I am?' She blushed. 'You did didn't you? I won't be able to show my face there again. I'll be known as the man whose wife has to keep tabs on him.' She looked angry again but realised he was teasing her. 'I don't know why you always have to think the worst. Why should I suddenly have an accident?'

'Must be when you really love someone,' she said thoughtfully. 'You always fear they are going to be taken away, just when you know you'd miss them most.'

'That's always,' he replied. 'I couldn't ever manage without you. And how's Carole today? She'll like this, don't you think?' His fingers continued to stroke the page where his own, special coronation mug was pencilled. He could see the finished object in his mind and could scarcely contain his excitement. 'The Canadians are going to love it. Americans too.'

'Carole's fine,' Dora interrupted, knowing he would continue his mental planning all night if she let him. 'Having trouble with some maths though. She'd hoped you'd be able to help her with her homework.'

'Has she left it out for me to look at?'

'Well, she did but it's far too late. It's gone midnight. And I bet you haven't had anything to eat?'

'Had a pork pie earlier. I'm all right. I'm sorry but I promise I'll be home early tomorrow night. Make up for tonight. We'll go out somewhere if you like. By the way, did I tell you, our William came in today? He wants a job. I can't say no but I'm not sure what he's going to do. Probably mostly labouring at first. He's a strong enough body.'

'I see. And how's your mother? Is he still staying at home with her?'

'Seems like it. She sounds as if she's the same as always. Our William doesn't seem to have any interest in girls. He's getting on a bit. If he doesn't hurry up, he'll be left on the shelf.'

'He keeps telling you. He's waiting for me,' Dora chuckled.

Archie stared at her.

'I hope he doesn't mean it,' he retorted almost fiercely. Dora stared at his unfriendly tone but he grinned again. 'You go on up. I'll just take a look at this homework.'

'But it's very late. Come to bed. She'll just

have to manage on her own.'

But it was too late, Archie was already trying to understand the complexities of proving Pythagoras's theorem.

## CHAPTER EIGHTEEN

John the mould-maker had made an excellent attempt to produce the little mug just as Archie had specified. Togther they worked on the lion shape, deciding exactly how best to produce the mould. It had to be a simple mould to make it viable to produce in large quantities. The two main pieces would be made to fit together down the sides of the lion and the third piece would form the bottom. With a bit of care, the last section was where the slip was poured in. It was tricky as the lion head was above the top of the rim. They worked hard on the piece, making several attempts to get it exactly right. Just a week later, the first ones came out of the kiln, ready for glazing. It had worked perfectly. Allowing for just a small amount of further shrinkage, the lithograph was going to sit perfectly on one side, with a smaller one for the back. Archie could hardly wait a further week for the next firing and wanted to make further moulds and begin production properly. He was persuaded to wait and complete the early stages first. He made a dozen or so and waited for them to go through all the processes, biscuit, glost and finally they were ready for the important part.

He personally applied the lithographs and put his most experienced gilder on the job of painting the lion handles. Several were completed, ready for the next firing of the decorated ware. The finished result was instantly approved by everyone and all the girls immediately ordered mugs for their children and families. He laughed delightedly.

'By the time this coronation happens, you'll be sick to the back teeth of the whole thing, just you wait. Now, that seems to be sorted. We'd better get on to the next line. I thought we'd try to make a scale model of the Coronation Crown. And the Queen sitting on the Coronation chair. What do you think?'

'Bloody hell, boss. You don't expect much, do you?' Vera, one of the paintresses told him.

'Oh but I do,' he said with a warning. 'Cancel anything you've got planned for the rest of the year. We're in business for real.' They watched fondly as he left their work-shop.

'He's really something that one, isn't he?'

'I'll have a job to cancel what's going on in my stomach,' said Betty, who'd recently discovered she was pregnant for the third time.

'You'd better discover what's causing it, right rapid,' chided Vera. 'He's not going to be best pleased that one his best paintresses is in the club.'

'I'm going to have a job to reach the bench in another couple of months. Do you reckon he'll let me work at home? I'll need the money.'

'If it goes like he thinks, he'll probably hold yer hand himself, just to make sure you paint and give birth at the same time.'

There was a buzz of excitement around the whole factory. Good humour and laughter could be heard in every shop and radios were playing the whole day. A new gas fired kiln had been installed and even this gave extra confidence to the work force.

'They mean business, sure enough,' the girls said to each other. 'I reckon our Archie's going to make it big. And we're all a part of it.'

William had joined the team some weeks earlier and was quickly learning what he needed to do to play his part. Much of his work was basic labouring, carrying the new heavy moulds up to the casting shop on the first floor when they were ready for use. He helped with making the moulds, though only in a very basic way. He mixed the slip, the liquid clay used for casting the pieces, and invented ways of mechanising some of the longer tasks. A simple paddle and motor was fitted into an old barrel and this kept the slip moving, preventing the solid matter from settling on the bottom and spoiling. His main task of the week was to load and unload the Monster, the name they had given to the big kiln. It was an extremely unpleasant task, hot and dusty. His arms soon became marked with small burn scars from occasional encounters with the sides. But he worked happily enough, glad to be away from mining and the pits.

Dora was not entirely happy with the disruptions to their family life but she understood Archie's needs, his driving ambition. Gradually, they made new friends and began to go out for Sunday lunch, a large party of them joining together. They would take turns to go back to each other's homes for games of cards and large high teas in the evening. For Archie, the new, affluent friends were a sign that he was successful. His life was full and busy. Carole teased him about what she called his golf-club voice, used for answering the telephone. He laughed it off, claiming that she was just as much of a mimic as he was. All the same, he knew she was right. The posher accent went with the new status. They regularly went to dinner dances at the North Staffordshire Hotel, forgetting how uncomfortable both of them had been that first time, all those years ago. He was happier than he ever dreamed possible and was always bringing home small presents and even fresh flowers appeared regularly each week.

When their new television arrived, Dora had even more visitors and had to admit that she was very pleased with the addition. They even sat watching the test card before the evening's viewing and remarked on the smart evening dress worn by the announcers. Mary and Harry visited more regularly, staying overnight, just to see what were fast becoming their favourite programmes. Harry had retired and they decided to move house to somewhere with a bit more garden.

As the Coronation drew nearer, mugs and other souvenirs were being dispatched all over the world, especially to the Commonwealth countries. The magnificent model of the Queen on the Coronation chair was an absolute triumph. When he brought home Dora's sample, she was speechless.

'I don't think I've ever seen anything quite like this,' she murmured. The young queen was dressed in a gold dress, the crown on her head and long purple robes, looking so like real velvet she almost expected to be able to stroke them.

'We had to guess at what she would wear and decided on gold. The whole piece is so expensive to make anyhow, what's a bit more gilding?'

'Why does it look as if some of the bits have broken off the chair at the back?' asked Carole.

'Because that's how the real thing is.'

'How do you know?'

'We had photographs to work from.'

Carole's questions went on, until she was

349

satisfied that the beautiful object was perfect in every way. 'It's pretty good,' was her final verdict.

'I'm glad about that,' Archie said with some amusement. 'There's only one thing,' he began, looking anxiously at his wife.

'Go on,' she said suspiciously.

'Well, I haven't got many of them finished and I need this one to complete an order. You'll get another as soon as they come out of the kiln. Promise.'

She shook her head in despair. So often she'd look at her shelf of figurines and find one was missing. It had been needed to make up an order.

'Well make sure you do bring another. I don't expect you'll make that many and I'll be very angry if we don't have one. It will be part of Carole's heritage. One of everything her father made.'

During school holidays, Carole often went into work with her father. She tried painting occasionally, but showed little aptitude for it. She managed to grasp how things worked in the casting shop, where she fettled and sponged away the seams left by casting the shapes from the moulds. Occasionally, if some items were broken during this stage, her Uncle William would attach the wrong heads to the wrong bodies and made highly comical figures as a result. It was part of the pleasure of being a small business. One task Carole did become adept at doing was fixing the lithographs and she often helped with this, managing to work almost as well and quickly as some of the girls. It became a source of pocket money, when she was able help her father.

Before the Coronation, a large exhibition was held at the Victoria Hall in Hanley. All the well-known names in the world of pottery were there as well as many of the smaller companies. Archie took a stand and Carole was delighted to help decorate it. Already, she showed some aptitude for creative needlework and she made white satin flounces, draped to hang down over the stepped stand. Strips of red, white and blue ribbon held it in place. It looked as good as any of the stands and was both patriotic and complemented the china very well. Samples of each of the special lines were arranged and spot lights made the whole thing shine gloriously. She felt very proud of herself and her father, when it was finished. There were several different designs of mugs, some with two handles and some with one, all lavishly gilded. The lion-handled mug attracted a great deal of attention and they took a great many orders. The magnificent Queen sat in pride of place at the top and Archie's other special design, the King Edward Crown, was beneath it. Some of the crowns had a musical movement added, playing the national anthem when the object was lifted. Carole was fascinated by the idea and ensured that it was demonstrated at every possible opportunity. There were several other items, busts of the queen, taken from the larger model and some small boxes and vases.

'It's a magnificent display,' Dora told him. 'As good as any here, including the big names. Makes all those late evenings worth while. Have you arranged for some photographs?'

'The press are taking stuff. We'll get one from them. Now, how about a pint? We've just got time before we need to get our little girl home.'

'I'm not that little,' she protested. 'If I was, I couldn't have done all this stand, could I?'

'No, love. You've done very well. You may not be much good at painting or drawing, but you've certainly got some creative talent.' Archie put his arm round his daughter. 'Makes it all worth while, doesn't it?'

'When it's finished with, can I have the satin? I can make things of it.'

'We'll see,' he promised.

'I hate it when you say that. It usually means you won't.'

The exhibition was a great success. It had been interesting to see what the 'big boys' as they were called, had come up with. There were many souvenir replicas of the Queen, but most agreed that Archie's was among the very finest. All the same, the price and time taken to create some of the pieces, limited the possible orders but on the whole, the little factory would be working flat out until at least May the following year. It was a time of expansion and success.

'You know, love, I think we should start looking for somewhere larger to live. I think we owe it to ourselves and our friends.' The search had to be postponed for some months, however, as they were simply too busy.

The Coronation was a great event for the whole family. Mary and Harry came over for the day itself and several other friends were dropping in during the day to watch the ceremony on the tiny television. There had been warnings given out for several days. Watching television for a whole day would be bad for everyone's health. Certainly, sitting in a darkened room was out of the question and several companies sold large quantities of small table lamps, designed to help prevent eye strain. The screens were rather small and not very bright, so it was impossible to see anything at all if there was much other light in the room.

Recipes were put out in the magazines for special meals which could be prepared in advance so the housewife could also be free to watch everything without starving her family. It was easy for the Potteries families. Lobby. Huge pots of the savoury stew were made the previous day and simply needed heating. Carole made a special cake and iced it, decorating it with the same striped ribbons as were used on the show stand. The obligatory die-cast model of the Coronation coach sat on the top. The fervour of patriotism rippled through the land as everyone who could watched the new young monarch as she became their very own queen. Street parties were organised everywhere and bunting hung from every possible place. Most windows held pictures of the Queen, decked round with red white blue in every possible combination of materials.

'Poor little thing,' Mary had said at one point during the ceremony. 'Her little neck doesn't look strong enough for that great crown.'

'It's quite like Dad's model, isn't it? Only a bit bigger, I s'pose. She should have had it made of china. That isn't very heavy, is it? It might have broken though, if the man had missed her head and it fell on the floor. Could have the music box in it as well. Save having all the bands and stuff.'

'Carole, why don't you just be quiet and watch?'

'Sorry,' she sighed, pulling a face.

Despite the poor weather, it was a day everyone would remember. The magnificent procession passed by, with the huge, laughing Queen Salote of Tonga, who insisted on riding in an open coach, despite the soaking rain. The ranks of representatives came from countries throughout the world. There was a glow of patriotism through the land. Sir Winston Churchill was in another coach, making his famous victory sign and receiving a rapturous welcome from the crowds.

'Bout time he was recognised properly,' Archie said. 'After all he did for us.'

It was a long day and once the television transmission was over, they all sat back, smiles on their faces.

'Why don't you take the dog for a walk?' Dora suggested. 'You could all do with some air. Mum and I can get tea ready.'

Back at work the next day, the girls came in with mixed feelings.

'What we all gonna do now? Now all the fuss is over?'

'We shall have a whole lot of orders any day now. Life goes on you know. I reckon we've only just started tapping the overseas market.'

'So I'm back on the flowers am I? Shame, I was just getting used to all the royalty as well.' The banter began again and soon, everyone was busy again, always working on something different. There were so many different pieces, nobody had the time to get bored. The little lion-handled mugs were given different badges and sent to the commonwealth countries to commemorate the visits made by the new queen. Badges of cities, especially London, were designed to appeal to the tourist trade and any other things they could think of. If there was any sense of anti-climax, it was soon dispelled as new orders came in. As Archie had hoped, the success of the Coronation memorabilia had spread his name and the quality of the work was appreciated by many of his customers.

For Dora, the social side of life became much more active. Some of the overseas buyers needed to be entertained and she was always a part of this. Meals out became a part of the routine and Archie became ever more determined to find them a bigger house. He wanted to be able to entertain at home, amongst other things. Once she overcame her initial shyness, Dora began to enjoy meeting people from all over the world. There was a system of barter beginning to grow and she received some beautiful lace table mats from someone living in Bermuda, following a visit they had made. They had returned home with some pieces of Archie's china.

'Just fancy,' Dora had told her mother, 'Me, having beautiful hand-made lace like that on my table and all the way from Bermuda. They asked us if we'd like to go and stay, would you believe.'

'Blimey. You won't be speaking to us soon. Holidays in Bermuda? Whatever next. You won't go will you?'

'Shouldn't think so. They said it wouldn't cost us a penny, once we were there but it would certainly cost a fortune to get there. We haven't even been out of the country.'

In the autumn of nineteen fifty-three, her parents told Carole they were going to move.

'But I can't, we can't,' she protested. 'What about school and all my friends?'

'We're only moving to Meir Heath,' Dora said. 'You can still go to the same school and your friends will easily be able to come and stay if you like. It's a lovely house. Very big and there's a lovely garden.'

For Archie, the whole prospect had become the achievement of his prime ambition. He'd wanted a big house, high on a hill overlooking green fields for as long as he could remember. *Greenacres* fulfilled this in every way. At the front was a large drive, bordered by a mature shrubbery. The back was mostly lawns and there was an orchard to one side, with space to make a vegetable garden. Mary and Harry were most enthusiastic and Harry looked forward to helping re-claim the land from under the weeds. There was a large double garage and a range of outbuildings. Archie had bought a new car, a large, slightly ostentatious model, Dora thought. He'd also decided that their old one wouldn't fetch much so decided to keep that for his wife to use.

'Two cars,' exclaimed Dora. 'Bit much for the likes of us, isn't it?'

'Nonsense. You'll be able to fetch your shopping and go to see your parents whenever you want to. I always aimed for my big house and two cars parked outside.'

Once there, Carole was also delighted. She had her own large room with a wash hand-basin of her own. It felt like living in a posh hotel.

'Now we really can entertain people properly,' Archie said with pleasure. 'But I want to decorate first. I always fancied a panelled dining room. I think I might have a go at it. What do you think?'

'I think you're getting carried away. Let's just settle in. We could do with a new lounge suite. The one we've got is the one we had at Branksome, really it's Mum's old one.'

'We can get it re-covered,' Archie suggested. 'That'd do the trick. There's nothing wrong with it.'

'It's just so dated. What was all the thing in the thirties is hardly right for us now. Here. But, OK. Let's see about getting covers made.'

The large lounge had a delft rack high round the edge and it was decided that this was the perfect place to display the china collection. The light walls showed off the colourful pieces perfectly. Carole spent many hours arranging everything and it became her task to take them down for washing every few months. At least the precious china was out of reach and safe from accidents. The only thing that still happened was that pieces still disappeared to make up orders or for unexpected presents. Archie usually remembered to replace them but there were

358

often large gaps. He even carried odd samples in the car and when he was short of cash, was known to barter with various tradesmen, even to settle bills. The local garage owner, also a good friend, had a good collection of pieces himself, in return for the odd tank of petrol.

When everything was finally finished the way he wanted it, Archie and Dora walked through the house with Carole. It was perfect.

'It's everything I ever dreamed of,' Archie said emotionally. 'I've got it all now. My own business, making the china I always wanted to make. My lovely home. My wife and a clever daughter who will go to University and have all the chances I never did. Thank you, Dora, for showing me how a miner's son could make it big.'

'Are you famous now, Dad?' asked Carole.

'It depends what you mean by famous. My china is in hundreds of homes all over the world. If they look at the bottom and see my name there, yes I'm famous. But the fact that particular piece of china was chosen by them, looked at every day by them, well that's good enough for me. My china will be around long after I am.'

'Unless someone drops it,' Carole laughed.

# CHAPTER NINETEEN

As Archie gained customers all over the world and plenty of trade in Great Britain, he bought jewellery for Dora, a gold cocktail watch, very elegant and very expensive. She was very thrilled with it and enjoyed showing it off when they went out with their friends. One day he handed her a box. It was a few weeks before her birthday but he couldn't contain his excitement to wait for the special day.

'Here you are, love. What I always promised you.' With shaking fingers she opened the box. Inside was a huge solitaire diamond on a platinum band. 'I always said you'd have the biggest diamond I could afford. Make up for the pathetic little one I bought you when we got engaged.'

'It's wonderful but you shouldn't have. I love my engagement ring.'

'Don't you like it then?' Archie said, hugely disappointed.

'Course I do. It's magnificent. But it must have cost a fortune. How can we afford it?'

'I did a deal. One of my customers from Brum. He knew a man who made up rings and I told him what I wanted.' Carole knew her mother felt uncomfortable but even she recognised that it was just another sign that her ever generous father felt successful.

'It's very posh, isn't it, Mum?' Dora gave a shrug and said it would be hers one day.

It wasn't long after this that Archie's mother came to stay with them. She'd had a fall and as with so many elderly people, had fractured her femur. Once the hospital had done what they could for her, she need looking after on a long term basis. There was no alternative but to take her into their home, despite their past differences.

'I hate inflicting her on you but there's nowt else I can think of,' Archie moaned to his wife.

'I'll just have to make the best of it,' Dora replied stoically. 'I dare say she'll be grateful enough, once she's being looked after and having regular, decent meals.'

'I wouldn't hold yer breath.'

Carole had never known her father's mother very well. Visits to her had always been short and stilted and though it was never mentioned, she gathered there had been some row in the distant past. The old lady had been cantankerous from the moment she'd moved in, banging on the floor for attention. Even Mary had found it hard whenever she visited, and she'd always got on with everybody.

For Carole, it coincided with her exams and she took very little notice of everything that was going on around her. Such was the self obsession of the young. Archie loved to help his daughter, especially with maths. She tried to hide her homework some nights, knowing he would want her to explain it all to him and let him share the work. It was rather too time consuming, however sympathetic she may have felt. It was as if he was still trying to catch up with what he'd missed himself when his schooling was cut short. As always, he had little sense of time and prioritising tasks.

Dora bore the brunt of the difficulties of having the old lady living in their spare room. The constant tramping up and down the stairs, carrying meals on trays and the demands of the old lady was wearing her down and her own health began to suffer.

'Eh, love, you look rotten,' Archie said one evening. 'I'm sorry. I've been so busy at work, I scarcely do anything to help.'

'I'd just like a night out occasionally. Maybe even a bit of a holiday.' Archie bit his lip. They'd been used to taking the odd weekend breaks and staying in nice hotels, often with their various friends. None of the cheap boarding house stays they'd once enjoyed.

'Yes, well. We'll make some plans. Once I'm over this patch. Maybe you'd like to go out for a drink? Carole will stay with Mum, I'm sure.'

For once, they managed to spend an evening talking properly instead of slumping in front of the television, where Archie tended to doze off, and Archie realised just how much of a burden the old lady had become.

'She'll have to go into a home. There must be somewhere she can go,' Archie suggested.

'William can't look after her and anyway, we've heard the old house is being compulsory purchased to make way for some new road. The landlord's given everyone notice.'

'Heavens. You never told me that,' Dora complained.

'Our William only told me today. Won't be for a while but it's on the cards. I dunno what me Mum will have to say about that. So, like I said, she'll have to go and stay somewhere else.'

It took several weeks for a place to be found and Frances was very grumpy about the whole business.

'You're just shoving me off like an old bundle of washing. It's your duty to look after the old folk but I s'pose you're too full of yourself these days to care. After all your Dad and me did for you. Expensive education. All them years of looking after yer. Putting meals on the table. Ungrateful wretch.' She went on and on for hours and eventually, Archie left her to it. He managed to contain himself and didn't challenge her about the years when he was always hungry and nor did he remind her that his so called expensive education had been cut very short when she found the need for more money. He could never forgive nor forget. The memory of his plate flashed into his mind. It was a loss in his life that had always been with him. At that time, it had meant so much. Now it paled into insignificance against what his future was threatening at this time. He sighed. Maybe there was still some way out of all the mess before Dora and Carole found out.

Exams loomed and Carole had gained a place at a teacher training college, believing that university might be beyond her abilities. Her place was guaranteed, whatever her results. She was so involved in her own life, teenage angst and what was happening to her, that she failed to notice any worries her father might have. She did accompany them one evening to visit her Gran in the old people's home. Visits were always uncomfortable and stressful to them all and they could hardly wait to escape again. To Archie's surprise, Billy Machin was waiting outside.

'Hallo, Archie,' said the scruffy man leaning against the wall smoking. 'Remember me?'

'Billy? Billy Machin? What are you doing here?'

'Heard your old lady was in the 'ome. Word gets around our parts. Reckoned as you'd 'ave to visit some time. Thought I'd wait around and catch you.'

'I see. You must have had a long wait,' Archie murmured. 'So, how's it going?'

'Pretty bad as it 'appens. You never came back to me with that job you promised. I've been waiting for you to come back to me.' His voice was coarse and seemed to hold some sort of threat.

'I'm sorry,' Archie muttered. He'd never given the man another thought.

'Can we get back to the car?' Carole asked. 'I'm freezing.'

'Your girl is it? Grown up now 'asn't she? And you must be his missus.'

'Sorry, love. This is Billy Machin. We were at the same junior school.'

'Oh yes. Your Mum kept the shop, didn't she? I'm Dora.' She held out her hand but he ignored the gesture.

'Yes. I remember. Posh car as well, is it? You've done all right for yoursen then.'

'I suppose so. Well, if you'll excuse me, I'd better get these two home.'

'I still need a job. You're the boss nowadays. Hirin' and firin' for yoursen. How about it? For old times' sake? I seem to remember my mum helpin' you out quite a bit when you needed it.'

'All right,' Archie said doubtfully. 'Call round at the factory. King Street, Fenton. Got the name over it. You can't miss it.'

Billy nodded. He looked shifty and nodded towards Dora and Carole, as if they shouldn't hear what he had to say. Archie frowned but said nothing.

'Thanks, Archie. There's a lotta things I'd like to talk over. I'll see ya tomorrow then.'

As they went back to the car, Dora turned to him in horror.

'Wasn't he the one who went to prison? You

365

can't seriously intend to employ him?'

'Poor bugger needs a chance, I s'pose. Maybe I'll find summat for him.'

'Thought you weren't s'posed to use words like summat?' Carole teased.

'I'm over twenty-one. That means I can do as I like.' Dad often joked about his past but sometimes he simply forgot about his old ways of speaking. 'Who's for fish and chips on the way back?

The tension for Archie was growing by the day. He tried desperately to keep it from Dora but she knew there was something troubling him and eventually, he had to admit the truth.

'I'm letting yer all down,' he said blandly. 'The thing is, I'm in a bit of bother at work.'

'What sort of bother?'

'I've fallen a bit behind with the paperwork.'

'What about your book-keeper? Can't she sort it out?'

'Truth is, she's left. A few months back. Said she couldn't manage any more.'

'Why didn't you get someone else?'

'I thought I could do it myself. Sort it out. Just a matter of going through the boxes. But the bloomin' government want all sorts of returns. Purchase tax stuff. Official this, that and the other. I haven't got it. They're threatening to close us down. Sell off the assets to get their money. Just so long as they get what's owing to them. Doesn't seem to matter that all the workers will have to go on the dole. There won't be a business for them and you know what jobs are like round here. Nothing. So many little factories are closing down or being swallowed up into the larger ones.'

'I see. And how long have you known about this?' Her tone held a note of bitterness and suppressed anger.

'Couple of weeks. Bit longer maybe.'

Dora pushed the tears back from her eyes. It wasn't so much the dreadful news as the fact he'd kept it from her. He put an arm out to her but she pushed him away.

'How could you know this and not tell me? I thought we were partners. In every sense.'

'I was trying to protect you. Thought I could maybe sort it out without worrying you. But I haven't. And Carole. What's she going to think? And Mary and Harry? And me Mum? Oh, no doubt she'll love it. Seeing me toppling from the high perch.'

'Forget about all that. Don't you ever, ever keep things from me again.' Her voice cracked as she finally allowed the tears to fall.

'Dora, don't cry. I'm sorry.'

'Don't keep saying you're sorry. It doesn't help.' They argued for the next hour, until Carole came downstairs.

'Mum? Dad? What's going on? Why are you shouting at each other?' Her parents were always the best of friends and this disturbance was both unusual and upsetting.

'It's nothing, love. Just a disagreement about something. Go back to bed. You've got school tomorrow.' Dora spoke almost calmly.

'If you're sure. I don't like to hear you arguing.' Slowly, she returned to her bed and Dora went to make some tea. When she returned, she handed a mug to Archie and sat down beside him.

'We have to decide what to do next. Make proper plans and not just drift along thinking it will all go away. We're in serious trouble here.'

'Well, I was thinking, I could bring some of the equipment home and start up again in the workshop out there. Just something small to start and then re-build the business once I've got going.'

They talked late into the night and decided that as soon as it was practical, they would organise the outbuildings. It would mean a good deal of work to clear out the junk and decide what should be brought back from the factory.

'Is it all right to bring stuff here? I mean, if the factory's closing down, won't the equipment have to be sold to pay the bills?'

'Don't worry yourself about details. It's all mine isn't it? I have every right to take it wherever I like. Besides, we'd get very little for it. Second-hand stuff never fetches much and I'd only have to buy again if I want to carry on.'

Over the next couple of weeks, a couple of

the kilns and all the smaller stuff took their places in what was called the new workshops. It all began to look viable. Gradually, as it took shape, Carole readily accepted that Dad had decided he would start making his china in the outbuildings of their home. She didn't really think much about it nor the fact that her parents might be trying to protect her from the truth. Though their arguments were far from over, they tried to keep them away from Carole's hearing.

'You'll stick by me, won't you, love?' Archie asked repeatedly. Dora reassured him but never let him forget that he needed to keep her informed about everything in future.

They all went to the factory to clear out some of the rooms one weekend. There were a number of items to be retrieved and things to be thrown away.

'Did you ever take on that awful man we met at the hospital?' Carole asked, as they worked.

'Who? Oh Billy? I gave him a few jobs. Labouring mostly. He wasn't capable of doing much else. I had to give him the push at the end. He wasn't very happy about it but there wasn't much I could do. Made all sorts of threats but he's all wind and bluster.'

'I expect everyone will be feeling sad that they won't be working here any longer. But it's too far to come to our house and there isn't enough room is there?'

The workers had been dismissed, all demanding he kept in touch and let them know if he started again. One or two of them agreed to make flowers at home and Archie arranged to collect them once a week. *It was just like the early days*, he often remarked cheerfully. Dora began to enjoy having him working nearby and sat watching him over endless cups of tea.

One night, the phone rang.

'Who the heck's that at this time?' Archie complained. 'It's three o'clock in the morning.'

'P'raps it's Mum or Dad been taken ill,' Dora said as she leapt out of bed.

The police were short and to the point. The factory was on fire and would he please get there as soon as possible. Archie insisted that Dora stayed at home and drove off anxiously. His once beloved factory was burning fiercely. The sign above the door was blistered and his name almost obliterated. Smoke poured out of the upstairs windows, already cracked and broken by the heat inside.

'What a mess,' he sighed. 'What started it, can you tell?'

'We were hoping you might help us with that,' said one of the firemen grimly. 'Would there have been anyone inside?'

'No, course not. We didn't have kilns firing or anything. Nothing I can think of. Maybe it was something electrical. Wiring shorting out.' He felt anxious, as he'd done a lot of wiring himself and probably it wasn't all entirely legal. Besides, most of the equipment was now stored in his garage. The lease on the factory would have run out by the following week.

It was daylight by the time the hoses had got the fire under control and clouds of steam mingled with the smoke. The stench of chemicals and paint filled the air. The largely wooden interior structure had completely burned out and most of the upstairs room had collapsed down into the ground floor. In the grey light, they looked inside. Pieces of blackened china, cracked moulds and the remains of painters' tiles littered the dark interior. Archie felt himself near to tears to see the destruction. Any remnants of the dreaded paperwork so necessary for inspection by the authorities had completely gone with the rest. He'd meant to clear out the last remnants of his business in the next few days.

'Mr Barnett, we'd like you to accompany us to the station,' the grim-faced policeman told him. 'We believe there are a number of questions you need to answer.'

'But I don't understand. What can I tell you there that I can't tell you here?' he blustered.

'There's evidence to suggest this fire was started deliberately. Haven't you heard of insurance scams? How's business at the moment, Mr Barnett? There's talk around that you've gone bust.' Archie felt his blood draining away. Business was indeed terrible.

The factory was closing. Things looked as bad as they could and he could understand the reason for the questions he was being asked. But whatever he might be guilty of, he knew he was innocent of setting a fire. 'So, can you tell me where you were last night?' the policeman continued.

'I was at home. With my wife and daughter.'

'Very convenient.'

The next few hours were a nightmare for everyone. Dora had rushed to the police station as soon as she knew what was happening. She wasn't allowed to see her husband but made a nuisance of herself to the duty sergeant, protesting her husband's innocence. As for Archie, he was grilled for the entire day.

'I have information here that says you're filing for bankruptcy. Convenient that all your records have gone up in smoke. And what about the contents of the factory? There's not much sign of all the equipment that should be there.' The detective was grim-faced.

'Aye, well a lot of it had to go. To pay off some of the bills,' he hedged. 'But I didn't set fire to the place. I'd never do a thing like that.'

'And what about the insurance?'

'I had to let it go. Couldn't carry on paying the premiums. Surely that must prove something? I'd hardly be doing an insurance scam if the bloody place wasn't insured, would I?'

They seemed to believe him. At the end of the longest day of their lives, he was eventually released. After he'd provided a list of all his employees and anyone who'd recently left, they had their suspicions allayed. They brought in Billy Machin, still stinking of petrol and as aggressive as ever. He caught sight of Archie and yelled out,

'I told you I'd settle your score, Archie Barnett. Got me own back this time, sure as hell.' Archie sighed in relief. Billie's confession had cleared him.

'Maybe you'll get something back from the insurance,' Dora comforted him. 'That would help.'

'I doubt it. Never paid the premiums. Didn't seem worth it somehow and money was tight. Seemed a way of economising. Good job I got some of the more useful stuff out before the whole lot went up in smoke.'

'But what about all the debts? You must owe hundreds one way and another.'

'I'll pay it off somehow.'

'Will we have to sell the house?' Dora asked in a small voice. She knew how much his home had meant to him. It was the symbol of his success and now it looked as if even that would have to go.

'It'll work out somehow, love. I'll soon be up and running again. We did it once. We can do it again.'

'You were a young man then and times were

373

a bit different.'

'We'll see, love,' was all he could say. With a heavy heart, they went home. The fire was the final straw for Archie. He tried to keep his feeling of dark depression from his family and worked away silently, his enthusiasm and love of his work completely drained. He spent little time planning and dreaming of his new lines and slogged away diligently at the repetitive tasks.

These events couldn't have come at a worse time for Carole. Wrapped up in her own world of revision and plans for the future, she had assumed a great deal. Everyone who was moving on to higher education was applying for grants and she had done the same.

'You'll only have to pay part of the fees,' she told them happily. 'The county will pay quite a lot. You'll have forms to fill in and everything. But I'll help with that . . .' She trailed off. 'What is it? What's wrong?'

Her parents held each other's hands as they told her what had happened. The business was finished along with the factory and though Archie was starting again, it would be many years before the debts were paid and they would probably have to leave their lovely home.

'It might mean we can't afford for you to take up this place at college.'

'We'll do everything we can. Maybe there's another way . . .'

'You'd better look at this,' she said sadly. 'It came in the post.' She was taking a practical course and this was a list of equipment she would need. 'I'd no idea it was all going to be so expensive. There's special clothing as well and it has to be bought from a store in London. They make it individually. And there's all the other stuff on the list. What on earth shall we do?' Her parents looked at the list with mounting horror.

'I'll just have to put in a few more hours, won't I?' Archie said resignedly.

'Don't be ridiculous. This is way beyond a few more china vases and kettles. You'll have to go and see your headmaster, Carole. Ask him what he suggests. Maybe there's some sort of extra grant you can get.'

The head was helpful enough, suggesting she contact the education department and explain the situation.

'They'll probably send a batch of forms to fill in and your parents will have to take a means test. I'll support you all I can, of course. Everything is all right, I take it? At home, I mean?'

'Of course,' Carole said, blushing furiously. No way was she going to admit any of their problems. She hadn't realised the full implications of the business failure nor the future prospects for herself and her parents.

When the forms came, it became clear that the means test section was not going to be easy. The grant would be estimated based on the previous year's salary. They filled them in as best they could and Archie wrote a letter to explain their problems. Then, they waited. Carole began to think that she might never be able to take up her place at college after all. The uncertainty made her bad-tempered and it seemed as if the whole family were arguing most of the time.

'And what do you expect to do if you don't get a grant?' the austere looking man asked at the dreaded interview, when Archie took Carole to County Hall.

'I suppose I shall have to get a job. I can always work in Woollies, I suppose,' she added angrily.

'And would that be satisfactory?' he asked.

'For whom?' she retorted. 'I suppose it would save everyone a lot of bother. After all, girls usually get married don't they? Why bother to get an education?' To her disgust, she then burst into tears. What did he know about anything? He sat there in his smart suit and tie, knowing nothing about ordinary people.

'I'm sure we shall be able to help you,' he said quickly.

'I'm sorry. It's just . . . after all the hard work.' She wasn't simply referring to her own efforts. It seemed so unfair that her father should have to face this final ignominy.

'Of course. I understand, my dear. Believe

me, I don't like having to ask all these questions but I have to be fair with everyone. You do have a case and it's rotten luck for you all that it came at this time. Now don't worry. I'm sure we shall be able to help. You'll hear from us soon.'

'You were very good,' Archie said to her, on their way home.

'What on earth do you mean?' she asked.

'The tears. Just at the right moment.' She said nothing but scowled at him through the driving mirror. As if she would play a trick like that. 'Listen, love, you know your Mum and me, well we'd do anything for you. We'll make sure you go to college. Whatever happens.'

'Thanks, Dad. I know. And, just for the record, those tears were genuine and not just for myself, either. I suddenly realised how tough it all is for you too. Maybe I should have forgotten about going to college and come into business with you. I could have looked after the books and kept you on the straight and narrow.'

'How do you mean?' he asked puzzled.

'Made sure you actually filled the orders you had and not try to fob people off with something else. Organised how the girls worked and generally made you a whole lot more efficient. You're too much of a dreamer, aren't you?'

'You'd have driven me mad, more like.'

'I suppose. But it does all seem such a

377

waste. You're such a good potter but a useless businessman.' He stared at his daughter. She was more perceptive than he had given her credit. For a few moments, he considered. It was obviously too late now, but might it have worked? He'd always promised himself that she should go on to university or college at least and never even given a thought to any other ideas. Maybe she would have been able to help and made it work. 'You're not exactly the world's best businesswoman, love, and you are useless at painting and most other things to do with potting.'

'I was as good as anyone at lithographing,' she reminded him. 'You said so yourself. And I could have learned other stuff.'

'You see, in a small business like this, you have to be able to turn your hand at whatever is needed. I can make moulds if I have to. I can do the casting, firing, painting. I know what's needed. What chemicals and materials we have to use.'

'But you don't know much about keeping books and records. This is the trouble, isn't it, Dad? You could never manage the business. I saw what passed for your office. I saw the boxes of bills and screwed up papers. How could anything work properly like that? Besides, it's all gone up in flames so what counted as records have gone. And what are you hoping to do now?' Archie flinched at her words. But she was right. He was too much of a dreamer. He'd had it all and lost it through his dreaming. He felt as if everything had collapsed and nothing would ever be right again. But he must never let his daughter see it. He drew himself up and took a deep breath.

'I'm starting again, as you know. At home. Fewer lines and then, eventually, a more modern place.'

'Oh, Dad,' she said fondly, knowing it would never happen and almost praying she was right.

'Oh Dad, what?' he asked. 'There are times you know, when you sound just like your mother.'

'Is that such a bad thing? I'm a proper mix of both of you. I've got something of your creative qualities and imagination. And I've got a lot of Mum's common sense. I reckon I'm pretty lucky. I'll make you proud of me one day.'

'I'm already as proud as punch.' Despite everything, he knew that was true.

A few weeks later, Carole was awarded the grant, just before they had to move from their beautiful house to a small rented cottage. Even working all hours, Archie could never earn enough to pay off his debts. There was an old wash house in the yard and a kiln and some equipment was moved over to the cottage. Though it was growing ever smaller, Archie Barnett China was somehow managing to cling to tenuous life. Her parents had been dreading telling their daughter about the move but as she pointed out, 'It'll always be home, as long as you two are there.'

Once she was away at college, Carole lost track of the daily goings on at home. Her exciting student life filled all her time. Between making his china, Archie had got himself some sort of travelling salesman job and arranged it so he and her mother called at her hall of residence most Friday evenings to take her and a friend out.

Three years passed quickly for Carole but less so for her parents. For them, it was a long drag of many hours spent working hard to make simple items of china and then taking them out to sell along with goods for other manufacturers. He was managing to make some sort of living. When he had been declared bankrupt and left *Greenacres*, he had felt the deepest shame. Most of his wealthy friends had disappeared and it was only a few of the group who had stuck by him.

'You find out who your real friends are, don't you?' Dora had said on many occasions.

When Frances finally died, they held a quiet funeral, not even bothering to call Carole back from college. Mary also died suddenly and left a feeling of despondency hanging over them all. Harry moved into the tiny cottage with them and his house sold. Despite it all, they kept up their spirits and fought their way through the difficulties. Dora often wondered how she could bear all the problems they kept encountering but her indefatigable spirit and good friends somehow kept her going.

Carole had met another student early on in her college life and they had fallen in love and become engaged. Her parents thoroughly approved of James and they looked forward to the wedding soon after she had finished her course. They wondered at times how on earth it would be paid for.

Archie fought on cheerfully enough.

'You've got grit, I'll give you that, lad,' Harry said one evening when they sat together to watch the television. 'I know I haven't got a lot behind me, but you're welcome to a bit extra to help with the wedding. Can't have our girl doing without, can we?'

'I'm going to make it up to you, I promise,' Archie said to them all. 'I shall do it, just you wait and see.'

When the business had folded, William had disappeared for a while. Nobody knew where he was and they all felt concerned. Out of the blue, he arrived back a few weeks before the wedding. It seemed he'd been working in various pubs around the country and had decided this was where he wanted to make the rest of his life.

'How do you fancy coming in with me?' he asked Archie and Dora. 'We could get a place together and then Archie can carry on working or whatever he wants to do and I can be the landlord. They'll only take on married couples,' he admitted. 'But as we all have the same name, I reckon we'd be OK. What do you think?'

It certainly gave them something to think about. Soon after Carole and James were married, Dora, Archie and William moved to a pub. At this time, Archie had given up his attempts to be a manufacturer and got a job in one of the big china producers. His reputation was known in the industry and he was given a good job in the research development department. It suited him perfectly and he felt happier than he had for many months. Dora and her brother-in-law managed the pub while he was at work and he shared the evenings, working in the bar with them. They loved the life and things were finally going well for them all. When Carole announced that she was expecting their first baby, Archie was absolutely delighted.

'I can't believe it. I'm going to be a granddad. You'll take care of yourself love, won't you?' Then he remembered all his old fears of pregnancy and held her very tightly. 'You've got a precious cargo in there. Make sure it's safe. They never did find a better way of producing babies,' he said with a wry smile. 'I'm so proud of you.'

'Oh, Dad. I'm proud of you too. All you achieved. All that beautiful china you made. You'll have some tales to tell your grandchildren. Best of all, you have something to leave behind you that very few people can claim as part of their heritage.'

'I always thought I wanted to be famous. Didn't quite manage that.'

'But you succeeded in doing what you wanted. Look at all the things you made. Surely that's success?'

'Is that how you see someone's life? Success is measured by what you leave behind?'

'In some ways. Much more important is what people think of you. The memories they have of you. But few people can also leave something as tangible and unique as you have done. You've created such beauty. Something that anyone would be proud to own. Best of all, there are so many people that love you as a person, for being what you are.'

'Then perhaps I might have been a success. But you know, the thing of beauty I'm most proud of, is you. My daughter. And all those who follow her. Including this bump.'

They stood side by side and turned to gaze at the unique display of fine bone china. Things of beauty from Archie's once dark world.

'The Fine Bone China of Archie Barnett. There's samples of it in homes all over the world. That's success. Such beautiful things coming from rough old clay dug out of the ground.'